Shadows
in
the Sky

Shadows
in
the Sky

MARY DE LASZLO

ROBERT HALE · LONDON

Robert Hale Limited
Clerkenwell House
Clerkenwell Green
London EC1R 0HT

www.halebooks.com

Typeset in 11/14½ Sabon
Printed in Great Britain by the MPG Books Group,
Bodmin and King's Lynn

For Thomas and Samuel
with much love

CHAPTER ONE

1940

The wind whipped up the sea and the troopship bucked and strained at its mooring like a wild horse fighting to be free.

Clemency, sitting in the grass above the beach, struggled to capture the scene with her pencil; the wind tugged at the pages of her sketchbook as if determined to thwart her efforts. She should have brought her camera, so that she could work on the scene at home, but then she wouldn't be left alone, always half-listening for someone to call her to help do something or go somewhere. It was easier to tussle with the wind than with her family.

She studied the pale faces of the soldiers while they waited to board the ship. She supposed that most of them had never been to sea before; the Pentland Firth on such a day would be a brutal baptism.

They were on their way to the naval base at Scapa Flow, the huge natural harbour ringed by the Orkney Islands. To get there they had to sail through the Pentland Firth, where the Atlantic and the North Sea met like two old foes, the waves crashing and pounding as they came together. There were fearful stories of the crossing, it was said that hardened sailors who'd sailed the world blanched at the very thought of it.

If only she were better at drawing. It was so hard to make the men come alive, show the wind huddling their bodies, hands gripping their kitbags as they waited to leave.

It was May. The lack of trees in this remote part of Scotland gave the wind a free run through the landscape. She loved it up here, loved the savage beauty with the soft, clear light and the rare days of sunshine, offered like an unexpected gift among the overcast days. They'd only ever come up here in midsummer and she wondered how they would cope with the bitter winter. Had Mummy, so set on her role as camp follower, thought of that?

They were staying near Wick with Aunt Mattie. They'd only been here a month and her family was driving her mad. She loved them but why was her mother so stubborn and so *stupid*? She felt guilty thinking it. She'd never fall in love: it stole your freedom, made you a slave to someone else's will.

Her mother, Nancy, was besotted with her father, Gerald, though Daddy didn't deserve her blind love, Daddy was a womanizer. She'd heard Tony Wakeham, her godfather say this to his wife Grace. He didn't know she was listening, they were discussing some party and Tony said,

'Gerald behaved true to form, he's such a womanizer, don't know how Nancy stands it.'

Her mother either turned a blind eye to it or – and this is where the stupid came in – didn't know. Since hearing Tony's remark Clemency had watched him surreptitiously, seen how at parties his eyes roved round the room before he'd pick out a woman and flirt with her. She was not surprised that women found him attractive. He was tall with an easy grace, oozing charm when it suited him. Now, he was serving in the Navy, a commander of a battleship, every inch the hero in his uniform. She was proud of having such a glamorous father, but if only he paid more attention to Mummy. His ship might be anchored in Scapa Flow now; no one knew exactly where the fleet was or where they were going.

Mummy's anxiety about him was the main reason for leaving their home in London and coming up here. Nancy'd heard that many of the RAF and Army wives had followed their husbands to Caithness, and as his sister, their Aunt Mattie, lived up here it seemed perfect sense to follow him. When Nancy had told them her plan she had been as excited as if she was offering them a treat.

'Daddy will be just over the water in Orkney,' she'd said, as if he was going to be permanently anchored there instead of going out on deadly convoys and battles in far off seas.

True to form her sister Verity made a fuss. Gone off the deep end, as Mummy called it. 'We can't leave London and our friends,' she wailed.

Clemency didn't think much of Mummy's plan either, if she kept quiet it might blow over and they'd stay in London. She was almost eighteen, Verity a year and a bit younger, and you'd think that if Mummy wanted to go to Caithness she and Verity could stay in London without her, but there was no chance of that happening. Neither parent would allow them to stay in London, unchaparoned.

When he came to London for a briefing at the Admiralty, Gerald tried to dissuade them.

'It is not safe up there. It may be a phoney war in London but it all started up there in earnest in October. Don't you realize the Huns are after Scapa Flow and the airfields in Caithness?'

Usually Nancy gave in to his wishes and he'd kiss and caress her, delighted to have got his own way. But to everyone's surprise, including his, she'd taken no notice of his scaremongering, and when he'd left to rejoin his ship she'd shut up the house in Kensington, given a key to the housekeeper to the family next door and set off for Scotland.

The troopship started off on its choppy ride. Poor boys: Clemency felt sorry for them. She packed up her sketching things, shoving them in her canvas bag, and hooked it over her shoulder. She wheeled her bicycle over the scrubby grass to the road and cycled on down to Aunt Mattie's house.

It was a good house, square and stalwart against the wind. It had belonged to Aunt Mattie's husband, who had died soon after their marriage. Aunt Mattie wasn't used to company, especially not young excitable women.

Verity was always 'in love'. Clemency supposed she took after Daddy, though she didn't think he loved the women he seduced; it was more a game for him. Verity loved 'her boys' as she called them, until the next 'smashing' one came along. Some of her admirers had been killed and that had shaken Verity and Clemency; this war wasn't meant to kill the people they cared for.

She bicycled almost to Keiss before turning down the track to Aunt Mattie's house.

'Don't you realize that Caithness is a key part of the defence of the country and a base for strikes against the enemy in the Norwegian waters?' Daddy had not been pleased that they had followed him; he tried to scare them back to London. 'There's a strong possibility that if the Huns invade they'll come in up here, where so much of the coast is deserted.'

'Nowhere is safe in wartime,' Aunt Mattie told him. 'There's plenty for them to do up here.'

So here they were and Clemency had to admit that there had been some scary moments. There were occasional dogfights in the sky, like a macabre kind of ballet, those great metal birds darting and dodging between each other, the sea and the sky, in for the kill. It was horrible to see them fall, shot down, spiralling into the sea, but she couldn't help envying those young pilots their freedom in the sky. Thanks to Tony, her godfather, she had learnt to fly and she longed to do it again.

If only she could do something more vital for the war than manning the canteen van at the ''drome'. She'd asked Daddy if she could join the Wrens with some of her friends who were the same age as her, but he'd refused, saying that she was too young to leave home.

'I want to do more than wind bandages and plant turnips,' she'd said, but he laughed, ruffled her hair as if she were a child being amusing. If only she was twenty-one and could do what she liked without his permission, but the war would probably be over by then, or they'd all be dead.

Verity didn't mind what she did as long as it involved men. She'd made enough fuss coming here but she was thrilled to find there were plenty of men from all the forces to choose from. There were dances most nights, at the 'drome or in Wick and army dances in Keiss or Halkirk, with vital young men living on the edge adding to the excitement, and for her there were aeroplanes . . .

She would be eternally grateful to Tony who had given her and his daughter Dory flying lessons at Brooklands as a birthday present. Daddy had disapproved, but Tony had laughed at him and said, 'Come on, Gerald, you wouldn't say that if she were a boy.' And that had been that. There was nothing in the world like the freedom of being alone up there in that vast sky; she'd been intoxicated by it. She longed to fly again, but stuck up here away from everything there was no chance of that, though the sky was often full of aeroplanes: Hurricanes, Spitfires, Wellington bombers. She watched them all, her thoughts flying with them, praying they'd all stay safe.

She'd volunteered to help out with the WVS canteen for the aircrew, and Verity teased her of caring more for the aircraft than the men, and perhaps she did. She had her share of admirers, it was flattering to have so much attention, but she'd rather talk to them about flying than about love. She'd become friendly with Angus, the pigeon keeper who kept carrier pigeons for the pilots to take with them so that if they were shot down they could send a message back as to their whereabouts. He knew more about the planes than anyone and she never tired of his stories.

She reached the house and parked her bike by the side of it, and then for a moment sheltered out of the wind in the lee of the house; she watched the wind buffeting the sea as the tide slipped out and the long, dark rocks appeared on the surface.

'Where have you been?' Verity greeted her from the window seat in the hall. She was curled up reading while watching the drive, hoping that one of her admirers would manage to slip away from his duties and visit her. She stretched and yawned, 'I'm bored, what's on at the cinema?'

'I don't want to go,' Clemency said. They were not allowed out in the evenings alone, unless they could find an excuse such as working in the hospital or handing out hot tea on the platform when the Jellicoe Express passed through. Aunt Mattie had scared Nancy with stories of rampant men scouring the hedgerows in the dark for women to ravish.

'Chance would be a fine thing,' Verity muttered, her water-blue eyes alight with mischief.

'Speak for yourself,' Clemency retorted. The men she'd met had been charming, some very shy. They had left their homes behind and all they wanted was a bit of kindness and she was happy to give it. Some wanted more, but they wouldn't get it from her. The girls up here often talked about, 'how far should they go?' But too far – and the exact meaning of that was rather shadowy – meant babies and no one wanted to be landed with one of those without a wedding ring on her finger. She imagined her parents reaction if it happened to one of them. Promiscuous though her father was, he expected his daughters to remain chaste and ignorant of such matters until their wedding day. Anyway, she felt she had some sort of block on her emotions; she wasn't going to fall in love until after the war, in case the man she loved got killed.

'What's bothering you?' Verity caught her expression.

She wasn't going to mention death, no one talked of it, it was better not to. She said the first thing that came into her head. 'Oh, just thinking what would happen if one of us got pregnant. Daddy would kill us.'

'Don't tell me you've found someone,' Verity exclaimed. 'Go on, do tell.' She hugged her knees, her face eager for gossip.

'No, I haven't. I've been sketching another load of poor chaps off to the Scapa Flow.'

'I think it's time we went there, check out the talent. I'm told that there are six hundred men for every woman.' Verity giggled. 'I'm bored with everyone here, most of the pilots and aircrew are on stand-by or out on reconnaissance all the time.'

'We are at war,' Clemency reminded her.

'Sandy will take us in his old boat. If you won't come I'll go on my own.'

'Daddy's ship might be in, and if he sees you there'll be hell to pay; you know we have to go together.'

It was irritating having to follow such draconian rules when women younger than they had left home and signed up to the Wrens or the FANYs. True, Daddy had seen terrible things in the last war and wanted to keep them safe, but what if she'd been a boy? He'd have expected a son to fight for his country, so why not his daughters?

She suspected that one of the reasons he had laid down such stringent rules was so that they could keep Mummy company and out of his way; though Mummy, who could be quite manipulative, did her bit by having one of her headaches, her 'heads' as she called them, whenever Clemency or Verity grumbled about Daddy's rules or, in Clemency's case, threatened to join the Wrens.

She often sneaked away to draw, but if they went as far as Orkney, where they might have to spend the night, they'd have to find a good excuse to go there, like knowing Daddy's ship was in; then Mummy would want to come too.

Sandy, who was older than God, with a Scottish accent as thick as marmalade, ran an unofficial ferryboat to Orkney and could surely be persuaded, war or no war, to take them on one of his crossings. The idea began to appeal to her. 'We could say we were going to visit Mrs Donaldson.' They had known her since childhood; she'd gone to live in the Orkneys when she married.

'Good idea, let's hatch a plan.' Verity hovered round her excitedly as Clemency changed her shoes and hung up her coat.

'Another time, not now.'

Verity was too impulsive. Their characters were different, and yet they looked so alike that people kept mistaking one of them for the other, though when you saw them together you could see the difference. They were almost the same height, with the same fine skin, fair hair, and the same water-blue eyes, but Verity's hair was slightly curlier than Clemency's, whose face was more oval. Verity loved chocolates – when she could get them – and her face and figure were more rounded. Verity was far more popular with the boys, teasing and flirting with them, while Clemency waited until she felt at ease with them. When they went to the dances it was Verity the attractive men flocked to, leaving the shy and gauche ones to her sister.

'Mummy's lying down with one of her "heads".' Verity followed her up the oak staircase with the carved banisters and pictures of Scottish scenery on the walls. Branching off from the landing was the main living room, the kitchen, a dining room, and a small study, which became the hub of the house when it was cold.

'Something to do with Daddy?' It couldn't be anything serious, not serious as in dead, wounded or missing, or Verity would have told her.

'She thought he'd got a few days' leave and was coming here, but he's been held up.' Verity put emphasis on the words 'held up'. Clemency'd told her what Tony had said about Daddy's reputation. She sighed with exasperation, though to be fair, it might not mean a woman: in wartime nothing ran to plan.

'There you are, Clemency.' Aunt Mattie appeared from the kitchen. Her face, criss-crossed with worry lines made her appear older than she was.

'Dried up and shrivelled, like you'll be if you refuse to fall in love,' Verity had once teased her. She wondered if it were true.

'Please could you both go down to the beach and get some seaweed? Angus McIver has bought us a salmon.' Aunt Mattie's smile lifted her careworn face. 'You know how moist seaweed makes it, especially when it's eaten cold.'

Clemency, tired after her bicycle ride, didn't feel like going. Surely Verity, who'd been reading all afternoon, could go down to the beach on her own, and not be ravished by some sea monster? But the thought of salmon for supper instead of some bland soup consisting mostly of potatoes and strange bits of greenery, cheered her. Fish was ration-free and they often had it, but wild salmon was her favourite.

'Oh and also,' Aunt Mattie sounded vexed, 'I've been asked to billet an airman here and—'

'An airman?' Verity shot an excited glance at Clemency.

Aunt Mattie swept on sternly. 'I've asked for a married man. I don't want anyone, since Wendy has gone. It will mean more work in the house, but we must all pull our weight at such a time.'

Clemency's heart sank; someone else to share the bathroom with and clear up after. Wendy, chief cook and bottle-washer as she'd referred to herself, had left her domestic work to join the land-army.

'What will Daddy say?' she asked.

'He'll expect us to do our duty.' Aunt Mattie's voice was firm as if to remind herself that despite her own misgivings it had to be done. 'I'll put him upstairs in the boxroom. You can help me turn it out. That's all he needs,' she finished sharply as if one of them might protest that the room was too small to sleep in.

'Goodness, what a turn-up,' Verity said as they went downstairs to get their boots on. 'Just because he's married it doesn't mean he'll be ugly.' She giggled.

'It will do if Aunt M has anything to do with it, and he'll have bad breath and smelly feet, so don't get your hopes up.'

As they climbed over the style to the grass sward that ran above the beach, a lone Hurricane flew over them. Clemency watched it, wondering whether it had got detached from the others or was the only one in the squadron to make it back, though it could also be returning from reconnaissance. She was overcome by a wave of dread, a deep sense of loneliness. Death stalked them all; almost every day it seemed to claim someone they knew. What were the thoughts of that pilot? Exhausted? Frightened? Relieved that he had almost made it home?

Women were not allowed to fly in combat, but there were some who flew planes better, or anyway as well as, men. Watching the Hurricane turning lazily towards the airfield at Wick, her longing to fly again was almost painful. She'd logged up over thirty hours' flying before war was declared; that must be good for something. She wanted to do more exciting things than working at the canteen, or helping in the hospital, but unless she could escape from here, and that meant being tough with Mummy and just leaving, there wasn't much hope of doing anything more challenging. There were plenty of organizations she could join up here, but her parents, especially Daddy if he didn't like it, would make it difficult. If she wanted to do anything with some edge to it she'd have to leave here and return south.

'I wish I could do more for the war effort,' she said as they scrambled down the bank to the beach. A bit of the barbed wire had been cut so they could get through: most of the coast round here was ringed with mines in case of an invasion, so they never went far, just on the rocks at low tide.

'I think we do plenty, being kind to the pilots, soldiers and sailors is very important.' Verity pushed back her hair, smiling up at the sky as if the pilot in the disappearing Hurricane could see her 'We must keep their spirits up.'

Clemency said nothing. How irritating Verity could be, thinking only of having a good time. It was pointless talking to her about joining one of the women's forces, but if the chance came she'd take it, whatever her parents said.

CHAPTER TWO

Wing Commander Harry Chatwin had lost his eye in a dogfight at the beginning of the war. He was married, almost thirty, well-mannered and exhausted, running on adrenaline. A suitable man, in Aunt Mattie's view, to be billeted in their all-female household.

Verity dismissed him as being 'too old'.

'Though his black eyepatch and dark hair are quite dashing, sort of heroic,' she reported to Clemency, who'd been working at the canteen when he arrived. He was stationed at Wick in some sort of advisory capacity which he refused, with his charming smile, to discuss if anyone asked him, but, to Verity's delight, he had a motorbike. Perhaps, she said with a giggle, he might be persuaded to give her a lift into Wick sometimes.

Clemency cringed whenever she saw how Mummy fussed round him, keeping the best scraps or an extra egg for him, making sure there was always a warm stone bottle in his bed.

'I know it's suppose to be hush, hush, but do you know anything about the battleships at Scapa Flow?' she'd say, cornering him when he came in. 'My husband is in command of a battleship there,' she told him proudly, as if she was entitled to know the secrets of their movements.

'Sorry, Mrs Franklyn, I don't. Aircraft are my business,' he'd say gently, as if regretful that he could not allay her fears.

'Leave him be, do, Nancy,' Aunt Mattie scolded her if she caught her at it. 'You can't expect the wing commander to put lives at risk.'

Harry was mostly at one of the 'dromes at Skitten or Wick; when he was at home he didn't do much more than sleep in the boxroom Aunt Mattie had assigned to him.

Clemency felt awkward about him being shoved in there when the 'best' room, overlooking the sea, was left empty. She asked Aunt Mattie why he could not sleep there, but Mattie said sharply that she was 'keeping it'. But for whom or for what was never revealed.

'Probably afraid he'll mistake his room for hers,' Verity said with a giggle. Aunt Mattie's room and the guest-room were beside each other along a short passage.

'But the boxroom is so small with all that mismatched furniture shoved in. He deserves better, he works such long hours.' Clemency ignored Verity's question: that would she care so much about his welfare if he hadn't been in the RAF?

News came through about troops being evacuated by an extraordinary fleet of boats and ships that had set off from Britain to Dunkirk. The Germans had cut through Europe like a hot knife through butter, trapping thousands of British and French troops on the beaches. This news aggravated the fear of a German invasion, convincing Nancy that any moment they would be overrun by Huns swarming into their wild landscape from the air and sea. To Clemency's annoyance she began to fuss about her going so far to do her sketching.

'You are not to go to any of that secluded coastline. They'd mow you down in a minute if they saw you.'

'I'd see them coming and get away. Anyway, they'd hardly come in daylight.' To her relief Harry came to her rescue and managed to reassure Nancy.

'Don't worry, Mrs Franklyn, our boys in the air will get them before they get within a mile of Caithness.'

But there wasn't much time for her to go on prolonged painting trips; there was so much to do for the war effort in Caithness. As well as her work with the WVS canteen van, Aunt Mattie suggested that she might help in the hospital in Wick.

'But I've only a rudimentary training in first aid.' Clemency protested, remembering herself and Dory getting the giggles over giving mouth-to-mouth respiration to a life-size doll under the stern instructions of a Miss Fletcher before they'd left London.

But there was plenty she could do, helping with washing and feeding patients and sometimes writing condolence letters to the families of any airmen or soldiers who died there. She hated doing that. How could she, a complete stranger, offer comfort to a parent, a wife, a sweetheart whose beloved man had just died?

But try as she might, her war work bored her, some spark was lacking and though she worked hard she felt she wasn't achieving much.

Apart from the first aid, she and Dory had taken part in a few exercises, lying about in the street pretending they were casualties of a bombing raid. They were often told off for gossiping and warned by the terrifying but competent wardens that when the Huns did bomb them there would be nothing to laugh about. Then she'd come here with the family while Dory stayed in London, no doubt having a wonderful time.

She'd received a dog-eared letter from Dory written over a month ago, saying that some of the women pilots she'd met at Brooklands had teamed up with Gerard d' Erlanger, known as 'Pops', to be trained as ferry pilots – taking medicines and supplies and possibly new planes from the factories to the airfields. Dory thought she might volunteer to do it herself, so if she could escape, might Clemency like to do it too?

The thought thrilled her, though surely she hadn't clocked up enough flying hours? Dory had flown many more hours than she had. But she'd written back saying she'd love to do it if they'd take her.

She was dog-tired; it was nearly the end of her shift at the hospital. She longed for fresh air, she'd bicycle back by the harbour and sketch the old steam drifter, *Lottie*, which was moored near the entrance, ready to be scuppered if the enemy approached.

A violent explosion rocked the building. For a split second everyone froze before snapping into the drill routine designed to protect the patients.

Clemency, upstairs sorting the bed linen, dropped the pile of sheets she'd been holding.

'Bloody Huns, tried to get the harbour,' Doctor McNeal came

puffing up the stairs, 'Best get ready for casualties; broad daylight too. Bloody cheek.'

'What if they drop their bombs on the hospital?' Clemency asked fearfully.

'Just pray they won't.' He dashed into the ward, barking out orders while Clemency hovered at the door wondering what to do. 'Come with me,' he said, running back down the stairs. She felt so inadequate, but she couldn't just stand here by the linen cupboard. *You wanted more excitement*, she reminded herself fiercely, *and here it is so get on with it.*

It wasn't long before victims were brought in.

'Bank Row took a direct hit,' one of the ambulance crew said as he helped a bleeding woman wrapped only in a blanket, into the building. Stretchers followed holding blood-covered casualties, others stumbled in, their clothes hanging off them.

It was like a scene from hell: the cries, the moans, the blood and shattered bodies, some already dead or close to it. Clemency swallowed a gob of vomit that rose in her gullet, leaving a sour sting in her throat. Doctors and nurses sprang into action, assessing patients, some for patching up, others for the theatre, others for the morgue. If only she'd paid more attention to those first aid lectures, but she'd never imagined she'd be faced with such a situation.

She'd faint with all this blood and torn bodies, some screaming for help, others for news of people possibly still trapped. The children were the worst, some frozen like statues with shock. She guided them in, checking as best she could for serious injuries, sitting them down, taking their names, offering words of comfort.

She lost all sense of time. Her head was bursting with the cries of the injured, and the smell of blood, urine and fear. How useless she was in the face of so much suffering, but on and on she worked into the evening, moving the dead away from the living, reassuring terrified people that they were safe while tensed for another bomb attack right here on the hospital.

If only she could get out, lie on the grass gazing up at the sky, she'd never grumble again. She'd seen suffering in the hospital, but then the patients were cleaned up, often sedated. This was the first time she'd seen such brutal injuries and such grief if someone loved had died.

She glanced up for a moment and saw Harry striding into the hospital, obviously on a mission. He looked so smart, so clean in his uniform, standing out like a film star among the rest of them now so tired and dishevelled. He caught sight of her; his face creased in horror then compassion. 'Clemency, were you caught in it? You're covered in blood.'

'No, I . . .' she looked down at herself; there was blood on her clothes. 'I've been helping; not that I can do much.'

He said gently, 'I think you've done all you can here. Give me a moment to check on one of my men who was there, then I'll give you a lift home.'

'I have my bicycle thanks.'

'I'll take you, wait there.' His voice was firm, commanding. He went to the stairs and ran up them two at a time.

He was back a few minutes later.

'More people have come in to help; they say you can go.' He led her outside to his motorbike and helped her on to it.

'Hold on to me.' He started up the bike and they sped off down the road. The grey dusk was swirling in; a slit cut in his headlight cover let out a line of light. Shyly she put her arms round his waist, but as they went on, the wind snatching back her hair, her body aching with exhaustion, she leant against his back. It felt so reassuring, solid and dependable that she closed her eyes, drifting into sleep.

The noise of the bike speeding up the drive alerted those in the house. Verity rushed out, brandishing a torch. They'd heard the explosion and found out that the raid had been over the harbour. Verity wanted to go to Wick to find Clemency, but Aunt Mattie stopped her, explaining that as Clemency was at the hospital she'd have to stay there and make herself useful. But seeing her sister lying against Harry's back, her hair dishevelled and blood on her face, she screamed, waking Clemency and bringing Nancy and Aunt Mattie hurrying downstairs.

'She's not hurt, just exhausted, having helped with the wounded,' Harry said.

Aunt Mattie's face was anxious. 'Is it very bad out there?'

20

'They fell in Bank Row, quite a few casualties.' Harry picked Clemency up, carried her inside and up the stairs to her bedroom, where he laid her gently down on the bed. 'Let her sleep. Now if you'll forgive me I must get back to the 'drome.' He ran down the stairs and roared off into the night.

Clemency kept her eyes closed, trying not to cry. She felt strangely bereft without Harry's arms round her. How safe she'd felt, so close to him after the horrors of the day. She was so tired that she never wanted to move again, but Nancy fussed in, talking of germs and poisons, ordering Verity to bring a bowl of hot water. Then she washed her, pulled on her pyjamas and tucked her up.

When Clemency woke hours later she heard that fifteen people, including seven children, had died. It was the first daylight attack of the war in Britain. Fear whirled round the scattered community: did this daylight attack mean the Huns had now got more ruthless, determined to strike at any time?

Two days later Verity insisted that Clemency should come with her to the dance in Castletown. 'Hitler won't stop *me* enjoying myself. You can't let him get you down.'

'You weren't there Verity, among all those poor people.' Her dreams were tortured with gaping wounds, piercing cries and the sight of the dead.

'I'm very sorry for them, but we can't let him stop us living our lives,' Verity insisted. 'Please come, just for a while.'

Verity was right; it did her good to roll up her hair, put on some make-up and a pretty dress.

Clemency danced every dance. There was no shortage of partners, a steady stream of airmen, soldiers and sailors laughing and struggling through the Scottish reels. The music lifted her spirits and to her surprise, for she hadn't seen him at dances here before, there was Harry. He hadn't seen her since he'd rescued her.

'Clemency, you look wonderful. I'm not a bad dancer. If you keep a lookout on my left we shouldn't knock into anything.'

'Thanks, I'd love to.' She took his hand. The band was playing a waltz as she went into his arms and he whirled her round the floor. She saw Verity slip out with a young pilot and sighed inwardly, hoping she'd take care.

'Do you still fly?' she asked him. She could see the ragged edges of a scar half-hidden by the black eye patch; she didn't like to ask how he had been wounded.

'If I can, but I'm not as good as I was, though I'm still useful, thank goodness.'

'I'd love to fly, I've had lessons.' She told him about Tony's birthday present and Dory's letter. 'I'd like to ferry the planes, perhaps, like Dory wants to do.'

The music stopped and he led her through the chattering throng of people, the air hazy with smoke, to a quiet corner where they could sit down.

'I know women who fly, they belong to the ATA, Air Transport Auxiliary, or,' he smiled, 'I think they call themselves the Always Terrified Airwomen, but believe me you'd never know it. I could put you in touch with them if you want me to.'

'Could you?' she said eagerly, then she slumped back dejectedly. 'Oh, but my parents wouldn't let me, Mummy would have one of her "heads" and Daddy . . .'

A flicker of impatience crossed his face; she felt ashamed that in this time of war she was still under her parent's thumb and would be for another three years.

'If you do hear of something I could do in that direction, please let me know and I'll get there somehow. I bet Dory is in the thick of it. I've written to her but letters take so long to get anywhere,' she said firmly.

He nodded, stifling a yawn; was he just tired or bored with her? Her spirits sank. He wouldn't do anything about putting her in touch with the ATA. No doubt he thought her just a silly, good-time girl like Verity. It was unfair, his thinking such a thing, but perhaps, she thought as she saw Verity coming back in, towing a glowing young man behind her, her sister did her bit by giving these scared young men a touch of love before they hurtled into the sky and often death.

She changed the subject, asking Harry where he lived and where his wife was. At the mention of his wife his face darkened and again she felt awkward: perhaps she had died?

He said, 'I live near Cambridge, my wife is there.'

22

She made some non-committal remark and his good eye fixed on something behind her, as if he were afraid that by looking at her he'd have to divulge more intimate details. 'These are hard times, hard for relationships,' he went on. 'It's probably best to stay single until the war is over.'

'I agree, I don't want to become romantically involved with anyone in case . . .' Her voice petered out as she studied the men around her, now so vital, laughing and flirting, though so many of them, perhaps even in a few hours, would be dead.

'Enjoy while you can,' Harry said. 'Ah, now they are doing an eightsome reel. Want to steer me though it?' He smiled, his face almost tender, and she felt an unexpected surge of warmth for him. Poor man, in charge of so many lives while his own injury had curtailed his flying; it must be a lonely job.

Two days later he was gone.

'Sent back south, but he wouldn't say where.' Nancy was baking scones when she returned from her stint in the hospital. 'He said to say goodbye.'

To her surprise Clemency missed him. Not that she'd fallen for him or anything; it had just been nice to have a male presence in the house. Daddy should be here, she missed him so much.

They'd heard from him last week. He was safe on his ship, based at Scapa Flow but he had not enough time to come across and visit them this time. She needed to see him; to have the comfort of his reassurance that they'd defeat Hitler and everything would be all right. It didn't sound all right from the news bulletins coming from the Bakelite wireless that was almost permanently on in the sitting room. But if he couldn't come to them, why didn't she go to him? Go to Scapa Flow; see what news she could get of him.

She put this to Verity as they struggled to put up the blackouts. 'We'll go over to Scrabster, find Sandy and visit Mrs Donaldson, but we won't say anything to Mummy or she'll either forbid it or want to come too. We'll just leave a note so they'll know where we are, shall we?'

'Oh, yes.' Verity clasped her hands with delight, her eyes shining. 'There are simply hundreds of men over there, we'll have a wonderful time.'

23

CHAPTER THREE

It was just like Verity having agreed to come to Orkney with her, to now moan about having to get up so early, curling up into a tight, unresponsive ball. Clemency felt grumpy enough herself at this early hour, but she wasn't going to be put off by Verity.

'Think of all those boys you will disappoint,' she snapped, lifting the blackout and peering out at the grey ribbon of sea moulding into the sky. 'Sandy will go without us. He can't miss the tide. Don't forget your ID card.'

Clemency crept down the passage to the bathroom, the lino icy under her bare feet. If Verity wouldn't come she'd go alone. She'd be able to sketch the rugged coastline and the Old Man of Hoy without Verity making inane comments about her drawing.

But the thought of seeing so many new men urged Verity on. They crept out of the house with their breakfast, a lump of bread with a scraping of jam. Clemency left a note propped up against the kettle, for Aunt Mattie to find when she came down for her cup of tea. *Gone to Orkney to see Mrs D, and Daddy too, we hope, back soon.*

They pushed their bicycles along the grass verge beside the drive so that Mummy wouldn't hear the crunch of the wheels on the gravel and put a stop to their adventure.

They reached Scrabster in good time, finding Sandy with his beloved boat. He grunted at them; he barely spoke when at sea, as if the sound of the waves and the wind was enough for him.

They were joined by two sailors, who staggered on board still intoxicated and stinking of vomit, and a large woman clutching a basket, who announced that she was going to be with her daughter whose baby was due any day.

'Surprised it hasn't come before with all this carry on.' She gestured to a line of Hurricanes above them, which had just taken off from Wick, on their way to the coast of Norway. Sandy, gnarled as an old tree, saluted them, muttering fearful curses for them to carry with them to the enemy.

Clemency was relieved that the sea was calm; unlike the bucking bronco she'd seen when she'd been here last. She wondered how many of those young men she'd sketched that day were still alive. At last they passed the Old Man of Hoy, a vast stack of rock standing on a lava flow looking out to sea as though watching for invaders, and a short while later Stromness harbour appeared like a mirage, misty in the morning light. Sandy nosed his craft into what he insisted, war or no war, was his corner of the harbour. He threw the rope to a boy who was mooching on the quay and they all trooped off the boat, the sailors now looking scared, thinking of the return to their ship and a likely ticking-off.

Despite knowing the whole place was a war zone, it shocked Clemency to see the amount of camps, guns and other signs of war dotting the bleak landscape, ready to defend the anchorage from the Luftwaffe.

'Perhaps Mrs D has moved away,' She said.

'Won't matter if she has. We only used her as an excuse.' Verity smoothed down her slacks and, unlike Clemency, looked around her with delighted curiosity at the paraphernalia of war that promised an inexhaustible supply of young men. As they passed the military checkpoint she threw a warm smile at the soldier in charge, making him blush.

'We'll go and see if she's here first. If she's gone we'll have to find somewhere else to stay the night,' said Clemency as they wheeled their bicycles alongside the harbour wall.

Sandy called after them. 'Are ye no askin when boatie goes back?' and went into a rigmarole about the tides and 'the watter', leaving them none the wiser, but they told him they'd be back in the afternoon if they wanted to return today; if not, tomorrow.

Mrs Donaldson's cottage was down a cobbled alley, sandwiched between two others and close to the water. The front door was newly painted, and some marigolds shone in a window box. They knocked. After a moment the door opened and Mrs Donaldson peered at them. She held a large and ugly baby on her hip. Her face lifted.

'Oh, what a surprise, Verity and Clemency. Have you come to visit your father?'

'Yes, if he's here, and you too.' Verity stared at the baby.

Mrs Donaldson flushed. 'He's Judy's. Her husband got killed.' She didn't look at them when she said this and Clemency felt for her. So many girls got left with babies from men who disappeared or were killed before they could marry them, or who had scurried back to their wives.

'He's a great boy.' Whatever had his father looked like?

'He's as good as gold. Judy's away in the WAAC and he's a bit of company.' Mrs Donaldson stood aside so that they could come in.

'We wondered if we could stay the night?' Verity glanced round the neat front room, the kitchen and scullery visible through the door. A basket of knitting stood by the sofa, a stack of knitted socks waited ready to be sent to the troops on the table.

'We've bought some home-made jam.' Clemency unpacked her rucksack and handed Mrs Donaldson a jar of blackberry-and-apple jam.

'Thank you. Nothing like home-made. You could sleep down here, I've turned the other bedroom into a room for him.'

'That's fine. Thank you.'

'Have a cup of tea, and a bite to eat, I've been baking.' Mrs Donaldson put the baby down on the floor where he stared at them balefully. 'It's a surprise to see you up here. I'd have thought you would have stayed down south.' She put the kettle on the stove and cut them thick slices of freshly baked bannock.

Clemency told her how her mother had been determined to follow her husband, as many other wives of the military had done.

'It's pretty lively up here. You heard about the *Royal Oak*? Hun crept in through a gap in the Flow, torpedoed it and slipped out again before he was caught,' Mrs McDonald said grimly. 'Lost over eight hundred men. Place wasn't safe, you see; gaps everywhere. Churchill came up himself to see to it and now they're going to build barriers, called after him, to keep the Flow safe. If you ask me it should have been done before, but 'spose it's better late than never.'

'Daddy told us about it. So lucky it wasn't him: he wasn't here at the time. Not many ships were, I don't think, but it must have been dreadful.' Verity shivered, then brightening went on, 'We must enjoy ourselves while we can. We hoped there'd be some dances. Are there any here?'

'Ask Betty next door, she's always gallivanting.' Mrs Donaldson frowned disapprovingly. 'I don't see much, stuck here with John.' She eyed the baby.

'I'm so sorry about your husband,' Clemency said quickly, remembering that he'd been killed at the very start of the war.

'It was a hard time. I don't even have the comfort of knowing he was killed fighting for his country. He fell off the ferry, got caught between the ship's side and the harbour. Crushed he was, drowned.' She took a fierce gulp of tea. 'I'm not the only widow, there are scores of us, some barely married either.'

To distract her from her grief Clemency asked how they could find out about their father's ship.

'Flow was nearly empty yesterday but it could be bristling with warships by now; we never know. But don't leave it until dark to come back or you won't find your way,' Mrs Donaldson reminded them. With no lights and no road signs it was easy to get lost. 'Ask Betty, she knows more about it than I do.'

Betty 'next door' – Clemency never got to know her other name – was a blonde bombshell, and with her carmine lips and curvy figure a magnet for the boys. She was thrilled to meet them and almost at once paired up with Verity. The two girls giggled together, both determined to do all they could to keep up the troops' morale.

They had nothing in common, yet Clemency could not help but like Betty's friendliness. The three of them went together to Kirkwall in a truck with some of Betty's army friends.

'The navy's virtually taken it over,' Betty said gleefully, ''spect you'll find your father there, if his ship's in.'

'How do we get back to Mrs D's if this truck's not there?' Clemency asked Verity quietly as they trundled along, squashed between two fresh-faced soldiers who kept throwing them nervous but appreciative glances.

'Stop worrying; there's a war on,' Verity joked.

It wasn't that Clemency wanted to put a dampener on the evening; she didn't want to be stuck for the night in Kirkwall without transport. But she kept quiet, ashamed of her mundane worries when she heard how unhappy the solders were, 'stuck at the end of the world,' as one put it; icy cold, living in dreadful conditions, with only card games and darts to amuse them apart from rare nights out like this.

They drove up the main street to a hall that was buzzing with people, girls in their glad rags, the men in their uniforms. Verity and Betty, their faces shining with excitement, clutching the arms of two of the men from the truck, were soon swallowed up in the crowd. Joe, another of the soldiers, took Clemency's arm and followed them. Once inside the hall she looked round for Verity, and there in the corner she saw her father. Smiling with pleasure she started across the room to go to him, then stopped. He was sitting close, too close, his arm round a woman, who was gazing at him with cowlike adoration. Clemency froze, her heart pounding.

'What is it?' Joe followed her gaze. 'Someone you know?'

Anger and shame whirled in her; how embarrassing to see her father leaning over that woman. How dare he betray Mummy while she waited so patiently for him at home? She must find Verity so that they could confront him together. She turned to Joe. If only he were older, was someone she could confide in.

'No . . . I thought . . .'

'A ghost?' His mouth drooped with disappointment. He was here for a good time, not to be caught up by some sad situation; there were far too many of those and this evening he wanted to forget them.

She understood his mood, but what was she meant to do? If she left now she had nowhere to go but hang about outside in the cold. If she stayed Daddy would be bound to see them. She must find Verity. They were all so anxious for his safety, with the perilous work he was engaged in, and here he was safe and sound and behaving far too intimately with another woman. She couldn't tear her eyes away from him. He kissed the woman, her red lips bright against his making her burn with fury. How dare he be kissing another woman here instead of trying to get to Caithness to see his wife and family?

There was no sign of Verity. Why couldn't she have waited with her instead of rushing off to goodness knows where and with goodness knows whom? She made an excuse to Joe and marched across the room, dodging through the dancers.

'Daddy,' she exclaimed as she reached his table. He spun round, snatching his hands away from the woman as though they had strayed there without his knowledge. He smiled, the smile that captured so many female hearts.

'Darling, whatever are you doing here?'

'Verity and I came over to find you. We haven't heard from you for ages. Mummy is so worried,' she said loudly, so that she could be heard over the music.

'Verity's here too?' He glanced round the room. 'How are you all?' She read the message in his eyes: *don't make a scene, it means nothing.* She ignored it. The woman wasn't even very pretty; not a patch on Mummy who loved him.

Gerald glanced at his watch.

'I have to get back.' He got up, tall and commanding. 'Excuse me.' He nodded to his companions. 'I must find my other daughter. Goodnight.' He did not look at the woman who lit a cigarette, staring with a hard expression at the wall.

'I'm ashamed of you, Daddy.' Clemency quickened her step to keep up with him. 'Mummy waits for you and you never come.'

He turned to her, a flicker of guilt in his eyes. He grabbed the top of her arm, giving it a little shake.

'You don't understand how hard we work, how many of the ships in the fleet have been blown to smithereens, men floundering in the water, some with terrible injuries and we cannot help them. We have so little time for relaxation.'

'But why don't you come and be with Mummy, or arrange for her to come here?' She was fearful of his anger but worse of losing his love. How could he have time for that woman and not for them?

'I'm only here this evening. We sail before dawn. Find Verity for

29

me, then I must go.'

Betty danced by. Clemency darted forward, startling Betty's partner, and demanded that she must find Verity as their father was here and had to get back to his ship. Betty's eyes appraised him with some curiosity. '*Now*, please.' Clemency stood beside her father as if she had him under arrest.

'I hope you'll not go unsettling your mother over this trivial incident,' Gerald said sternly; then his face softened as he saw Verity, twisting Clemency's heart. He preferred Verity to her; he always had, he and she were two of a kind. *she* never made him feel guilty.

'What a lovely surprise, darling.' He embraced her.

'Daddy, we hoped we'd see you. We came to see Mrs Donaldson and . . .' she giggled, clutching the arm of the sailor she'd been dancing with, 'have some fun.'

The sailor, seeing this older man of high rank, slipped away and Gerald, his face slightly darkening, said, 'Does your mother know you are here?'

'Oh, yes, we are with Mrs Donaldson. We go back tomorrow. We haven't heard from you for ages. Mummy will be so pleased that you are safe. Have you a message for her?'

He did not look at Clemency. 'My love; send her my love.' His voice became sterner.

'It's very dangerous here, I don't like you coming. Stay where you are in Caithness with Aunt Mattie.' He went on to remind them of the dangers from the Luftwaffe, but Verity laughed, saying it was the same in Caithness; they'd even bombed Wick. She never mentioned that Clemency had had to deal with the aftermath, but then Verity wouldn't want to dwell on something so unpleasant when they were here supposedly 'having fun'.

Gerald left soon after, kissing Verity warmly and Clemency less so. He squeezed her shoulder.

'Be sure to give your mother my love.' His eyes bored into her, demanding her silence.

The words, *just the dregs of it, I suppose*, hovered on the tip of her tongue but she suppressed them, saying firmly instead, '*You* must come and see her.'

He nodded curtly and then he was gone, leaving her tortured with the thought that she might never see him again. His ship might be blown up and his shattered body left to drown in the sea, as had happened to so many others before him.

CHAPTER FOUR

Clemency was still haunted by the carnage and suffering that afternoon at Bignold hospital. She wanted to do something more vital to help win the war. There was plenty to do up here, but as she had no proper training for anything she could only do menial jobs. She tried to telephone Dory, but there was no answer. Clemency would be sick with envy if she heard that Dory was flying with the ATA while she was stuck up here, handing out tea and cakes to the pilots and aircrew at the 'drome, the nearest she got to flying.

She recognized each type of plane by the sound of the engine. Sometimes they were scrambled many times a day, the Spitfires and the Hurricanes valiantly fighting off the Huns, the sky buzzing with dogfights. So many were lost in that treacherous sea. She'd talked about it with Angus. Even if his pigeons came home alerting him to the positions of the downed pilots, if they'd ditched in the sea the cold usually finished them before they could be rescued. She longed to be part of the easy camaraderie of the pilots, to be up there sharing the vast freedom of the sky. She wrote to Dory again.

She became increasingly impatient with her family, which made her feel guilty. It was hardly Aunt Mattie's fault that food was scarce, but she seemed to find pleasure in their austere way of life, cooking soups or scraps of unidentifiable animal – Verity swore they were rats – under a pastry cover. And if she had to knit another pair of socks for the troops she'd scream, she was so bad at it. Any poor soldier who had to wear her socks would probably end up with deformed feet. Verity hid notes in the pairs of socks that waited to be sent, adding her address as her way of 'offering support'. She'd had letters back, which she sometimes answered but mostly discarded, leaving Clemency grieving for the possibly lonely solider reading Verity's note and imagining a loving girl to come home to.

Verity annoyed her most: the party girl with her string of boys and the hours she spent dressing up. Stockings were scarce so the girls painted their legs with a line for the seam down the back when they went out, but Verity would do it even for cooking at the canteen. 'I don't know why you don't bother, Clemency. Your legs look like uncooked sausages,' Verity would say when Clemency turned up at the 'drome when it was almost time to pack up. Though Clemency had the last laugh when it rained and the colour ran down Verity's legs, giving her skin an unsightly look as if she had some disease.

It was mid-September when a letter arrived from Dory. When Clememcy and Verity returned that evening, it lay there waiting for her on the brass dish on the hall table.

Verity snatched it up.

'A letter for you. Who's it from?' She held it away from Clemency laughing. 'Have you a secret lover?'

'Don't be silly; it's probably from Dory. Please give it to me.' Clemency held herself in check, knowing that if she tried to wrestle it off her Verity would tease her further. She might even tear it open and tell everyone what it said. If it contained anything about joining the ATA, it would scupper her chances.

She forced herself to go upstairs, as if the letter meant nothing to her, though inside she was churning with impatience and anxiety. To her relief Verity tired of her teasing and threw it at her.

'Have your silly old letter, then.'

It lay on the dark wood of the step. Clemency picked it up.

'I'm popping,' she said and darted upstairs to the lavatory, locking the door before opening the letter.

Dearest Clem,

You must come here to White Waltham to do the ATA training course with me. We desperately need more people. I cannot bear to tell you how many young pilots are lost trying to defend us, especially during that terrible time in August – masses of them killed or seriously injured. When

*we've passed our test we deliver – at the moment only light,
single engined aircraft – typical! to the airfields, or the MU
(stands for Maintenance Unit where planes go to be fitted
with instruments etc.) or act as a 'taxi' service – but it's a
great joke. Can you escape the clutches? Come as soon as
you can.*

*I'm in love with a flying ace, Johnny Elliot; he looks like
a matinée idol (teased about it by his friends) and he's got
eight kills to his name and rising. If we ever get through this
we might marry and fly off together into the sunset.*

The letter rambled on, Dory's writing getting increasingly
untidy, making it difficult to decipher, but Clemency worked out
that when Dory was not at White Waltham she was living alone
in her parents' flat in London. Her mother was in the country and
her father was serving in North Africa. Clemency must get away as
soon as possible – and as her home in Kensington was shut up she
could stay with Dory in the flat – what fun they would have.

She enclosed her address at the training base and told her to
send her a telegram to let her know when she'd arrive, but to do it
quickly while there were still places.

Clemency shoved the letter in her pocket, elation followed by
despair chasing through her. She stared out of the lavatory window
at the wide, open sky strewn with skeins of cloud. A small snapshot
of a tranquil view: who would guess from it that they were at war?
The longing to fly again took hold of her like a fever. Dory seemed
to think it was possible for her to fly *if* she could get on the training
course. She felt wild with despair, how could she get there?

Daddy would forbid it; he'd never let her fly. He'd once remarked
that flying was men's terrority, women would only make a mess of
it, be a nuisance and need rescuing all the time. There were plenty
of other things for women to do; they had some cheek thinking
they could take over the men's jobs. Mummy would side with him;
would get one of her 'heads', filling Clemency with guilt. She knew
all their arguments; it exhausted her just thinking of them.

But nothing could be worse than that day at Bignold hospital.
She'd coped then, after a fashion, and if Dory could ferry planes

then so could she. Somehow she'd escape their clutches and get there under her own steam. She daren't confide in Verity, she might let something slip to one of her boys and Mummy or Aunt Mattie might hear of it when they worked at the canteen.

She unlocked the lavatory door, remembering to pull the chain, but Verity was not there, so she went into their bedroom and hid Dory's letter under her mattress. Verity was always going through her drawers, borrowing things, and this was the only safe place, for although Aunt Mattie expected everyone to turn their mattresses once a month they rarely did.

The obvious way to get to London was to take the train from Wick down to Inverness and catch the sleeper on to London. She wouldn't be able to take much luggage as she'd attract the family's attention, but she could do it. She had money, not a lot but enough. Daddy gave them both a small allowance and she hadn't spent much for ages. She wondered if she'd be paid to ferry planes, but if, as Dory seemed to suggest, they lived in some camp she assumed that her living expenses would be catered for.

She needed to discuss it with someone she trusted. She thought of Alice Weaver, a girl whom she particularly liked, who was in the WAAF and worked at the 'drome. She saw her the following evening when she and Verity were at the Pavilion to see Flash Gordon. Alice saw her, waved and came over. Verity saw a man whom she knew, and walked over to him, leaving Clemency free to tell Alice of her plan.

'Alice, I want to ask you something important. Keep this to yourself.' She turned her back on Verity in case she could lipread. 'I want to get down south without my family knowing, meet up with a friend who is training to be a ferry pilot and see if they'll take me on.'

Alice's eyes shone with admiration. 'Gosh, could you really do that? Do you know how to fly?'

'Yes, I had lessons before the war. My friend Dory is in the ATA and training to be a ferry pilot. They are taking on women so I'm hoping they'll take me.' She sighed. 'But my family will forbid it. I want to see if they'll accept me and if they do, then I'll tell them. Once I'm there they'd probably let me stay. It's just that if I asked first they'd panic and ... you know how it is.' She lowered her voice even more. 'I'm not even telling Verity.'

'I won't say a word,' Alice promised. 'But do be careful, Clemency. I've heard that the ferry pilots have no ammunition to protect themselves if they meet enemy planes, and have even been shot at by our people. It's frightfully dangerous.'

'Everything is frightfully dangerous in wartime.' Clemency reminded Alice of the bombs that had been dropped in Bank Row.

'Well, count on me, of course I'll help. You could hide your stuff in my room, or I could pick you up in the truck.'

'What are you two whispering about?' Verity joined them, her eyes flicking from one to the other. 'Secrets? Do tell.'

'No secrets, just gossiping,' Clemency said. 'Come on, we'd better get back.'

It was infuriating that she couldn't talk it over with her family, that she couldn't leave with their blessing. She'd turned eighteen at the end of July, they were at war, and it was time they stopped treating her like a child.

'I feel badly about leaving my mother,' Clemency told Alice as they wandered round Woolworth's before going to the Chic Café for a cup of tea. She'd confided in her and told about her father and the woman she'd seen him with in Orkney.

Alice, examining the lipsticks, said, 'It's their marriage, not yours. You must do what you think is right for you, Clemency, and if your flying skills can be used to fight the war, then do it.'

'You're right, I shall.' She was filled with determination.

They made a plan for the following week, the middle of October. Alice would come by with the truck and wait on the road outside the house for Clemency to join her, then she would drive her to the station. When the train had gone she would put Clemency's letter, explaining it all to her family, in the box outside the house.

Clemency spent the days leading up to her departure in a fever of anxiety. She'd bicycled over to Scrabster to send Dory a telegram at the post office there, saying she'd arrive at her flat on 15 October. Now there was no turning back. It was fortunate that Aunt Mattie and Mummy were very occupied with the WVS and didn't notice any change in Clemency's mood. Verity noticed and grumbled about her distraction, but she was 'in love' again, with a soldier and was more intent on finding ways to meet him than deciphering her sister's moods.

She managed to pack her suitcase without Verity seeing, hiding it in the back of the gun cupboard the evening before she was due to leave.

She could hardly eat that last supper with her family. She'd felt so irritated with them, but now the time had come to leave them she dreaded it. What if she never saw them again? What if they were caught up in some bomb raid like the one in Bank Row? But she must not think like that. Ever since Dory had told her about the ATA she'd wanted to be a ferry pilot more than anything. If they wouldn't let her fly, she'd come back here and carry on as she was.

'You look peaky, Clemency.' Aunt Mattie studied her as she pushed her food round her plate.

'I'm not feeling too good.'

'You need a dose,' Aunt Mattie said. Verity suppressed a giggle. Their aunt put all moods down to needing a good 'clear out' and left a bottle of syrup of figs on the windowsill in the bathroom, with a spoon beside it.

Clemency barely slept, and at dawn she crept out of bed to dress in the bathroom so as not to wake Verity. There was no time for breakfast; she didn't dare to go into the kitchen to make some tea so early and disturb them.

She ran down the stairs to the hall and unlocked the door, holding her breath, fearful they would hear the click of the lock, the rattle of the chain. She waited, listening for a moment in case she had disturbed one of them, before putting on her coat and retrieving her case from the gun cupboard. A car crunched up the drive and stopped outside the door. Surely it wasn't Alice? Her stomach clenched, she'd expressly told her to wait in the road where she could not be seen from the house.

Through the window, to her horror, she saw her father get out of the vehicle. He must have caught her expression for he frowned. He opened the door and came in.

'I'm here for a night,' he greeted Clemency, his eyes hard on her, his voice defiant as if she'd start on about that woman she'd seen him canoodling with.

37

'You could have warned us,' Clemency blurted in despair. However could she get away now?

'Thought I'd surprise you. Your mother here?'

'Of course, she's upstairs, still in bed.'

'Visitors?' He glanced at the suitcase.

She'd been caught red-handed.

Seeing her confusion he demanded, 'What's going on?'

Her heart fluttered with anxiety. Alice, who was breaking rules by doing this and would be severely punished if she were caught, could only come by in the next ten minutes.

'Just things for the laundry,' she said.

'I think you are lying.' He took a step towards her, his hand out as if he would snatch up her case and open it. 'Are you running off with someone?'

'Of course not,' she retorted, mortified that he would think such a thing.

'Who is he? Is he coming here? Well, he'll find me and then he'll be sorry. I'll report him to his commanding officer, I'll—'

'I am not going away with a man, I'm going to join Dory and fly planes.' The words shot out of her. 'I'm sick of making tea and winding bandages, I want to do something important, and she's joined the ATA and so can I?'

His expression hardened, she saw a flash of something bordering on panic in his eyes.

'I forbid it. We are fighting a war and no one has time to pander to silly women who want to play at flying. They will never take you on and then what? You'll be all alone in London.'

'I'm going. I must go now and if you try and stop me . . .' Alice could only wait a short time before she'd have to abort their plan.

'I am going to stop you. I am your father and you are not yet twenty-one. I will not allow you to be alone in London.'

'I won't be alone, I'll be with Dory and the other women at the base and if you won't let me go I will tell Mummy about that time I saw you in Kirkwall, let her know about *your* war work,' she said in panic.

'You will not bring your mother into this. You don't understand about life. Why should you hurt her with something that means

38

nothing to me?'

There was logic in his words; it would destroy Mummy, she might choose not to know, or be entirely in the dark about his womanizing, but Clemency didn't want to be the one to make her confront it. The minutes ticked by; the grandfather clock in the hall sounded each second slowly and methodically, each one striking her heart, counting down an end to her dreams. There was a movement above and Verity called out.

'Is someone there? It sounds like Daddy.'

'Yes,' Clemency called. 'It is. Such a surprise. Get Mummy.'

'Gerald?' She heard her mother's voice. 'Is it really you?' There was the sound of footsteps running down the stairs.

'I'll tell her now,' Clemency said quietly. 'It is you who's responsible for hurting her, not me.'

He threw her a murderous look. 'Stay there, I forbid you to leave.' He started up the stairs to meet his wife. 'My darling, I'm here.'

Clemency didn't wait; she snatched up her handbag, picked up her suitcase and ran out down the drive without looking back. A few planes roared overhead, as if egging her on. 'Soon it will be me, up there.' she thought, running down the drive, her suitcase banging against her legs. To her great relief Alice was there. She threw her case in the truck and jumped in.

'I was just about to leave; thought you'd changed your mind. You're quite sure you want to do this?' Alice started up the truck.

'Yes. Go quickly. Daddy's just come home and has forbidden me to go.'

They got to the station just as the train was about to leave. She jumped in, convinced that Daddy would arrive at any moment and stop her. But the train started off without hindrance. She found a space in a crowded carriage and sat back with relief, watching the station slip away, and caught one last glimpse of Alice waving.

At Inverness she stayed out of sight, afraid that Daddy might have sent someone to stop her, but no one took any notice of her and she boarded the sleeper for London.

CHAPTER FIVE

After many freezing hours and one last belch of steam the train shuddered to a halt at Euston. Clemency stretched, drowsy from the rancid atmosphere, the smell of unwashed bodies and nicotine. The train was bursting, mostly with military people snatching a few precious hours of leave, their faces ashen with exhaustion.

Her heart ached after that scene with Daddy; it was just her luck that he'd arrived on a rare visit at the very moment of her departure. Why had she been such a fool as to tell him where she was going? It had been his unfair insinuation that she was running away with a man that had thrown her, made her blurt out her destination. Would he play the heavy father and contact White Waltham and insist they turn her down? She must not let her imagination spin away with her but wait and see what happened. The ATA might not want her. But maybe he'd be relieved that she had gone and so could not carry out her threat of telling Mummy about that woman? It was no good speculating, but if only she had left with his blessing and his love.

This was the first time in her life that she'd been alone without a member or a friend of her family making the choices for her. It scared her and yet beneath that fear shone a glimmer of elation. It was too late to back out now.

She shrank into the crowd, keeping her head down in case Daddy had sent someone to meet her and take her home, but no one took any notice of her; everyone was too intent on their own lives. She relaxed, but contrarily felt disappointed that he had let her go so easily.

Dory's flat was in Victoria; Clemency had known it since

childhood. Grace, Dory's mother, preferred the country life, so she mostly stayed in their house in Hampshire. Clemency knew Tony better; he had given her flying lessons and that alone would make her love him for ever.

She took a taxi to Dory's flat, shocked by the devastation all around her, the piles of rubble where buildings used to be, their skeletons stark against the sky. The taxi driver, a dour man in a tin hat, told her with grim detail about the raids.

"spect you wish you 'adn't come now,' he finished.

'We had bombs too, but not on this scale.' She shuddered; how terrible it must be to face this night after night.

The driver skilfully negotiated his way across London, bypassing streets that had been closed by bomb damage. But despite the devastation the streets were busy, people seemingly going about their business as if they barely noticed their beleaguered city. A couple of officers in uniform with girls in evening dresses passed her, laughing together as if they had not a care in the world. There was Big Ben stoically standing there and her heart lifted, the Hun would have a difficult time breaking the Londoners' spirit.

They were nearing the flat now. Clemency felt excited, yet guilty too. How would Verity get on without her? She'd write to her tomorrow. And Mummy? She swallowed a lump in her throat; perhaps she shouldn't have done this, but how else would she have got away to follow her dream?

She arrived at the block of flats, went up to the first floor and rang the bell: two sharps bursts, as Dory had told her. There was a scuffling inside and she heard Dory's voice close to the door.

'Who goes there, friend or foe?'

Clemency giggled, relief flooding through her.

'Friend.'

Dory opened the door and pulled her inside. Wellington, her Norfolk terrier, barked a welcome, his claws skittering on the wooden floor.

'You came! I never thought you'd get away.' With her arm tightly through Clemency's, Dory led her through the hall where two elephants' feet – which had shocked Clemency as a child, held a collection of walking-sticks, umbrellas and tennis racquets, into the more feminine drawing room with its blue silk curtains and cream-and-blue chintz upholstery.

'I so nearly didn't; Daddy arrived just as I was leaving.' Clemency dropped down on a chair and told Dory what had happened, telling her about the woman she'd seen her father with in Orkney.

'That's mean, with your mother so near,' Dory exclaimed. 'But the war, you know, it changes people.'

Clemency didn't like to say that he'd been like that before the war, instead she said, 'You've cut your hair.' Dory's unruly curls were now tamed into a short bob.

'Looks better under the forage cap. You'll have to cut yours too, or tie it back. I'll take you to my hairdresser tomorrow.'

'But the ATA might not want me. I haven't flown for ages.' Clemency couldn't believe that she was actually here, about to go to White Waltham with Dory. She thought she had better not get too excited, as they might not want her.

'Oh they will, you fly well. I told them all about you and who our instructor was and he has the best reputation. You're needed, that's the thing; there's a great shortage of pilots.' Then Dory's sparkle faded. 'Too many young men in Fighter Command have been killed; they can't spare a single RAF pilot to deliver planes, so that opens the way to us. Anyway . . .' she brightened, 'you're going to be trained. There's a flying test, but you'll easily pass that, and a dirty old doctor who makes you take off all your clothes for the medical.'

'Oh, horrors!'

'Take no notice of him, he's a sad old man. I firmly kept my undies on and gave him such a look he didn't insist. But listen,' she grabbed Clemency's hands excitedly, 'I've got two days' leave before we must go back. I'll telephone a couple of chaps and we'll go out, London is buzzing, Hitler can't stop us having fun.'

Exhilaration surged through Clemency. Dory was only three months older than she was, and since the outbreak of war she had managed to break free of her family. Clemency was now determined to do the same; she was eighteen for goodness' sake; old enough to live her life as she pleased.

'Is your father back?' she asked, wondering whether Tony might turn up any moment.

'Sadly no, he's miles away, still in North Africa.'

Dory took her to Bruno, her elderly hairdresser, who told her he considered his war work to be keeping the women pretty to cheer up 'our brave boys'. His remark reminded her to write to Verity.

Clemency suppressed a sigh as the first gleaming strand of her hair fell to the floor. What if they turned her down? It would take ages to grow again.

Dory lent her an evening dress for the evening, in turquoise silk. It was far more glamorous than the one she'd pushed in to her luggage at the last minute 'just in case'.

She managed to scribble a quick note to Verity.

Sorry I had to rush off but need to do more for war effort. I suppose everyone is furious with me and sorry to leave you in it, but am well and will send my address later. Use Dory's otherwise, but we are leaving there tomorrow.

Two fighter pilots, Teddy Osborne, and Charles Evans appeared at six o'clock. Charles, a stocky man with an infectious grin, was in love with Dory, but, as Dory had told Clemency in great detail, she was in love with Johnnie Elliot, whom she hardly ever saw as he was stationed in Wales.

Teddy was tall, with auburn hair and though Clemency found him attractive, she sensed that there was a ruthlessness about him that unsettled her. But tonight was for having fun; tomorrow she was off to White Waltham and if she was taken on she would soon be flying.

They went to the Berkeley for cocktails finishing up at the Savoy for dinner and dancing. The men joked about their flying exploits, light-hearted banter glossing over the dangers that stalked them. Clemency soon got the hang of it; nobody dwelt on the painful things, friends who would never come back. If they were shot down you drank to them and moved on, it was a vital part of self-preservation and keeping up the moral of the squadron. Successful pilots kept their emotions and imaginations firmly in check; it was a lesson she had better learn if she was to be any good at her job.

'You girls aren't allowed to fly in combat, but I bet you'd give old Jerry a run for his money,' Charles said to her. 'How long have you flown?'

'Dory's father gave me lessons as a birthday present with her. I think I have clocked up over thirty hours.'

Teddy looked dubious so she went on, 'Dory thinks I'll soon pick it up again and there's training.' Now she had broken free and was here in the thick of it, mixing with fighter pilots, talking about flying as if she were one of them. She could not bear to go back to Scotland.

'We need every pilot we can get, so now even the most stuffy of the top brass accept that women ferry pilots are essential.' Charles smiled encouragingly at her.

Dory drove them to White Waltham in her Humber. 'I managed to get a few extra petrol coupons, but Wellington and I often take the train,' she said. They picked up Jane Glover, another flyer, a cheerful ginger-haired girl and the two of them regaled Clemency with stories of their flights.

'We're not allowed near anything too fast, it's mostly Proctors and Lysanders, or Tiger Moths with an open cockpit, and people say that in the winter pilots have to be chipped out of those with an ice pick.'

Earlier that morning Clemency had gone round to her London home off Kensington High Street. It had been shut up for the war but Mrs Paxton, the next door neighbours' housekeeper, had a key and Clemency, Dory and Wellington went in to find Clemency's flying-boots and helmet and a few of her mother's evening dresses. The rooms seemed ghostly with the furniture covered in dustsheets. Wellington dashed about sniffing madly, making her anxious that mice or, even worse, rats, had got in.

'He's just showing off,' Dory said, calling him unsuccessfully to heel.

The empty house depressed Clemency; she was relieved to lock the door behind them. Her old life seemed to be suspended in the past, like a stage set waiting for the actors to bring it alive. Would her life ever the same again? Once the war was over would they just go back to what they had been before or was that style of life lost for ever?

Dory had brought her fur coat. Clemency wished she had one, but Dory gave her a thick blanket. 'You can wrap yourself up in that in bed, and in the plane if it's really bitter.'

Dory was part of the group of women pilots at White Waltham who had flown with the Brooklands flying club. It was Dory's influence that had got Clemency here in the first place. They'd taken her word that Clemency could fly and Clemency prayed she wouldn't let them down, but she would not go to get her uniform at Austin Reeds, 'just in case they don't want me,' she said when Dory suggested it.

'It was a scream,' Dory said, shrieking with laughter. 'The tailors had never measured a woman for a uniform before and kept as far away from us as they could. They tried not to touch us as they measured us and only looked at the tape measure when they had moved away. You can't imagine what the trousers looked like.' She rolled her eyes. 'The crotch was at our knees. We had to measure them ourselves and send them back to be altered.'

They arrived at the base and Clemency struggled to hide an attack of nerves. How dare she come here among all these experienced people? Dory reassured her, introducing her to the head of her unit who, to Clemency's amazement, after asking her a few questions seemed happy enough to accept her for training.

She passed her medical; to her relief the voyeur doctor was not there. Then she signed the secrets form, which made her realize how serious this job was. The training was tough, with intense classes covering everything from meteorology to how to steer clear of church steeples and barrage balloons whose lethal cables tethered them to the ground. Whenever they could they went to London to meet friends. She became accustomed to the battered buildings, some ripped open as if by a giant cleaver, exposing rooms like snapshots of people's lives. She became familiar with the wails of the 'moaning Minnies,' as the sirens were nicknamed, and the sound of bombs falling. It was a tough, unreal kind of life but she thrived on it.

Johnnie, Dory's love, appeared for a few short hours on leave. It was obvious why his nickname was Matinée Idol. He was beautiful without being effeminate, sending a flutter of desire through them all, but he had eyes only for Dory.

Many of the men – their uniforms adding to their glamour – attracted Clemency, but she was determined not to fall in love until the war was over. Besides it was all such fun, meeting so many amusing people, dancing every night you could get off, and even if there was a raid it still all went on, most people not even bothering to go into a shelter.

She received a letter from Verity, and one afternoon she telephoned her. Verity was breathless; Clemency imagined that she'd been sitting on the window seat in the hall watching for visitors and had bolted up the stairs to answer the telephone on the landing.

'There was such a fuss. Why did you go? Surely there's enough to do here, and besides you're missing so many parties,' Verity said.

'Are you allowed to go on your own? I was worried that by leaving I'd put an end to your social life.'

'I've got other girls I can go with. Can you get out or are you stuck in your training place?'

'There are parties here too, when we can we go to London and—'

'London. I wish I was there.' Verity sounded wistful; then she perked up. 'I often go to the Orkneys to see Betty and I'm in love with quite a few people, but as Betty says, safety in numbers.'

Their minutes were running out and Clemency managed to hear that Mummy, after having hysterics at her leaving was, with Aunt Mattie's support, getting on with life. Daddy was furious, swearing that as she'd left the house after being 'expressly forbidden' not to, he would not speak to her again until she returned and apologized.

'Oh, and there was another hit on Wick,' Verity said just before the pips went. 'I think they were meant for the 'drome but they fell in Hill Avenue.'

'Take care.' It was as if an icy hand touched her; would they ever all be safe together again?

To her dismay Dory and Jane, having started training before her, left White Waltham for the ferry pool at Hatfield, leaving Clemency without their support. Some of the other girls kept themselves to themselves, or moved in little cliques that excluded her.

46

It made her even more determined to work hard so that she could rejoin Dory.

Christmas, her first away from home, was hard; they only had a couple of days off. She met up with Dory in London and went to parties there. She rang home and her mother answered, the anxiety in her voice filling Clemency with guilt.

'Are you all right, darling? I can't help worrying about you.'

'I'm fine, Mummy. I'm sorry I had to leave like that, but you wouldn't have let me go otherwise.'

'You're too young and women can't fly, shouldn't fly. Your father forbade you to go and . . . he knows best.'

'If I were a boy he'd have expected it of me,' Clemency answered quietly. There was not much more to say, the silences between them said it all.

'Daddy hopes to come tomorrow.' Nancy sounded excited.

'Give him my love.'

There was an ache in her throat as she rang off. She pictured them all sitting round in the study, a fire in the grate, the curtains drawn tight against the cold. Perhaps they would be doing a jigsaw or playing a board game, with the gramophone on or the wireless. And later, when Daddy would be there, being proud of her, but that was a luxury she'd have to wait for.

Four days after Christmas, when they were safely back in the country, London received its worst hit so far. All night the city blazed with incendiary bombs. So many people lost everything and three of the girls at the base lost people they loved, fighting in action. Everyone's life was so precarious that Clemency felt she had no right to indulge in self-pity.

CHAPTER SIX

She'd been expecting it, it nagged at her at odd moments, but when Clemency's final flying test came, it shocked her. She'd put in the hours of flying cross-country, following rivers and landmarks to familiarize herself with the terrain, but this was her last hurdle before she could get her wings and become a ferry pilot. She'd passed her practical and learnt to fly the Tiger Moth and one plane in the class from the aircraft she'd be permitted to fly, though the 'First Eight', the women pilots who were at the forefront of the ATA, were gradually breaking down the prejudice against women pilots so that they were being permitted to fly other classes.

One of the 'First Eight' came over to Clemency. 'Meet you there in half an hour,' she said.

'Fine.' Clemency gulped down her tea, her heart fluttering, yearning for a moment of commiseration, a smile of encouragement from one of the other women sitting here, but they seemed too preoccupied to notice her. There was no sentiment here among the pilots: you couldn't afford it with so many people not coming back; especially the fighter pilots they felt close to through flying their planes. She'd known the flying test would be imminent, was impatient for it so that she could join Dory and Jane at Hatfield, but now it was here she was scared she'd fail and be chucked out.

You left your family for this, get on with it, she reminded herself firmly, wishing Dory were here to tease her out of this mood.

She was dressed in her ATA uniform, but she went and changed into trousers. Some of the top brass had insisted the women fly in skirts, though later, when a woman had had to bale out in her skirt and complained at how immodest it was they had relented. They could fly in trousers or their Sidcot flying suits as long as they

48

changed back into skirts when they were safely on the ground.

How she loved the power of flying, the freedom of the wide, clean sky, but now, with the possibility of having to use her skills to ferry a vitally needed plane alone to some faraway airfield, she felt like running away. Dory would understand her fear, her feeling of inadequacy. It would be like that which she'd experienced in Bignold hospital when the bomb victims were bought in, though her flying skills were far superior to her nursing ones.

The airfield was alive, the aircrew were busy with the planes. A plane started up and set off. Every pilot had to go through this test and she could not expect their sympathy. The eight women who had started this group had fought so hard to prove that women were as competent as male pilots; in fact they had to do better, as they were not excused even minor accidents. She could not let them down.

Curbing her agitation she made her way to the aircraft. A man came towards her, walking smartly, glancing at his watch. He wore an eyepatch: it was Harry.

'Harry.' Her heart leapt at seeing him, a reminder of home, where she'd been safe. 'What are you doing here?' What a stupid question; he was part of the RAF, why shouldn't he be here and what business was it of hers anyway?

'Clemency?' he exclaimed in surprise. 'So you made it. I thought . . .' Well,' he looked embarrassed 'that you . . .'

'Preferred parties and love affairs like my sister, Verity,' she finished for him.

'Yes . . . if you like. But well done, I'm so pleased you got here.' His warm smile touched her heart.

'I'm just about to take my test, and if I pass I'll be off to Hatfield to start work,' she told him. She heard the fear in her voice and cursed herself; she'd meant to sound joky but her nerves had got the better of her.

He laid his hand on her shoulder, his good eye gazing down at her. 'You'll be fine, you'll see. Look forward to hearing about it when we meet again.' He squeezed her shoulder, then he was gone and she heard him calling for his driver.

Her examiner was waiting; she got in the rear seat and Clemency climbed into the cockpit, her insides churning with apprehension.

Talking down the speaking tube her examiner gave her her instructions. She familiarized herself with the controls and taxied off down the runway. She had the feel of it, the controls seemed safe in her hands, her fear left her and it felt so right to be here. Gently she eased the throttle, the nose rose up obediently and she was airborne. She climbed to 2,000 feet, the wind rushing past her, but she didn't notice it. She turned right and then left: easy, smooth turns; she repeated the same manoeuvre again but more steeply.

It was done but she waited for the last thing. Her examiner would cut the engine and she must make a forced landing. Although she was tensed, waiting for it, it shocked her when it came and it needed all her control and nerve to land safely.

'Well done. Now report back after lunch for a lift to Hatfield,' her examiner said. She got out of the Moth and strode away.

The rigger fussing round the Moth winked at her. 'Another one to put the wind up the Jerries,' he joked and she smiled back, elated. She'd done it; now she really was a member of the ATA and was at last doing something important to help win the war.

As she entered the mess she looked round for Harry before remembering that she'd heard him call for his driver; she felt a pang of disappointment. His moment of kindness had saved her, helped her to pass the test.

Later she was dropped at Hatfield. Eagerly she looked round for Dory, but she didn't turn up until much later, looking exhausted.

'Had a terrible journey back in a freezing train, but so glad you are here,' she said, giving Clemency a hug. 'You'll probably have to do a spell of taxiing, but they'll soon find you a plane to deliver, there are far more coming out of the factories than there are ferry pilots.'

Clemency was shocked to see how tired Dory looked. She'd heard enough stories to know of the dangers they faced. Ferry pilots could be shot down by a passing Luftwaffe plane, or even by someone from their own side mistaking them for an enemy plane. They were supposed to fly low, under the cloud, as they did not carry enough fuel to go too high and land safely at their destination. Flying low was supposed to keep them away from the Luftwaffe who, on the whole flew high to avoid being shot at, but it didn't always work. Ferry pilots could become disorientated in bad weather and get snared in the cables of the barrage balloons, or crash into the sea, or into the brooding mountains in Wales. They all knew pilots who'd been killed but no one could afford to dwell on it.

'I must catch a few hours' sleep and catch up with Wellington before I'm wanted again,' Dory said. 'I take him with me sometimes on short flights; he loves it, I think he could almost fly himself.' With a cheerful wave she was gone.

As Dory had predicted Clemency's first assignments were as a taxi driver, flying a Fairfield Argos or Avro Anson round the airfields, picking up ferry pilots and taking them back to base, or dropping pilots at the factories to collect a plane to be delivered. These flights were social and chatty, the pilots were glad to relax before they took off again – sometimes delivering four or five planes a day. At other times she flew military personnel about; she had hoped that Harry might be one of them, but she didn't see him, though Dory said she had flown him a couple of times.

'I remember him because of his eyepatch, and also because he was so complimentary about my flying,' she told Clemency. 'Some of the men are impossible back-seat drivers.'

When Clemency checked the board for her work schedule one morning she saw that she was down to deliver her first plane. There was her name chalked on the board to fly a Miles Magister to Wattisham in Suffolk. At last she was doing the job she'd left her family for.

They were dropped by truck at the factory. The sky was overcast, and the day appeared to be a 'wash out', when no one could fly. She collected her chit and joined the others waiting impatiently, hoping for a change in the weather. Some women stubbed out endless cigarettes before lighting another as they paced the floor and stared at the sky, as if the power of their eyes would shift the cloud. She suspected that this waiting was one of the worst trials of the job.

At last one woman, Audrey, got up. 'I'm off,' she said. 'I'll fly above it. See you all later.'

Clemency felt a surge of panic but she braced herself. For hours she'd been idly sketching the planes waiting like huge tethered birds outside, but if everyone followed Audrey's example she'd feel she had to go as well, She didn't want to fly blind; they had no instruments to help them. Sometimes they hadn't yet been installed in the plane, or if they had they had not been shown how to use them. But, to her relief, no one else followed Audrey. Voices just said goodbye as if she were merely going safely to the shops.

Two hours later the skies cleared, giving them just enough time to arrive at their destinations before dark.

'Good luck. See you later.' Dory blew Clemency a kiss as she went to her plane with Wellington trotting beside her.

Clemency had a quick look at her Ferry Pilot's Notes which were printed on ringbound cards, containing all the information she needed to fly each aircraft. She tucked them into the top of her boot, and went out to her plane. She settled herself in the cockpit, her map close by, started up, taxied down the runway and took off. Remnants of cloud drifted around like skeins of cobwebs. She must keep her wits about her and strengthen her flying awareness, sense if anything was wrong before it came upon her. There was plenty to occupy her attention: keeping a watch-out for enemy planes, keeping clear of the heavy cables that tethered the barrage balloons floating above sensitive areas to deter enemy planes, and watching the weather which could change in an instant.

To her relief she saw the airfield of Wattisham beneath her. She made for the runway, holding the plane on its course, lowered wheels and flaps and landed. The ground was bumpy and the plane skewed a bit to one side, but she'd made it. She taxied towards the dispersal area and a young airman ran to greet her and help her out. He gave her a saucy grin.

'Great landing,' he said. She did not tell him it was her first delivery, though she glowed with pride.

She took her delivery chit to the operations room beside the airstrip. There was nothing to report on the plane and she spent a few moments chatting to the airmen before she was driven to the station and put on a train back to Hatfield.

All the carriages were full, so she sat in the corridor on her parachute bag and closed her eyes. She'd done it, delivered her first plane; she was suffused with a warm sense of achievement. Each plane she delivered would be one in the eye for Hitler.

CHAPTER SEVEN

In the spring Clemency, Dory and Jane were sent to No. 15 Ferry Pool in Hamble by the Solent. Their hours were gruelling and often ended with a long and uncomfortable train journey back to base. When they had any free time they went to London, slept at the flat, had lovely hot baths, drank cocktails and dined and danced the night away. Sometimes they managed to snatch an hour or so of sleep before catching the dawn train back to base to report for duty.

Dory was spending this evening with Johnnie. By a miracle they both had a twenty-four-hour pass at the same time. Clemency was annoyed with herself for feeling excluded, wishing she had someone; but then, she reminded herself, hadn't she sworn not to fall in love until after the war?

There were times in the lonely hours of the night when she wondered if something was wrong with her, that she was incapable of falling in love. She'd met some wonderful men and she enjoyed being with them, but she didn't love them. Many of them didn't make it back and she supposed she'd unconsciously built a wall around her emotions; if you didn't love you didn't suffer so much if they were killed. She was so different from Verity, whose letters were full of her 'new love'. This one, this time, really was the 'one'.

Teddy was in love with Clemency and they often went out together. He was good company and, not wanting to play gooseberry to Dory and Johnnie she was going out with him this evening with some of their friends. They were meeting at the Berkeley, and then going on for supper and dancing at the Savoy.

Usually Teddy was the life and soul of the party, but this evening he seemed subdued. All the pilots, but especially the fighter pilots, suffered from exhaustion and if you weren't careful that let in the fear.

He held her close while they danced, his cheek against hers; she closed her eyes letting her body follow his and the music.

When the dance was over he kept hold of her hand.

'Let's get some air,' he said. He led her outside and across the road to the river. Other couples were doing the same, chasing fresh air and space after the crowed ballroom. They were often interrupted by an air raid but tonight all seemed quiet, the sky was heavy with clouds. They stood together listening to the movement of the river beneath them.

Teddy said gravely. 'I love you, Clemency, will you marry me?'

The words came out fast and a little indistinct and for a moment she wondered if she had misheard them. He grabbed her, holding her to him, she could feel his body shaking against hers.

'Please, darling.' His voice was desperate. 'I think of you all the time and when this bloody war is over we'll make a wonderful life together, won't we?'

He released her while he lit a cigarette, and in the flare of the match his face was eager, hopeful.

His proposal shocked her and yet why was she so surprised? Everyone was getting married or engaged, trying to beat death, have someone to love, to live for. She was fond of him, he was a great companion, a good and decent man but she didn't love him. Did it matter? Wasn't friendship enough? Perhaps it was a better bet than the more demanding love?

He threw away his half-smoked cigarette and withdrew a small box from his pocket.

'This was my grandmother's. She left me this to give to my future wife.' He opened the box, took out a torch and shone it over the cluster of diamonds glistening there.

'You will marry me, won't you?' he pleaded and before she could sort out the words in her head to refuse him without hurting him, he had pushed the ring on to her finger. 'My darling, my own darling, I love you so much.'

He kissed her lips, he was suddenly passionate, his tongue pushing into her mouth, his groin gyrating against hers. One arm held her in a vice and the other hand crawled up her skirt. She was standing with her back to the wall, which was hard and unyielding, hurting her through her thin dress. She gave a little cry, tried to move away but he held her so tightly that she couldn't move.

She didn't want this onslaught; did he think that now she was wearing his ring he could do what he liked with her? Panic rose in her and with a superhuman strength she wrenched herself free.

'What's the matter? We're engaged and you . . .' His voice was harsh with disappointment.

'It's all too fast,' she said lamely, knowing she could never love him as he wanted her to. His almost animal hunger frightened her, and the situation was not helped by her being pressed so hard against a stone wall.

'But . . . I want you so much—' He made a grab for her again but she jumped aside.

'Teddy, take me home and we'll talk about this tomorrow.' She was afraid of him now, afraid of his sudden strength and what he might do if she upset him.

'It's too early. We'll . . . have a drink, then we'll discuss it.' His voice was cold. 'I don't know what's the matter with you, Clemency; I thought you cared for me. Don't tell me you're one of those frigid girls.'

'I think I must be.' She was near tears. She crossed the road to go back to the Savoy. A group of people she knew came towards them.

'The Hun seems to have given us a night off,' Dickie, another pilot said. Some of the others joked with Teddy and she went inside to the ladies' room, her back sore from being pushed against the wall, her mind disturbed by his desperate sexual passion, such as she had not experienced before.

'You all right, dearie?' Martha, who sat in the cloakroom ever ready to sew on a button or stitch a fallen hem, asked her. She'd seen it all over the years: tears and laughter, and treated them both the same.

'Fine thanks, Martha.' Clemency smiled though she felt like crying. Were all men like Teddy so charming and amusing until they wanted to sleep with you? He wasn't the first man to have tried it on but he was the first to have assaulted her so roughly.

She retouched her lipstick and went reluctantly back to the ballroom, wanting to go home. Teddy was with a group of other pilots from his squadron based at Biggin Hill. He saw her and came towards her. One of the men called, 'We're leaving now.'

'We've had a call to return to the airbase. I'll be back in a few days,' he said.

It was dark where they stood, his face was in the shadow. His friends joined him.

'Come on Ted, got to go.' They were all fighter pilots; their minds were already switched to scrambling and dogfights, far away from nightclubs, girls and love. There was no chance to say any more; he squeezed her hand, his eyes boring into her, before he was swept away by his friends leaving the girls bereft in their pretty dresses. Clemency wanted to leave too, to take off this beautiful dress, put on her uniform and get back to work.

'Clemency, what are you doing hiding there?'

She turned and there was Harry, a cigarette in his hand, smiling at her.

'Harry.' She wondered why he hadn't been called away with the others but perhaps it wasn't his squadron and, after all, he wasn't a fighter pilot. It was getting late and she must catch the dawn train to get back to Hamble in time. 'I've got to go, snatch an hour's sleep before the early train.'

'I'm just leaving myself, I'll see you home.' He slipped his hand under her elbow and led her towards the ladies' room. 'Fetch your coat, I'll wait for you here.'

'Is your wife with you?' she asked, assuming that that lady had gone to collect her coat and that he would drop her off on his way to wherever they were staying.

'No, she's not. I came here with friends, but I too have an early start.'

'You are always rescuing me,' she joked. She felt glad his wife was not with him. She wanted to be alone with someone kind and comforting so that she wouldn't have to think about Teddy going back to the base in the dark, cold night, ready to scramble at dawn, wondering whether she'd accepted his proposal or not.

Harry flagged down a taxi and they got into it. He gave her address, then his, which was in Chelsea.

'So, how's the flying going?' he asked as they set off through the dark streets.

She told him about the long hours, though of course he knew all about them.

'But I love it, that wonderful freedom of the sky.'

'I was back in Wick the other day,' he said. 'I saw your sister at the Pavilion.'

'How was she?' Clemency was engulfed with a surge of homesickness, wishing she could be instantly transported back to Caithness, gossiping with Verity in their bedroom.

'She's well, she asked if I'd seen you and wished you'd come home, but she also envies you being in London.' He smiled. '"All those men and parties," she said.'

'She'd cope better with all that than I do.' The words came out unbidden.

Harry frowned. 'Don't you enjoy it, then?'

'Yes, usually but . . .' She pushed her hair back from her face and he caught the glint of her ring in the glow of his cigarette.

'Are you engaged? You have a pretty magnificent ring on your finger.'

'Oh, gosh, I . . . I forgot it was still on my finger. I must give it back, I didn't realize I . . .' She stared down at the ring as though it were a monstrous growth that had suddenly appeared there.

'My dear girl, surely you know you have such a ring on your finger? I mean . . .' he regarded her intently, 'you don't seem drunk or anything.'

'No, but . . .' She wanted to confide in Harry; he was like Daddy, like Daddy was *sometimes*, kind and sensible. 'I was with this man whom I like very much; he said he loved me, asked me to marry him and put this on my finger – it belonged to his grandmother and then . . .' She stopped, embarrassed to relive the frantic scene that had followed, but Harry seemed to understand.

'And you don't want to marry him?' His voice was gentle.

'No. I don't love him . . . he . . . he's a brave, a decent man but . . .'

'I needn't tell you how difficult these times are, how emotions run high. If he's a fighter pilot you know what pressure he is under. I'm sure he didn't mean to . . . frighten you.'

She couldn't look at him; not that she'd see much in the dark, but his voice and the bulk of his body beside her comforted her. She remembered how he had taken her home after that terrible bombing in Wick, and then he had been there just when she needed him before her flying test. But he was married and much older than she was, and so he was used to such situations.

'Will you tell me his name?' he asked.

'Teddy Osborne.'

'Ah, Teddy, he's an ace pilot and a good man. You could do a lot worse than marry him.'

'I know, but I don't love him.'

Harry said nothing, staring out into the darkness. She wished he'd say something to soothe her guilt for not loving Teddy, but they had arrived at her flat. He helped her out, asking the taxi to wait to take him on to Markham Street.

'Love is the devil if it doesn't work out; friendship stands much more of a chance, but don't be too hard on him or yourself.' He kissed her hand lightly as if in jest, opened the main door of the flats for her and wished her goodnight.

The flat was empty. Dory must still be out with Johnnie. Clemency was engulfed in a flood of loneliness. She went to her room and took off the ring, the diamonds winking at her under the lamp, and hid it in her undies drawer. As soon as possible she'd give it back to Teddy; she'd probably see him next week; or she'd tell him when he telephoned. Perhaps it would be better to write, a kind letter saying how honoured she was to be loved by him. Maybe after the war they'd have more time to be together and would not feel so pressed and she would realize that she did love him. But now was not the time for commitment.

But despite her concerns for him she slept late and was woken in a rush by Dory, who'd also overslept, and Wellington who, sensing a drama, jumped about barking.

'We've got ten minutes before Alf comes.' Dory pulled on her clothes. Her make-up from the night before was still on her face.

Their 'pet' taxi man, Alf, wearing his tin hat, who always arrived whatever the situation: fog, sirens, shrapnel hurtling about, drove them to Waterloo and they just made the 4.20 a.m. train. All the way back to Hamble Dory talked of Johnnie and how they were going to get engaged at his next leave. Clemency, not wanting to spoil Dory's excitement, didn't mention her time with Teddy, but she wrote her letter to him in her mind, telling him how she cared for him but thought it better to take things more slowly.

She got round to writing the letter a couple of days later, but before she could post it she saw Dory coming into the mess, looking frantically round for her. Her eyes were red-rimmed; she clutched Wellington close to her face as if she was using him as a shield to hide her tears. Clemency rose to go to her, her stomach tight with fear. Not Johnnie, oh no, please not Johnnie? She reached Dory, conscious of the curious glances from the other pilots who were sitting round waiting to fly. Dory pulled her outside.

'Oh Clemency, Teddy's been killed. I've just heard from Charles, he saw him shot down. I can't bear it. He was such fun, the best of friends. Oh, where will it all end?'

CHAPTER EIGHT

Dory's news hit her like a body blow; the two of them huddled together outside the mess in the biting wind. Teddy could not be dead, she had to talk to him, give him back his ring. She said the words in her head as if he could hear and would come back.

Pilots came past them to take advantage of the gap in the clouds, pulling on their flying-coats, strapping up their helmets. She must go too, but she stayed beside Dory, sick with shock and riddled with guilt, thinking of that evening only a few days ago when he had asked her to marry him. If only he hadn't had to leave before she'd had a chance to say goodbye properly, to explain that she couldn't think of marriage just now. She still had his ring and the letter – thank God he had not seen her letter.

'The ring.' The word slipped out.

'What ring? What are you talking about?'

'Last Wednesday he proposed to me and—'

'Oh, Clemency, I'm sorry.' Dory hugged her. This was too much for Wellington, who wriggled to be free. 'You never told me or I'd have broken the news better – I knew he cared for you, but you never talked of him and so . . .'

'It's not what you think.' Clemency was aware of the disapproving glances of the pilots as they passed them on their way to the airfield. Work must go on and sorrows must be put aside. She must join them; she had a Moth to fly to Tangmere. Dory was on taxi duty and didn't have to leave for another hour.

The cloud had been dense all morning and the pilots had become edgy with hanging around; most of them must know of Teddy's death by now; he'd not been the only one: two others from his squadron had gone down too, but you didn't show your emotions all over the place, it was bad for morale.

'What do you mean?' Dory said. 'He proposed and you. . . ? Well, did you accept him or not?'

'He took me by surprise. I'm fond of him; we have fun together. I didn't realize he loved me enough to want to marry me.' The tears rose in Clemency's eyes. She bit her lip; she had to go: she could not allow herself to be overcome with grief.

'But he did? What did you say?'

'I said I wanted to wait, but by then he'd put the ring on my finger. Oh, Dory, it's so awful, it belonged to his grandmother. I must give it back to his family. I was going to give it back to him that evening and explain, but there wasn't a chance, they'd all had to leave in a rush and then . . . as you know, Harry saw me home.'

She told Dory about the letter she'd written to Teddy but, mercifully, had not posted.

'His parents live not far from here; we'll go over when we're free. But why didn't you want to marry him? He is . . .' Dory swallowed, 'was, such a special man.'

'I know.' The guilt of not loving him twisted in Clemency. There had been so much to love about Teddy: good looks, charm, everything a girl, a *normal* girl would cherish, but not she. When he had grabbed her, squirming against her, his hands all over the place, she'd felt sick, even fearful, and that was surely not normal. Not if Verity was anyone to go by – she, who so obviously enjoyed all that stuff.

'But did he think you were engaged?' Dory persisted.

'I don't know, I suppose he did. When I came out of the ladies' room he was surrounded by the other pilots. They'd been called back to base and there was no chance to say any more. He said he'd telephone, but when he didn't – well, I didn't think much of it. You know how difficult it is to get through.'

She wasn't going to say that she'd been relieved that he'd had to go, that his thoughts had been directed to the task ahead, and she, with the other girls, had been smiling and waving goodbye, knowing that no one wanted to see tears and suffer regrets before they left for their dangerous missions.

'I must go now. Talk when I'm back.' She pulled on her flying helmet and walked over to her plane, feeling the pull of that eternal sky. Up there she'd feel free, able perhaps to come to terms with her time with Teddy.

The next few minutes were a flurry of activity then, at last, her plane lifted into the sky. She wondered how his end had been; he'd confessed that he was terrified of burning to death and would rather hurl himself from the plane to certain death than burn.

She felt closer to him up here. He'd told her of the dogfights he'd been in, seeing the German enemy clearly in the plane beside him, as they fought to the death, even admiring his opponent's flying skill. He'd explained that a pilot could not allow himself to think of the Luftwaffe pilot as a man he might like, a man the same as he was, only on a different side. As you shot him down and watched his plane fall like some giant sycamore seed twisting its way, burning, to the ground, you mentally crossed off one more enemy, not a young man with the same hopes and dreams as you had.

A few days later, Dory and Clemency were back in London. They had dinner at the Dorchester and then danced at the 400 Club where they drank a toast to Teddy. Perhaps all of them were secretly pretending that he would turn up and join them on some other night.

It was May masquerading as November as it was so cold. Their work had kept them busy and they were often stuck at some far off airfield for the night, when the weather closed in or it was too late for them to fly back. Ferry pilots did not fly at night, but whenever they could they came to London. This evening Clemency sensed a restlessness about the city, an edginess as if people were waiting for something momentous to happen.

'There hasn't been a raid for weeks,' they heard from friends who lived and worked in London, carrying on defiantly enjoying themselves in the face of the enemy. They'd got used to having a raid most nights: it had become routine, but there had not been one for so long their nerves were taut to breaking while they waited.

They were meeting friends at the Savoy for dinner. Johnnie's squadron had been posted to West Malling and he and the rest of the squadron were confined to the airbase, which disappointed Dory.

'Let's go anyway,' she said. 'We could do with a night out and to dress up in something glamorous instead of this uniform.'

Titch's Bar was full when they arrived at the Savoy but none of the RAF crowd was there. A few journalists had made the bar their own, to the extent that it used to be known as the American Bar, until Titch, the maître d'hôtel from the River Room, put his seal on it. Peter Seymour, an American journalist whom they knew, with saggy jowls and tired eyes, bought Dory and Clemency a drink and asked them about their work.

'The same as ever, that's all we'll tell you. Sorry.' Dory smiled, lifting her glass of champagne to him.

'My duty to scout for a story,' he answered good humouredly.

Many of the men and a few women were in uniform, but some, like Dory and Clemency, wore evening dresses, jewels sparkling on silk and satins. Wellington, who'd been sleeping contentedly under the table, suddenly jumped up and began to bark.

'Shh Wellington.' Dory scooped him up, holding her hand over his mouth though he still emitted little barks from his throat. 'Must be a raid coming; he always knows,' she said to Keith, her dance partner.

'Let's hope you're wrong.' Keith back on leave had been looking forward to an amusing evening; now, it seemed, it was going to be cut short.

The wail of the siren cut through their chatter and Carroll Gibbons's piano playing.

The sound of the first bombs thudded outside, Carroll Gibbons played louder. Overhead could be heard the buzzing of planes. Dory's knuckles were white as she clenched her glass; she caught Clemency's eye, trying to smile. She was thinking of Johnnie; was he up there, dicing with the enemy and death? Clemency squeezed her hand; there was nothing she could say. They both knew, perhaps more than most, the possible fate of the planes they ferried into the airfields; theirs was a non-stop job to replace the ones that didn't make it home.

Keith and a couple of his friends said they wanted to go outside and see the damage; Dory and Clemency went with them to the riverside, where Clemency had last been with Teddy. The other side of the river was a flickering inferno; flames appeared to die down, then spring up again, eating their way through the warehouses with a ferocious appetite. The sky was thick with planes picked out by the roving beams of the searchlights. The water hissed as burning debris hit the river. Added to this cacophony of noise was the clanging of the fire engines. No one spoke. Clemency felt numb. London, their beloved London, was burning to death. After a while they went back inside, the bar was full; Titch, as unflappable as ever, was serving drinks as if the world outside was not coming to an end.

'We'd better stay here, we'll be as safe as anywhere,' Dory clutched Wellington to her. 'At least we're among friends.'

The night went on, people came in from the street, their faces caked in soot, their feet black from walking through mounds of ash. 'It's like a black snowstorm out there,' a young man who'd just staggered in reported. 'Burnt muck floating about, so much destruction, bodies everywhere, dazed people . . .' He called for a drink, unable to go on.

Peter Seymour questioned him, then said he was going on to the roof, to see the devastation for himself.

'Can we come too?' Dory said.

Peter shrugged. 'Don't see why not,'

The four of them followed him to the roof. Like some macabre film the searchlights picked out the planes as they chased their targets, such huge enemy planes with the smaller Spitfires darting among them like silver fish, twisting and turning, dodging the bullets and firing their own. Beneath the whine of the plane engines they could hear the deadly whistle of bombs as they fell. The horizon was like an inferno; here and there the buildings that were still standing were gaunt and stalwart against the cruel beauty of the red-and-orange fire-filled sky. The earth shuddered as more and more bombs hurtled down, exploding as they hit their targets.

None of them spoke; there was nothing they could say. They just watched stunned and helpless as their beloved city, the heart of the country, was destroyed around them.

CHAPTER NINE

That night changed them all; they had all been through other raids but none of them had been as relentless as this one. They had survived and yet so many had not. Johnnie had come through, but only just; he'd had to bale out: 'take silk', as it was known. He laughed as he told them how his boots had clicked off as he parachuted down, chasing his bullet-riddled plane to the ground.

A month after that terrible night, Clemency and Dory managed to get away to visit Teddy's parents.

The two women had barely seen each other during these past weeks. They had rented a cottage near the base at Hamble, with Jane and Audrey, and all of them were working flat out delivering planes, but at last they both managed to get a day's leave together.

A fellow pilot had seen Teddy's damaged plane struggling to get home before it had crashed into the sea. His body had not been found, so there was no funeral, though there had been a church service, which neither of them could make both being stuck on the other side of the country at the time.

'Teddy told his parents about you,' Dory said, having telephoned them. 'Be careful what you say.' They drove along the country lanes to their house, with Wellington on the back seat jumping up and barking at anything that caught his fancy.

'I will.' She dreaded meeting them, witnessing their pain. 'I must return the ring. I have no right to wear it. Perhaps, after the war, if he hadn't been killed but . . .' She had a stack of excuses for not loving him. The war had deadened her feelings; she wasn't brave, like Dory, to fall in love in case she lost them. They weren't strictly true, but how could she explain that to his bereaved parents?

Hearing their car in the lane Teddy's parents came out to greet

65

them. They were both older than her own parents; his father was dressed in a tweed suit and his squadron tie. His mother was round and comfortable.

Clemency struggled with a rush of tears for these decent people. Should she lie about her feelings, pretend a love that wasn't there? She hung behind Dory, who hugged them both, Wellington greeted them with enthusiasm before making off round the garden to investigate the tantalizing smells there.

'This is Clemency Franklyn.' Dory ushered Clemency forward, her hand firmly on her back as if she were afraid that she might run off round the garden like Wellington.

'My dear,' Teddy's mother clasped her hand in both of hers, 'we are so glad to welcome you. Teddy talked of you so much.'

Clemency couldn't speak. Mr Osborne shook her hand vigorously; the pain of his son's loss was etched into his face. They went into the house, Dory chatting away, answering Mr. Osborne's questions about the ATA.

'Must say,' Mr Osborne turned and studied them both gravely. 'I never thought I'd live to see women flying in wartime.'

'We can't fly in combat, we only deliver planes,' Dory said airily. She clamped her mouth shut, throwing Clemency an agonized look. Clemency guessed that she'd been about to say there were so few male pilots now that if the women didn't deliver the planes there would be a severe shortage.

'All the same.' Mr Osborne sounded disapproving. Both girls had come across this prejudice. The women pilots, some from rich families in society, had attracted a lot of attention and some of the men found this hard to take. There'd been stories of women having their planes sabotaged by male pilots. They'd had a few jokes played on them, a large spider left in one cockpit, a dead mouse in another, but neither woman had taken any notice and had just flung them out on to the grass.

Teddy's mother produced tea, cake and meat paste sandwiches. Clemency struggled to eat, though Dory tucked in. They sat in the drawing room overlooking what had once been the lawn, and which now held rows of vegetables. The ring lay wrapped in a handkerchief in her handbag and every so often during a lull in the conversation she slipped her hand inside to take it out to give it to his mother. Then the conversation started again and she lost her nerve.

They talked of Teddy quite freely, Teddy alive, not dead. Perhaps they didn't quite believe it. It was easy to imagine he was off flying somewhere and would return. With the constant ebb and flow of people being posted all over the place there was nothing unusual in not seeing someone around for a while, and then they'd turn up again.

But though his mother smiled at her and his father regarded her with interest, neither mentioned love or marriage. The tension tightened as she waited for one of them to broach it. She tried to compose a sentence that would explain the truth without hurting them.

It was getting near the time to leave, Dory started throwing significant glances at her and at last she turned to his mother, her stomach churning.

'Mrs Osborne . . . I . . . I have a ring Teddy gave me, I believe it was his grandmother's and . . .'

Mrs Osborne exchanged a look with her husband, half-joyful, half-sad. If only she could disappear, leave them with their dreams, but she forced herself to take it out of her handbag, unwrap it and hold it out to Teddy's mother. The rays of the late sun shining through the window caught the diamonds, making them dance with light.

She sensed Dory sending her warnings to take care, but she wanted to be honest too. It was a valuable ring and not hers. Teddy had an older sister, Pauline, who was in the Wrens and overseas. She had more right to it than Clemency did.

'It was my mother's,' Mrs Osborne said quietly. 'Do you not wear it?'

She took the ring from her and studied it. The diamonds glinted back at her. 'Teddy gave it to you. I know you were hardly engaged before . . .' she stopped, took a breath, her eyes shining with tears, 'but he gave it to you.' She held it out to her.

What should she do? Take it and say no more, let these kind and bereaved people think that she had been their dead son's fiancée? She must do the right thing, but what was the right thing? Keep a ring she didn't deserve or give it back?

'I . . . I was very fond of Teddy and—'

'He adored you,' Mrs Osborne said, 'and so we . . . ' she gestured towards her husband, 'will love you too. It must be so hard for you, his . . . not coming back, so many dreams of family and . . .' She broke down and her husband got up, put his arm round her shoulders,

'Come on, old girl, don't fret,' he said gruffly

Tears swam in Clemency's eyes. Not for lost dreams; she hadn't had any with Teddy, but she was even more certain that she couldn't keep the ring.

She touched Mrs Osborne's arm. 'I want to explain how it was,' she said hesitantly. Dory prodded her foot with her own and Clemency almost succumbed to saying nothing and keeping the ring, but she wouldn't feel right if she did.

Mrs Osborne looked into her face, her eyes red-rimmed, her face in soft folds with deep creases round her mouth. She appeared beaten, diminished by her son's death, but she said gently, 'Tell me how it was.'

Clemency started to cry; this was the hardest thing she'd ever had to do. Dory thrust a handkerchief at her and she blew her nose. To distract herself she studied the comfortable room, the antique furniture gleaming in the evening sun. There on the piano stood a phalanx of photographs. She snatched her eyes away, not bearing to see Teddy as a little boy, growing up to that handsome fighter pilot, proud in his uniform.

'I was very fond of Teddy,' she went on. 'But I am a coward and when he asked me to marry him I was afraid to accept, afraid to lose him, so I asked him to wait until after the war. But he put the ring on my finger . . .' She had a flashback of him grabbing her and her fighting him off. 'I didn't have a chance to return it, as he and the other pilots were called back to base and then . . .'

'So you didn't want to marry him?' Mr Osborne glowered at her for turning down his son.

She wanted to say yes, of course she did, but the words would not come. She muttered feebly, 'I wanted to wait, I . . . we both had such dangerous jobs, he worse than me of course, and . . .'

'I understand,' Mrs Osborne broke in, 'it was just too much at that moment, but if you had both got through the war . . . you would have . . .' Her eyes were alight with hope and Clemency could not disappoint her.

'Yes, if we had both got through,' she repeated.

'Then the ring is yours.' She gave it back to her.

No, that was not how she wanted it, she could not take it.

'Teddy gave it to you,' Dory said and Clemency knew that behind those words was a plea to take it and shut up: stop tormenting this kind couple, but still she could not do that.

'I'd like you to keep it safe,' Clemency said. 'We are always in different places, don't know where we'll end up next; it could so easily get lost.' She put it in Mrs Osborne's hand. 'It will be safer with you.'

To her relief Dory broke in, 'That's the best idea. We're not allowed to wear jewellery when we're working and there are thieves everywhere. When this war's over then she can come back for it.'

'If she hasn't married someone else,' Mr Osborne said darkly.

Clemency felt ashamed; he knew that she hadn't loved his son enough to marry him, but Mrs Osborne – no doubt more romantic – thought differently.

Dory took charge of the situation, saying they must go as they had an early call in the morning. 'We'll come and see you again when we can,' she said. 'Meanwhile the ring will be safe with you.'

Clemency wept all the way back to Hamble. Wellington sat on her knee, licking away her tears. 'I wish I had loved him. I don't think I'm capable of love.'

'Nonsense.' Dory had been shaken by the meeting with Teddy's parents. Their grief was too real; you didn't see much of the families at this time, so perhaps the deaths did not register so deeply, but seeing a family torn by grief bought you up close to it and it was hard to take. 'You just haven't met the right person.'

'But Verity is always in love and I've never been,' Clemency sobbed, furious with herself for causing the Osbornes such pain by returning the ring. She'd meant well but in the circumstances it had been wrong. She should have waited or, better still, found his sister and given the ring to her.

CHAPTER TEN

Clemency used to love autumn, with its feeling of nostalgia as the nights drew in, the carnival colours of the changing leaves heralding images of winter parties, but this year she found it heartbreaking. So many people had died, and she dared not think too deeply of them, or rage at the futility of war, in case she lost her nerve or, worse, put other people's lives in danger.

So much of London was reduced to piles of rubble, like monuments to the dead and injured, yet the dome of St Paul's Cathedral stood strong and defiant, keeping the city's spirit burning. And still they went out dancing.

She missed Teddy more than she'd imagined; he had loved her and been a good companion, and now he was gone. There was no shortage of attractive and amusing men to dance and flirt with but since Teddy's death she felt she was flitting about rather aimlessly. She couldn't even blame the numbing of her feelings on exhaustion; everyone was exhausted, but some of the others managed – even went out of their way – to have love affairs as well.

She rang home, seeking reassurance, hoping to hear that, despite her escape, they still loved her. Verity answered, snatching up the receiver, her voice excited until she realized it was just her sister.

'Oh, it's you. Everything all right?' She didn't wait for an answer but prattled on. 'Daddy came last week and went all peculiar when I talked about you. Surely it can't be because you're flying, even though he thinks that women flying is obscene?'

Clemency stifled her irritation; she'd craved comfort, wanting to tell Mummy about Teddy. What could she do about Daddy's philandering? There was no point telling Verity about seeing him with that woman in Orkney; she, so like him, would not believe it was anything serious, and talking about it would only resurrect that last painful scene she'd had with him before she left for London.

'I'm working very hard and it's so sad; some of my friends have been shot down and—'

'Quite a few of my boys have gone too; it's hateful, I wish it would stop,' Verity broke in. 'I'm often in Orkney with Betty. Mummy's met her – she came over for a dance. I'm in love with a soldier there: a gunner called Jim, Jim Harris and . . .' On she went, not picking up Clemency's need to talk. Clemency managed to break in and ask to speak to Mummy, but Verity said she was not there, leaving her feeling childishly excluded. She made an excuse and rang off.

She'd expected too much, even if Mummy had been there she'd have gone on about Daddy. Neither Mummy nor Verity would understand how draining and yet exhilarating her work was. As long as she was 'all right' she'd get little sympathy. After all, they'd remind her, it had been her choice to join the ATA. If she found it too arduous she could always come home.

The weather had been bad all day – a wash-out day, with heavy cloud sitting tight over the airfield, but at last in the afternoon there was a break and Clemency set off to deliver a Spitfire to Prestwick, Glasgow.

They had now progressed from the Tiger Moth to fly any plane there was to be delivered and the Spitfire was her favourite; it was so responsive and compact, with an intimacy that made her feel as if the plane was an extension of herself.

She took off into the gap in the clouds and for a while the visibility was good, but then the weather started to close in, meaning that the flying taxi wouldn't make it and she'd have to stay put or find a train to get her back.

The airfield lay beneath her and she landed smoothly and taxied to the delivery point. Lugging her parachute bag, her maps and her overnight bag with her she made her way to the operations room to hand in her chit. The work had become so routine, but there were still moments of exhilaration in flying alone in a wide, clean expanse of sky.

The casualties among the fighter pilots increased, leaving huge gaps that threatened to become impossible to fill. They worked relentlessly on supplying the pilots with aircraft, keep going for the country and for Teddy and Charles who'd been shot down a month after Teddy, and all the other friends, and for people she'd never know who'd died trying to defeat Hitler.

She went into the mess room and sat down with a cup of tea and a cigarette. It was late afternoon and quite dark, the cloud having now completely closed in. She doubted the flying taxi would make it; she'd have to return on the train.

'Clemency, how good to see you.' Harry stood before her. 'So you were the pilot who landed that Spit so perfectly.'

'I hope I did.'

'You look exhausted. Don't we all?' He smiled. 'I was just going to the town to get a very late lunch. Like to join me?'

His voice was light but she thought she detected an undercurrent of defensiveness as if he were arming himself for her refusal. She was glad to see him; so often he turned up just when she needed someone to reassure her, to make her life feel worthwhile. What should it matter that he was married and older than she was? She wasn't going to fall in love with him, or sleep with him.

'Thank you,' she said, 'but I'd be a poor companion. I'm exhausted and . . .'

'Then we'll fall asleep together over our Woolton pie or whatever other concoction we're given. I've a car outside. When do you have to get back?

'A flying taxi was meant to come but now the cloud's come down. I better ring Hamble.'

'Nothing else will get in for a while,' he said, but she rang to confirm. She could do with a good lunch.

She relaxed with him over the meal – something warm under pastry. He was easy to be with. You could be fond of someone without hurting their marriage. His good eye appraised her, looking tenderly at her, and she was tempted into breaking the rules that kept their morale strong by telling him about two friends who'd been shot down the previous week and the funerals she'd attended.

Somehow the conversation got on to Teddy.

His face darkened, a slight tic twitched at his mouth. 'Such casualties, you can't take it in. I feel I should do more, I don't fly enough with this . . .' he gestured impatiently at his eyepatch. 'But we have to keep going: we cannot be invaded, let them win.'

'When it's over, however, will those of us who are still left get back to normality?' she said. 'So many people lost, leaving such huge holes in our lives.'

'Maybe new people will fill them.' He took her hand as she fiddled with the cutlery on the table. She started, surprised at his gesture. She should disengage it from his with a smile – a joke if she could think of one – and yet the touch of his hands on hers comforted her. Then, to her surprise and mortification, she was enveloped with a fierce longing for his arms to be round her, holding her, his face against hers. She dared not look at him, afraid that he'd guess at this sudden yearning to be loved.

He felt the tug of her hand as he clasped it and almost let go, but then it lay quiet, like a bird in his own.

'I love seeing you.' His voice was rich with emotion. ' I watched that plane coming in serenely like some proud eagle and land so beautifully. I was curious to see who the pilot was, and when you got out and walked across the tarmac, pulling off your helmet and shaking out your hair, my heart lifted.'

His words slipped into her, soothing her, releasing a beam of joy. He's married, she repeated to herself like a mantra; there can be nothing between you. If you get involved with him, it will destroy you. Either he'll be killed or after the war he'll go back to his wife.

'You're worried that I'm married,' he said as if reading her mind.

She saw the tender longing in his face and to her surprise she felt it echo in her body. She'd never gone to bed with anyone, not because she disapproved of it as her parents, especially her wayward father, did, but because she felt she'd have to love someone and be loved by them before she did, and love was doomed by the war. Yet could there not be little interludes of love, snatches of happiness enjoyed just for that moment without their being part of the future?

'Yes I am. It must be so dreadful for your wife, waiting and worrying. I see it with my mother waiting for Daddy and . . .' With

73

difficulty she suppressed the anger that rose in her, thinking of her father's constant betrayal of her mother, who loved him too well.

She went on, 'If you are fighting, or even supporting like us in the ATA, we're so busy caught up in the real thing we don't have time to think sensibly about the consequences, and even if we do we're usually too tired to delve into it too deeply.'

'But what if she's not waiting and worrying?' His face was etched with pain.

'What do you mean? Is your wife bound up in it too? Driving ambulances or in one of the services?'

'No, she . . .' his mouth tightened. 'I suppose you could say her war work is sleeping with . . . well, not quite the enemy, but I expect she would if they invaded and were good-looking enough.'

'Oh, Harry. I am so sorry.' What could she say? She knew women like that, Verity wasn't far off it, though she was generous with her love, handing it out like sweets with the enthusiasm of an affectionate puppy; but she was not a marriage wrecker. Clemency didn't know how far she went or if she was involved with married men, but Verity herself was not married, with a husband out there putting his life on the line every day and night for the country.

'I should have known when I met her; there were enough rumours about her. She's very beautiful and she acted as if she loved me. I loved her, still do in a way.' He sighed. 'I should have realized the temptation of all those fired-up young men would be too much for her. She's taken to staying in London – we also have a house there – and going out most nights, having the most riotous time.'

'Do you ever see her?'

'If I go to the house in London. I send a telegram now if I'm coming and just hope she's there to see me. But I've had enough of it.' He still held her hand. 'I despise her for doing so little for the war effort when so many courageous women like you are doing more than their fair share.'

'She sounds a little like Verity. She does try to do something, being in the canteen and such, but she too can't help getting caught up with the boys.'

'And you?' He studied her face. 'Have you someone to love?'

She laughed awkwardly, foolishly abashed that she had no one.

'No. I've seen how love has dominated my mother's life, and been a torture to her. My father is a womanizer.' She told him about their time in Orkney. 'I want to live a bit before, if ever, I fall in love. You know how difficult I found it with Teddy; I didn't love him but I miss him now he is gone. I'd rather not risk it until the war is over.'

'But love, real love,' his voice was soft, 'helps you through. Even if you lose it, it touches you with . . .' he laughed, a little embarrassed at his sentiment, 'magic, stardust, whatever romantic name you choose to call it. You know the old saying "better to have loved and lost . . ."'

'"Than never to have loved at all",' they chorused together.

'Maybe you're right,' Clemency allowed, 'but it's not something I'm looking for now.' Even as she said it she felt she'd been too abrupt, had cut off any chance of a relationship with him. There was something between them, waiting to be picked up and cherished, and she had killed it before it could go any further. He released her hand, calling for the bill, his good manners and maturity smoothing over the cracks. She wished she could get back to those moments that had just passed. She might not love him or he her, but they could have spent an hour together giving each other much-wanted comfort. To sleep with him, her first time: he'd be gentle, not impatient like some less skilled impetuous youth; she could almost feel poor Teddy's clumsy gyrations on her body. With Harry it would have been a kind of lovemaking to remember always.

'A girl never forgets her first lover.' She remembered a friend of her mother's saying that when she'd thought Clemency wasn't listening. Watching Harry pay the bill, chatting easily to the elderly waitress, she wanted it to be him, but it was too late. She'd slammed the door in his face and she did not know how to open it again.

CHAPTER ELEVEN

In June Clemency managed to get a week's leave. For the first time since she'd started work she was to deliver a plane to the 'drome in Wick and she decided to take some overdue leave and see her family.

America had entered the war in December and some American women pilots had joined the ATA, as had women of other nationalities, swelling their ranks and making it easier to get time off.

'I hope your father won't lock you in some dungeon and throw away the key,' Dory joked, though Clemency saw the anxiety in her eyes. It worried her too but she longed to see her mother and Verity; her sister might annoy her but she missed her.

'He's probably relieved not to have me there spying on him.' The familiar band of tension tightened in her as she thought of his betrayal.

She was flying a Spitfire that was to be used for reconnaissance, so it was lighter, not fitted with heavy guns, and it was painted a glorious blue.

As she approached the 'drome, the light played on the sea as it tumbled against the rugged coastline. She made for the runway and landed, wondering if Mummy or Verity were working there and had seen her land and would be impressed enough to take her job more seriously.

As she clambered out of the cockpit two mechanics whom she knew from when she'd worked at the canteen greeted her.

'Clemency, we had to watch you come in. Great bit of flying; good to see you back.'

She was touched by their welcome. 'It's wonderful to be back. How beautiful it looks from the air.'

Alice was waiting for her in the mess; she hugged her. 'Very impressive landing. How's it all going? Have you time for a drink? I can run you home in the truck.'

'Thanks. I'd like that, unless my mother is here with the van?'

'No, she and Verity only help here if there's no one else.'

Clemency hoped she'd hidden her disappointment. Couldn't they have come here today to see her arrive? Alice had waited, and Kenny and Bill had welcomed her too, and here was Angus, the pigeon keeper, coming to see her. Why couldn't her family have made the same effort? But it was good to see Alice, and the people she knew here would be far more interested in her work than her family would.

It was nearly eleven and the blackout was down when Alice dropped Clemency at Aunt Mattie's. She breathed in the sharp, salty air, listening to the rhythmic sound of the waves breaking on the shore, watching the sinuous gleam on the water, black as oil under the moonlight.

Aunt Mattie opened the door to her, hugging her awkwardly.

'Clemency, good to see you.' She ushered her in to the darkened hall, shutting the door quickly behind her. She studied her in the dim light. 'Your uniform looks nice.'

Nancy ran down the stairs and kissed her, holding on to her as if she was amazed she was still in one piece.

'I've been worried sick about you. I'm sure girls shouldn't be doing such a dangerous thing as flying. Isn't it far too difficult for you? What would you do if the plane fell from the sky?' On she went and Clemency struggled to reassure her, wishing Verity would come and calm their mother down. She asked where Verity was and Nancy said she wasn't there.

'She's in Orkney; she'll be back tomorrow. She does a lot of good works over there now, mainly helping in the hospital.' Nancy added the last bit brightly, as if determined to dismiss Verity's reputation of just having a good time

Surely Verity had known she was coming only for a few days and could have given up whatever boy she was after to spend some time with her? Clemency felt hurt; they had no idea how hard she worked, neither did they seem to care.

After an hour of listening to Nancy telling her how worried she was about Gerald and the squadron leader who sometimes billeted with them, and her war work, Clemency fell thankfully into bed. She didn't feel that she belonged here, though had she ever, anyway since the start of the war? And as for Verity – she glowered at her empty bed – could she really not give up her partying to welcome her sister home?

Her irritation increased when Verity returned the following evening, glowing with excitement. Her mother, Aunt Mattie, and the neighbours whom Clemency had seen were pale and exhausted, worn down with the anxiety and the general hardships they suffered, but Verity seemed to be flourishing.

'I've met this wonderful man. I've never been so in love,' Verity started after she'd hugged Clemency.

Clemency pushed her away. 'Can't you ever think of anything else? Really good people are being killed or badly injured every day and all you think about is falling in love.'

Verity recoiled as if her sister had slapped her. 'So ferry pilots don't have the same feelings as the rest of us?'

'We wouldn't be much good if we fell in love all the time,' Clemency replied. If only she was back at Hamble among the pilots, women like her. She'd been looking forward to seeing Verity, but now that she was here she found that Verity infuriated her: again the spoilt child showed itself in her. They hadn't seen each other for ages and so couldn't she just for one moment stop talking about her rackety love life and show a little interest in *her*?

'Well, I'm sorry for you,' Verity burst out. Her eyes shone as she added: 'I won't talk of him again, but this one is different.'

Clemency sighed, she knew what Verity was like and it would be foolish to fall out with her in the few days she was here. 'Aren't they always?' she said wearily.

'This one really is.' Verity said seriously, as if he were Adonis. 'He's Italian, a prisoner of war; there's a whole lot of them in Orkney. He's in a camp on Lamb Holm, they are helping build barricades, or causeways they call them, to make the Flow safe from any more enemy subs getting in.'

'A POW certainly is different.' Clemency's heart sank,

remembering Harry's remark about his promiscuous wife who'd sleep with the enemy if they were attractive enough. 'What about the German POWs?' she said acidly. 'Have you fallen in love with one of them yet?'

Verity scowled. 'My, you've changed into a really bitchy creature. Love is love; you can't help who you fall in love with. They're not all bad. Some are like us, having to fight, but normally they'd be our friends.'

It was pointless to argue with her. She should have guessed that Verity wouldn't have changed. It wasn't anyone's fault, her life was so different from theirs; she shouldn't blame Verity for being how she was.

'I'm sorry.' She threw her sister a wan smile. 'I'm not used to having time on my hands, but be careful, Verity. They are our enemies, and many people, especially if they have lost someone close, will not think well of you for fraternizing with him. How did you meet him? Surely they are kept away from the Orcadians?'

'Well, yes, when they are in their camps. But during the day you see them working on the causeways.'

'But how were you able to get to know one of them enough to fall in love with?' Clemency asked with exasperation.

'Betty is training to be a nurse in Balfour hospital in Kirkwall. I help her sometimes. He came to the hospital with a friend who was badly injured and—'

'But surely there's a military hospital?'

'There is, and a hospital ship, but his friend needed X-rays and as he doesn't speak any English, Stephano came with him to interpret. He speaks good English, as he studied here before the war. He had to wait in the waiting room until he was needed and I . . .' she blushed, 'I saw him going in, alone. His guard was not around so I went in to . . . I . . . made an excuse that I was looking for something. It was a *coup de foudre*,' she said joyfully. 'Oh but it's so awful; do you know they had to sew red discs on their clothes as a target to shoot at if they try and escape? Isn't that terrible?'

'Verity, he is the enemy, he and any of the others might try and kill us,' Clemency retorted. 'We are at war. This is not a garden party.'

'But he's a good man. He can't help having to fight for his country, just as our men can't. He's so kind and so artistic – look what he made for me.' She held out her arm, showing Clemency a bracelet. 'He carved it out of wood just for me. Look how delicate it is, flowers intertwined with leaves and a tiny heart.'

To please her and make up for her bad humour Clemency inspected it. It could not have been more beautiful if it had been made in gold.

'It is exquisite,' she said as she studied the petals and leaves. 'But be careful, Verity.' She experienced a sudden dart of fear for her sister. 'Don't get hurt. He'll go back home at the end of the war and he may have a wife and family there.'

'All sorts of things change in wartime,' Verity went on defiantly. 'He had to marry his cousin and—'

'There can be no excuses, Verity; he is married.' Clemency blushed thinking of Harry; she could so easily have gone to bed with him that afternoon if she hadn't ruined it with her abrupt manner.

'Maybe he is, but the war may go on for years and he'll be stuck here and she might marry someone else or even . . .' Her voice petered out, as if she knew she was going too far.

'Die,' Clemency picked it up. 'She might, so might any of us, but I still think we should try our best to live honourably.' She winced as she remembered the pain in Harry's expression. His wife hadn't even the decency to keep faithful to him while he risked his life in defence of his country.

Nancy appeared in the doorway. 'Verity. You're back. Did you see your father?' Her voice was eager, hopeful, making Clemency's heart bleed for her.

'No. I don't think his ship was there.'

'He never seems to be there,' Nancy said sadly.

Clemency hugged her. 'He's winning the war for us, Mummy. He'll be back soon.' She smiled encouragingly, swallowing the fury that surged up in her. 'When did you last hear from him?'

'Oh, a fortnight ago, I know he's busy, but . . . at least you're back.' Nancy put her arm round Clemency's shoulders. 'Tell me more about it. Isn't it frightfully dangerous, especially for a woman?'

'Not really. The pilots need us to keep them provided with planes. We have lost so many of them and men are needed to protect the convoys, go out on reconnaissance, drop the bombs. It couldn't be done without us. Besides, we are good at it and we love it. We women can't go on sitting about at home, Mummy; there's a whole world out there for us to share in.'

'I'm sure, dear, but after the war things will go back to how they were.'

Guessing her mother wanted nothing more from life than being at home with her husband and family, Clemency stayed silent. She would certainly never be the wife sitting at home while her husband played the field.

A couple of days later Verity said she must go back to Orkney. She insisted that Clemency must come with her. 'There's so much going on there and I want you to meet Stephano.'

Their mother and Aunt Mattie were out most of the day, helping to teach the children in the church hall, as many schools had been disbanded or their buildings taken over by the military. The two women also worked with the Red Cross.

Verity spent a lot of time in Orkney, 'doing her own war work'. She'd giggled when she said it, which made Clemency despair of her. But Clemency had not come home to spend hours alone in the house, though she could spend the time sketching. She could do that in Orkney too, and maybe Daddy's ship would be in and she could make her peace with him.

They bicycled up to Scrabster and found Sandy. Today they were his only passengers and he ignored them, setting his craggy face to the wind, lost in his own world. Verity prattled on for most of the way.

'Betty thinks she may be having a baby; she hoped to marry him but he hasn't come back. She might come and stay with us if she is, then go back home and pretend she's a widow,' she went on, as if it was easily settled.

Clemency was shocked. 'But you can't expect Aunt Mattie and Mummy to deal with her if she is having a child. There's no room now that there is the squadron leader.' She had not met him, but Verity had told her he was dull and plain. He had been put in the best bedroom, so he must have impressed Aunt Mattie, or perhaps he'd been neutered or something, to make him safe in the night.

'There's *your* bed. You've been away ages and will probably be so again.'

'My bed! You can't put her there.' Clemency was outraged; she might have left home but she didn't want her place to be taken by Betty and her unborn child.

'Why not?' Verity shrugged. 'You're not in it. Anyway she might not be, then everything will be all right.'

'I do hope so.' None of this was anything to do with her any more, she reminded herself. Flying was her life now; she must leave her family to their own devices.

Clemency offered up a prayer to keep Verity safe. She glanced at Sandy to see if he had overheard their conversation. He had his pipe in his mouth, his hands on the wheel. He seemed like part of the boat, part of the sea, only showing his irritation with them if they disturbed his communion with them.

They arrived at Stromness, and Sandy tucked his boat into his usual place. Verity was obviously a popular figure at the check post and they passed through with their bicycles. A lanky youth jumped from the cab of a truck, blushing with excitement.

'You are a brick, Andy,' Verity greeted him, giving him her bike to put inside. 'This is Clemency, my sister.'

Andy nodded at Clemency but his eyes stayed on Verity.

'Andy will take us to Kirkwall, but first we'll leave our things at Betty's.'

'Betty's? I thought we were staying with Mrs D?'

'No, it's too noisy there with the baby. Betty's mother doesn't mind, she goes to bed early and doesn't care if we bring people back.'

Clemency said no more; this was Verity's world and she was not part of it, any more than Verity was part of hers. They left their bags in the porch of Betty's house.

As they drove Verity kept up a cheerful chatter, Andy kept turning to gaze at her, swerving this way and that, and once or twice nearly hitting a sheep or another vehicle.

They arrived at Kirkwall and he dropped them near the

harbour. Clemency, feeling rather sick, was relieved to have arrived unscathed.

'Thanks Andy.' Verity blew him a kiss.

'So now what? Is this man at the hospital?' It surprised her that Verity worked there, though not that men were involved. One of Verity's many men had been a patient here and it was while she had been visiting him that she'd met Stephano; now, as far as she could gather, she hung about, doing small jobs, hoping to see him again.

'No, not the hospital,' Verity said, 'We're going to Graemeshall House.'

'Graemeshall House? Why there?' She'd assumed that Stephano worked in the hospital interpreting for the Italians who needed medical treatment.

'Stephano helps there in the gardens sometimes.'

It was irritating having to chase this man around. With so many British, Canadian, Polish and now American men to choose from why did Verity have to fall for a POW? She could only hope the relationship would be as short as her others had been. This thought was hit by another concern: would they be breaking some law by fraternizing with POWs, which could end in her being expelled from the ATA?

She put this to Verity, who just shrugged. 'Of course not, some of the Orcadians have taken pity on them and help them with small gifts of food and things. It's not their fault that they had to fight.' She started off on her bicycle and Clemency followed her. Once she'd seen this man she might be able to persuade Verity to give him up.

They arrived at Graemeshall and Clemency saw a group of men with red disks sewn on their clothes just as Verity had described. Despite their being the enemy, it shocked her. They looked a sad bunch, with hardly the energy or the will to turn on their captors, and anyway, where could they escape to?

Verity had worked her magic here. The British soldiers 'escorting' the Italians greeted her cheerfully, the Italians more flirtatiously, their admiring glances including Clemency. She turned away haughtily; she would have none of it.

'Come on, this way,' Verity said, going down a path among

some shrubs. Clemency saw a man with his back to them, sitting on a tree trunk. He got up as they approached, putting down something he'd been working on. Verity took off, running towards him. Clemency studied the horizon; how embarrassing Verity was with her unseemly enthusiasm.

'Stephano, this is my sister, *mia sorella.*' She giggled. 'Clemency.'

'I am pleased to meet you.' His voice had an attractive lilt in the way he pronounced the words. Clemency composed her face into an expression of indifference. This man's country was at war with them and the Italians had killed and maimed thousands of her compatriots. She hoped Verity didn't expect her to shake hands with him: that would be too much. She turned to look at him, her gaze straight, now with a touch of arrogance. He was tall and slender, his hair blue-black and his eyes deep and dark. He smiled at her hesitantly, as if he guessed her animosity towards him.

'Bellina. Beautiful like your sister.' He said it as if he meant it and it was not just an empty compliment dashed out without a thought.

'She flies Spitfires; she's only here a short while. I wanted her to meet you,' Verity prattled on, placing one arm on his shoulder and leaning against him.

Clemency had meant to give him a civil greeting and then leave them together, but it was as if he were a magnet, gently but firmly drawing her in. Her eyes devoured his lean face, his full mouth that seemed to curve so readily into a smile. He was dressed in a collection of clothes to keep out the cold, and yet he seemed elegant, wearing them as if they became him. An unfamiliar warmth spread through her body, shocking her. She wanted to be the one leaning against him with one of his arms encircling her waist, to be close to him, touching him.

'You both look very like each other, shall I know the difference?' He laughed, his eyes holding hers. He must know of the passion that raged inside her. She felt ashamed; he was their enemy, how could her body betray her so?

'She's thinner than I am,' Verity said, giggling, nibbling at his ear.

Clemency wanted to be in his arms, to feel the softness of his earlobe against her mouth. She wrenched her eyes away from him.

'Don't be long. It's getting late. I'm going to draw the garden.' She forced herself to walk away, overwhelmed with her emotions.

Was this love? No, surely not, for she didn't know him and he was a prisoner of war, an enemy, and married. But none of that, moments ago so important, seemed to matter now. Her body, her very spirit had recognized him as if he were part of her being. She must be suffering from some sort of madness, bought on from working too hard and for so long without leave.

Their parents would be horrified. As one of the enemy, a POW and a married man, he was completely out of bounds. Verity professed to love him, though no doubt, as she had with all the others, she'd soon become bored with him. What a mercy it was that she, Clemency, would soon be back down south and need never see him again.

CHAPTER TWELVE

Parts of the garden at Graemeshall House could make people forget there was a war on and that the islands had been invaded by military camps and batteries. Some land had been turned over to growing vegetables but there were also clumps of colourful flowers that cheered the spirit and brought hope of better times ahead.

Clemency found herself a corner and sat down on the grass. She forced herself to concentrate on her drawing, struggling to quieten her raging emotions, willing her eyes to take in the shapes of the bushes, the play of light on the sea and the glimpse of ships anchored there. If Daddy were there he'd soon put a stop to this unsuitable romance.

Her pencil stroked the paper, quick faint marks feeling the lines of the land, the sky and the warships that waited there, then becoming stronger, more sure as her eye connected what she was seeing with what she was drawing.

'*Bellissima.*' She jumped. She had not heard his step on the soft ground. She blushed, forced herself not to look at him, but now she knew he was standing behind her she could feel the heat of him radiating towards her. That was just being fanciful. Why must she behave like Verity, who reacted so violently to any half-attractive man?

'Thank you.' She heard the harshness in her voice. Three more lines and she'd done enough to work on later. She snapped her book shut and pushed it into her bag. Then she wished she'd kept on drawing; he might have left her alone to work.

'I draw too, it helps to pass the time.'

'I suppose it does.' She could not trust herself to look at him. Where was Verity? Why couldn't she come and take him away?

'So you fly Spitfires? Do you kill us?' The undercurrent of anger in his words stung her. She whipped round to face him.

'No, I don't. I'm a ferry pilot, I deliver the planes from the factories to the airfields.' Why did she feel she had to explain herself to him, the enemy? She was shocked by the depth of sorrow in his eyes. He took a long draw on his cigarette.

'War is a bad thing, a stupid thing. Nobody wins.'

She was hit with compassion. So many people were pawns in the hands of their governments, their lives shattered by the whims of tyrants. Had Verity seen this in him, realized that he was a decent man who didn't want to inflict such destructive pain on others? But before she could examine such thoughts Verity appeared.

'I just popped behind a bush,' she said and wound her arm though Stephano's.

'I must go back now,' he said. Verity clung more tightly.

'Sandy says storms are coming, so we may not get back to Caithness. Will you be here tomorrow.' She nuzzled into his neck.

Clemency hadn't heard Sandy say anything of the sort. 'We must get back tomorrow,' she said sharply, 'I've only a few days' leave and—'

'Daddy's ship might be in; you'll want to see him,' Verity retorted. She kissed Stephano saying, 'We'll see, but please be here, same time.'

Stephano shrugged. 'I may not be here, we have too much work on the causeways, but Marius's leg is hurting, so perhaps I must go with him to the hospital.'

Verity pouted, 'I wish I could come over to your camp; it's barely a mile by boat. I could borrow one and row over.'

Stephano laughed, hugging her to him.

Clemency said sharply, 'Of course you can't, you'd get shot, it is a prison you know.'

''Course I know,' Verity snapped, 'but . . .'

'*Cara*, see sense,' Stephano turned to Clemency and perhaps to charm her out of her bad humour, he said, 'You draw so well, might you draw me a picture of your sister, and yourself too, give it to me next time?'

'I doubt I'll have time.' The disappointment in his expression made her feel ashamed. She could imagine the bleakness of the camp; they could not have many, if any, of their own things with them. She said, to make up, 'Your carving is exquisite. I saw that bracelet you made for Verity.'

'Thank you. We work in the quarry, build these barricades, but we have many hours when we cannot sleep, when the thoughts of home are too painful.' His eyes were so eloquent, brimming over with the sorrows that an English man would keep hidden, locked away tight inside him so he would not have to face them.

She yearned to comfort him, kiss that troubled mouth. Impatiently she dashed away such nonsense. 'Your English is very good,' she said.

'My grandmother lived here. I came to study here, but now she is dead, bombed in her house in London.' His mouth clenched with fury. 'How stupid it is that the side I am meant to be on killed her.'

'It is stupid. I'm sorry.' What else could she say? She hardened her heart, they were still at war and soon she would be back flying more aircraft to the airfields, among them Wellingtons for the bomber pilots to carry bombs to drop on other innocent families. But she could not go on with her work if she allowed herself these sentimental feelings. British cities suffered just as badly too. 'I'll see if I have time to draw the picture.' She walked away, calling to Verity to hurry so they could get to Kirkwall to see if Daddy was there relaxing with his Naval colleagues.

'So,' Verity said as she caught up with her, 'is he not the most beautiful man you've ever seen?'

'He is good-looking.' She hoped Verity couldn't see her lust for him, for surely that was what it was? 'But you know how charming Italians are said to be.'

'It's more than that.' Verity stopped her bike, planting her feet solidly on the ground. 'English men, Polish and Americans are attractive too, but there's something about Stephano that singles him out from them all. It was a *coup de foudre*, for both of us.' Her face was glowing in wonder that such a thing had happened, surprising Clemency. Verity was always in love; Clemency had been irritated by the repetitiveness of it, but this time she saw it was different, for she, for the first time in her life, felt it too.

'Be careful.' She tried to ignore the bite of envy. Why did Verity have to find him? She, who thought love was a game, interchangeable among the many young men she met. Perhaps, as before she would find someone else next week to divert her and yet Clemency had a feeling that this time she would not. Verity's whole being seemed to be different, changed by this man. He was the one and Clemency could not bear it, for she wanted him too.

CHAPTER THIRTEEN

They met Betty after her shift at the hospital, she and Verity giggled together but Clemency felt apart from them.

Meeting Stephano had unsettled her; surely she was a traitor to feel so strongly for one of the enemy, however noble and decent he might be?

She hadn't liked it when Teddy had ground himself into her like that and whenever other men got fresh she soon put them in their place. She'd been rather hazy about what happened between men and women. She'd heard a few things from some of the racier girls, mostly innuendo that she didn't understand, but since meeting Stephano, though she felt ashamed of her feelings, she longed for him to kiss her, hold her to him, to be with him naked. She blushed thinking of it. Verity, turning to speak to her, noticed and exclaimed, 'Look at you all flushed like that. Don't tell me you're coming down with something.'

'I'm just hot after all that cycling.' How mortifying that her feelings were so obvious. She must stop this madness; never think of him or such things again.

'That was ages ago.' Verity studied her sister, then went on, 'Betty knows one of the sailors on Daddy's ship and it's anchored in Kirkwall Bay. We can go there for cocktails, then stay on dancing.'

Clemency's stomach churned; she wanted to see her father and yet she was afraid of his reaction. Would he embrace her or cut her dead?

'Are you sure we can go?' she asked.

'Of course, these things are laid on to amuse the men and they love to have pretty girls to lighten them up.' Betty caught Verity's eye, both girls glowing with excitement.

Later that evening, when the three girls had changed, an easily persuaded Andy drove them over to Kirkwall and Gerald's ship, where he was taking advantage of being temporarily anchored in the Bay, and giving a cocktail party.

Betty and Verity hurried aboard, towing Clemency behind them. Clemency looked round for her father. There were other women on board, some Wrens in uniform among the sailors. Then she saw him, such a glamorous figure in his uniform, her heart surged with pride. He caught sight of her.

'Clemency?' There was a flash of joy in his face, before he banked it down. 'So you've come back.'

Her heart lifted: he was pleased to see her even if he pretended that he wasn't.

'Only for a few days. We're here for the night. What luck you're in, will you have time to go and see Mummy?'

'I hope to.' There was a flicker of guilt in his expression; he added, almost as an afterthought, 'I heard from Tony. He says you and Dory are doing a good job. Well done.'

His praise warmed her. 'I love it, though it is hard work.' She hesitated. 'I had to go, you know that. I've found my ideal job.' She studied his face, it seemed leaner, harder, a clutch of grey hairs at his temples, ageing him, smoting her heart.

He stared down at the deck. 'I hope you are behaving yourself.'

'Why wouldn't I be?' His statement stung her, reminding her of his accusation of running off with a man when she was leaving for the ATA. What would he say if he knew that Verity was in love with an Italian POW?

Verity rushed up to them and kissed him enthusiastically.

'Daddy! I've missed you. This is Betty, and isn't it good that Clemency's here.' On she chattered, occasionally throwing warning looks in Clemency's direction, forbidding her to mention Stephano.

From the corner of her eye Clemency saw a woman watching them. She realized with a sickening jolt that it was the woman she'd seen with her father the last time she was here. Without thinking of the consequences she approached her. 'We've met before, what is your name?'

The woman was younger than her mother and quite attractive,

though a more vulgar woman than her, with her low-cut dress and too much make-up. She said defiantly, 'Joan Milton, and you . . .' her mouth quivered, 'are Clemency, Gerald's daughter.'

'You know my father is married and my mother waits for him to return. She's only over the Firth; he could get there without much trouble. You should not stop him going, you—'

'I don't stop him going.' Joan's bright scarlet mouth was tight with defiance. 'He wants to be with me. He's often not here long enough to get across to Caithness.'

'I'm sure he could get a lift over in a plane.' Fury consumed Clemency, thinking of Mummy waiting so patiently at home. 'You should be ashamed, keeping a man from his wife, especially in times like these when he could be killed any day.'

Before Joan could answer, her father strode over, his face hard and stern. Verity and Betty followed him, flashing flirtatious glances at the sailors who stood around.

'Clemency, what's going on?' His voice was low so as not to attract attention, but she was chilled by the look on his face.

'Hello,' Verity said cheerfully. Then sensing something was wrong, she frowned. 'What's the matter?'

'Nothing, my darling.' Gerald tried to steer her away.

Clemency said, 'This is Joan Milton, Daddy's mistress, and the reason he never comes to see Mummy.'

Verity and Betty gasped; Betty, overcome with nerves, almost giggled. She stared at the woman and then back at Gerald.

Gerald had his arm tight round Clemency, his voice was menacing in her ear.

'Don't you dare make trouble. You don't know anything about it, so stop poking your nose into things that don't concern you.'

Joan was pressed against the ship's rail; her eyes rolled as she searched for a way to escape, reminding Clemency of a trapped sheep. Verity turned to her father in consternation.

'Don't you love Mummy? Don't you want to be with her?'

Gerald, taking each of his daughters by an arm, wheeled them round towards the gang plank. 'Of course I love your mother,' he said, still under his breath but at the same time smiling and nodding at anyone who caught his eye. 'Time for you to go though, everyone will be leaving soon.'

'But I've hardly seen you,' Verity wailed.

'I'll come home soon, I promise.' He firmly steered her on to the gangplank then, with more force, his fingers tight round her upper arm, manoeuvred Clemency on to the gangplank behind her. 'I told you I will not have you making trouble, upsetting your mother,' he hissed through gritted teeth.

She shook his arm away. 'It is you who upsets Mummy, no one else.' She marched off behind Verity, who kept glancing back, her face anxious.

Betty followed them, grumbling that she hadn't had time to speak to anyone, but Gerald must have said something, for two of his sailors moved to stand in front of the gangplank, their faces impassive, blocking their way back.

'How do you know that woman is Daddy's mistress? She's too common, she can't be.' Verity raged as they stood on the quayside staring back at the warship.

'I saw them together the last time we came.' Clemency described the scene on that evening and how furious their father had been with her.

Verity was stunned, disbelieving. 'But he couldn't. Does Mummy know?'

'I don't know.' Clemency was defeated by it. If only Mummy lived in the real world instead of imagining some fairyland where Gerald was Prince Charming. She'd seen it countless times in London: the sense of urgency among people that life must be lived to the full in the short time that may be left, combined with loneliness and the longing for human comfort. It was too easy to slip into someone's arms if one's wife or husband was far away. But she didn't expect Daddy to do it, not when their mother was so close. But hadn't he always chased after other women, war or no war?

'I don't want to think about it any more. I wish I could get home tonight, get a good night's sleep,' Clemency said.

'You can't, we're going on to a dance.' Verity linked arms with her. ' I'm sure he doesn't mean it.'

They were interrupted by a group of soldiers who had been relieved of their duties for the evening and were thrilled to come upon three pretty girls all on their own. Clemency went with them, not wanting to be alone tortured by her thoughts. The soldiers were good company, but she kept seeing Stephano in their place. Compared with him she felt that they were lacking in looks and charm, but that was nonsense, and surely lusting after a married man made her just as bad as Daddy? She was overwrought from that scene with him; it was impossible that an Italian POW could seem more attractive to her than an English man.

CHAPTER FOURTEEN

Clemency felt she had just fallen asleep when Betty's clattering downstairs to get breakfast before going to her shift at the hospital woke her. She was sleeping on the sofa in the front room and she tried to go back to sleep, but she was soon disturbed by Verity.

'I'm going to the hospital with Betty in case Stephano is there,' Verity perched beside Clemency on the sofa. 'That party was fun, wasn't it? Though I thought you seemed a little bored.'

Clemency gave up any hope of more sleep. 'It's difficult to adjust to another way of life, not being on call,' she said, though Verity wouldn't understand. She hadn't shown much interest in her sister's work, apart from asking how many fighter pilots she'd fallen in love with.

'Well, you are on leave now. Do you think we can stay here another night? If I don't see Stephano at the hospital I'll go back to Graemeshall and see if he's there.'

'You can do what you like but I'm going back with Sandy this afternoon. I've only got another twenty-four hours and I want to spend them with Mummy.' This was true, but she also didn't want to see Stephano again. The sooner she was back at work at Hamble the better and safer she would be.

Verity frowned. 'Well, if I stay you can tell Mummy I'm with Betty? Because I am.'

Clemency pushed back the blanket and got up. 'I've said, you do what you like, but I will go back with Sandy.'

Verity sighed. 'Will you come to the hospital? I'll be helping there. We can get a lift with Betty's neighbour who also works there. You could draw the people or the view or something,' she added as a sweetener.

Sandy wouldn't leave until the afternoon and the alternative was to stay around Stromness. The town had some curious little streets to explore and she would be content to spend the morning sketching there, but she felt reluctant to be alone. She wanted to be with Verity, but was it Verity she wanted to be with or did she hope to see Stephano?

'I'll come with you until it's time to go to Sandy,' she said, thinking she would take a taxi back to pick up her things.

When they arrived at the hospital Clemency said she'd stay outside to draw and meet them later.

'Ask for me and I'll come at once.' Verity was easily distracted from her work. 'If Stephano is there to interpret for his friend and I see him I'll come back with you. If not I'll see you tomorrow.'

'Fine.' Clemency wandered off to find a comfortable place to settle. She began to sketch the houses and a group of children playing near by.

She worked until the cold wind distracted her; then she went back to the hospital to find out if Verity was coming back to Caithness with her.

She glanced round the reception area for someone she could ask where to find Verity. Stephano was sitting on a chair by the wall. He saw her and smiled. Her heart did a tiresome flip; she frowned at him, determined he should not guess how his presence affected her. Perhaps he took her expression for one of disapproval that he, a POW was sitting here alone without a guard, for he said reassuringly, 'I was escorted here with my friend Marius; his leg is not good, so I wait. My guard,' his eyes twinkled, 'has someone to see.'

'I'm leaving now, going back to Caithness. I'm looking for Verity,' She heard the sharpness in her voice and felt ashamed.

'So Verity is here?' His eyes shone, stabbing her with jealousy, 'I have not seen her and I cannot ask for her.'

'I'm going to find her to see if she's coming back with me.'

A nurse approached and Clemency asked her where she could find her sister.

'She's upstairs. I'll tell her you're here when I go up again. Sit there and wait a moment.' She gestured to the short row of chairs where Stephano sat.

There was nowhere else to sit. If she waited outside the hospital Verity would become embroiled with Stephano and she'd forget her and they would miss Sandy.

'Please sit, I won't bite you,' Stephano seemed amused. He shifted in his chair as though she might feel contaminated by his proximity. She sat down, feeling dizzy, hoping Verity would hurry up and yet, perversely, she did not want her to come and dash away this strange and unsettling moment.

Stephano didn't seem to notice her discomfiture. 'It is good to leave our camp, and the work, it's hard, but harder still to be away from home.' He turned to face her. She had never seen such sorrowful eyes and yet there was a liveliness there that excited her.

She studied the wall opposite. She would not allow herself to be caught up with him. She wasn't used to men discussing their emotions as he did. It was a flamboyant, 'foreign' thing. English people kept their feelings buttoned up, did not strew them all over the place to evoke the sympathy of others. She felt sorry for him; naturally she did, being here in the bleak, grey North instead of being with his family in the golden tones of Italy. But he was still the enemy.

Her eyes were drawn to his hands, lying still on his thighs; his fingers were long and slender, though the skin was rough and pitted with cuts and bruises, no doubt from his quarry work. Enemy or not, he was a human being and had suffered, was still suffering.

'It must be hard for you,' she said at last.

'War is hard for all of us, but I am lucky, people are kind here. They cannot help the cold, the icy winds . . . and the mud!' he exclaimed. 'But we grow flowers round our huts, making the place more cheerful.'

The tenderness in his eyes was like a caress. 'But you have a family back home?' she asked brusquely, to remind herself that he was married.

'Yes, Donata, my wife, and Sabina, my daughter.' His eyes misted over and she had to clutch her hands tightly together to stop herself touching him with a gesture of comfort. 'I have not seen them for two years, I was fighting in North Africa, then we were captured and after many months travelling came here.'

'You hear from them, get letters?'

'Yes, but not enough.' He sighed, then added with forced cheerfulness, 'And you, Spitfire lady, you are married?'

'No, I don't want any commitment until the war is over. Too many wonderful people have been killed.' She had worried that she was incapable of loving but now, here with Stephano . . . but she was being foolish. They were not touching, there was an empty chair between them and yet she felt the warmth of him, everything about him from his scuffed and dusty boots to his thick, dark hair attracted her in a way she'd never thought possible. It *wasn't* possible; he was married and a father, but what was Verity doing with him? She'd get very hurt unless she'd moved on to the next man before the end of the war, when Stephano would go home to Donata and Sabina. Just saying their names brought them to life, confirming that Stephano was out of bounds.

'Surely you have loved someone?' His eyes probed into her. Could he see that she had never been in love or, worse, guess that she imagined that she loved him?

She turned away, afraid he would read the truth in her eyes and pity her.

He broke into her silence. 'You are not like your sister; she has so much love to give.'

'Too much.' The words shot out before she could stop them.

He frowned, 'How can you love too much?'

'I . . . I meant she loves so . . .' She wanted to say *freely, indiscriminately*, but that sounded unjust, though it was true. 'She loves without thinking of the consequences,' she finished lamely.

'How can we think of the consequences? When I married Donata I didn't think I'd be taken away from her by war. No one knows what life will throw at us; we cannot be nervous as an old woman watching at the window, afraid to live and love.'

His eyes, dark as sloes, probed into her. She was about to protest when he went on, 'The English are a cold race, afraid of passion. Perhaps it is a safer way to live, but so unexciting, without courage.' He smiled now, a little pityingly as if she would never understand the tumult of passion, never allow her deep emotions to run their own course, unfettered by strict discipline.

'Stephano! No one told me you were here.' Verity burst upon them. He jumped up and went to her, greeting her quietly, warning her not to draw too much attention to them in case he got into trouble.

'How long have you two been here?' Verity's expression held accusation, as though Clemency had kept him away from her.

'Not long. I've been outside drawing. I'm just leaving to go to Sandy. What are you going to do?'

'Stay. Oh, there is Marius. Why didn't I know you were here before?' She pouted as Marius came towards them on crutches, a new plaster on his leg. A nurse and a man who was obviously the guard accompanied him. 'They'll take you away now. Will you be at Graemeshall later?'

'No, not today,' Stephano answered. 'Next week perhaps, or maybe here if Marius has to come back.'

The group reached them. Marius said something in Italian, Stephano spoke encouragingly to him, taking his arm, glancing down at his leg. The guard, a weak-faced man, said sharply, to show he was in charge, 'Come on, back to camp.'

'So when will I see you?' Verity stretched out her hands to him.

Stephano took them but held them away from him as if shielding off an embrace. 'Soon, but let me go now.' He eyed the guard. 'Don't make trouble, *cara*. I see you soon.' He kissed both her hands, quick kisses one after the other, then turned away and went out with Marius and the guard.

Verity stared after him in anguish. 'Why didn't someone tell me he was here?' she wailed. 'Now I don't know when I'll see him again.'

Watching the party leave, Clemency was engulfed in a moment of intense loneliness. She'd felt this sometimes while flying when she was deep in the cloud, or in a storm. She always tried to shake it off, afraid it meant that she or someone she loved was going to be killed.

'I'm sure you'll see him again soon.' she said briskly. 'Are you coming to Sandy with me?'

'I suppose so,' Verity said ungraciously.

'Verity,' Clemency laid her hand on her sister's shoulder, 'remember he is married with a little girl, and when the war is over he'll go back to them. Have you thought of that?'

'What have you said to him?' Verity demanded, her eyes blazing with indignation.

'Nothing; it's what he said to me. He misses and worries about his family, Donata his wife and Sabine his daughter. He longs to go back to them.' Clemency said this firmly, to convince herself as well as to warn Verity not to get too involved with him.

'You can't help who you fall in love with,' Verity retorted. 'And who knows if he will go back? I'm going to find Betty to tell her I'm going.' She flounced off, leaving Clemency alone.

Clemency went outside to wait for her. It had taken Marius some time to reach the truck to take him, Stephano and the guard back to the camp. She watched how tender and patient Stephano was with his friend, who obviously found it difficult and painful to climb into the seat. When he was in, Stephano turned round and saw her. He smiled and lifted his hand in a wave before getting in to the truck himself.

She waved back. *Goodbye ... my love.* The words slipped silently into her thoughts and she turned away from the scene, annoyed with herself for being so sentimental.

CHAPTER FIFTEEN

Clemency said goodbye to her family, hugging her mother close. It wasn't their fault that she no longer fitted into the family, but hers. She'd broken free and now lived an independent life. If she survived until the end of the war it would be hard, if not impossible to slot back in as before.

The train journey back to the cottage was long and exhausting; if only there had been a plane flying out of Wick going her way. She'd barely opened the front door when Dory and Wellington appeared, Dory's Humber careering up the dirt track. Dory, too, had been on leave and had gone to visit her mother in Hampshire.

'So glad to be back?' She greeted Clemency with a hug and dumped her bag on the floor beside Clemency's. 'No one else here?'

'Don't think so, unless they are asleep upstairs.'

'So,' Dory turned to her, her face expectant. 'Did you have a good time? I was afraid they wouldn't let you come back and we'd have to send out a rescue party.'

Wellington, having jumped up and given Clemency's hand a hurried lick of welcome, ran around the cottage sniffing at his territory to make sure it was the same as when he'd left it.

'Yes, I did, but . . . I couldn't help feeling that I don't fit in there any more.'

'Me too. Mummy was hardly there, busy with her war work. She has some Belgian refugees staying in one end of the house, very commendable but not the home I knew. Still,' Dory shrugged, 'no good moaning about it, others have it far worse.'

She went out to the car and returned with a sack stuffed with vegetables. 'I saw a friend of yours, Harry Chatwin, at a lunch we went to. He asked after you.' She threw Clemency a look that

101

suggested she thought that there might be something between them. Clemency did not rise to it; her emotions were too tangled up elsewhere.

The cottage consisted of a hint of a hall, a sitting room leading into an alcove used as a dining room, a kitchen and a bathroom and four small bedrooms upstairs.

They cobbled together some sort of supper and took it with half a bottle of wine into the sitting room, where they curled up at each end of the sofa, facing each other, with Wellington contentedly asleep on the cushion between them.

'On parade at dawn.' Dory yawned. 'I missed flying, though it does get a bit relentless at times.'

'What will we do when the war is over? Maybe we can carry on flying in some civilian capacity?'

'If they still let women fly after the war,' Dory said darkly. 'They need us now but they may not in peacetime. Look how hard we had to fight to be allowed to fly Spits. Some men are afraid we are better pilots than they are.'

'There's that, and it's true in some cases.' Clemency felt relaxed for the first time since she'd gone on leave. She felt closer to Dory than she did to Verity, but then they were more alike, both flying, both here in the thick of it.

They talked of Johnnie who was off on some secret mission. Dory had not heard from him for a fortnight.

'I'll know if he's dead, I'll just feel it,' she said. She was a little maudlin now. Every day the causality list was put up on the board at the base, or a name on the board of the daily ferry flights was rubbed out. It was best not to dwell on it, but to mourn their passing in private.

'He'll be fine; he'll suddenly turn up like he does,' Clemency said with a smile as if just by saying it he would be kept safe.

'I hope.' Dory changed the subject. 'Did you meet anyone nice in the cold, cold North?' She said it to tease and to lift the pall of fear that Johnnie might not come back. It surprised her when Clemency blushed and looked away.

'So you did? Come on, do tell.' Dory leant forward eagerly, disturbing Wellington, making him grumble. She poked Clemency's side playfully, relieved that there was something exciting she could focus on.

How foolish she was to react so blatantly to Dory's question, a question Dory had just thrown in, not expecting anything more exciting than the description of a party in Wick – with no alcohol unless you had access to the secret whisky store. Dory knew her too well; she would not be able to fob her off with some vague story, but sitting here in the semi-darkness, lulled by the familiarity of being with her friend, she felt a sense of release. She could tell Dory about Stephano, Dory would laugh, put it in perspective and her ridiculous crush would be over.

'I did meet someone, someone different, in Orkney.' She tried to make a joke of it. 'Verity's fallen in love again and—'

'Verity's always falling in love. Which of the forces is it this time? Land, sea or air?'

'None. Any of them would have been fine but he's . . .' Clemency paused, conjuring up Stephano's face, his expressive eyes and that mouth, that gave her an absurd longing to kiss him, 'an Italian POW.'

'Oh gosh, that is a bit much. But, you know, the Italians are so seductive,' Dory rolled her eyes. 'Remember Daddy sent me to Florence to study art and learn Italian? The men were so warm compared to the English boys I knew, comfortable with themselves, with women.' She sighed. 'I understand it, but she must know he's out of bounds.'

It would be embarrassing to admit to Dory that she too had fallen for him. 'He's married, too, with a daughter.'

'It won't last; you know Verity. She's like a child in a sweet shop, she'll be on to the next one soon. But how can she see him? Isn't he in a camp or something? Did you meet him?'

The colour flooded Clemency's face. Just the thought of him made her heart race. Whatever was the matter with her? Perhaps she was having a breakdown, like some other pilots had – though they were mostly fighter pilots, burnt out by their endless sorties and the tension of the dogfights.

'Don't tell me you fell under his spell too!' Dory exclaimed. 'You did, didn't you?'

'I don't know what came over me, I felt as if I ... well, it sounds so stupid, like those cheap romances, but I felt I knew him, belonged with him.' Clemency felt hot and ashamed. 'Perhaps I need a long rest; we've certainly been working hard.' She got up and paced the room. Wellington lifted his head, growled half-heartedly at another disturbance, then lay down again with a disapproving sniff. 'I've never felt like that before with any man and ...' She turned to face Dory, 'it scares me.'

'It's only because he's Italian and possesses their inbred art of seduction. What was he like? Did he fall in love with you?' Dory drew up her knees and watched her expectantly, like a child waiting for a fairy story.

'No, he didn't.' Clemency ignored a stab of regret as she told Dory how it had happened. She remembered everything about him, the way his hair swept back from his forehead, his eloquent eyes and soft, mobile mouth and the air of sadness about him that lingered in his smiles. She described his slender, elegant hands, bruised and cut from working in the quarry. Dory watched her, a little spellbound herself.

'Well,' she said when Clemency had finished, 'looks like you've fallen in love at last, but you know it won't do. You won't get up there again for ages and he might be moved on. If he's married he'll go back to his wife. He must find the Orkneys a very bleak place after Italy.'

'I'll get over it now I'm back here with the flying and the life here. This is where I belong.' Clemency was determined to forget him; there was no other option. 'But Verity loves him; I really think she does this time.'

'We can only hope she's not stupid enough to sleep with him, but I wouldn't worry, she's never stayed with the same person for long before.'

'I hope you're right.' Talking about it with Dory added to Clemency's conviction that as there was no future in it there was no point in fantasizing about him. She changed the subject and told Dory about Daddy and Joan and the scene on his ship.

'What a cad! How could he cheat on your mother when she's just over the water while he's in Scapa Flow?'

Audrey and Jane came back from London, creeping in as if they might wake Clemency and Dory. When they found them gossiping on the sofa, they joined them before they all went to bed to snatch a few hours' sleep before they had to report at the base for duty.

CHAPTER SIXTEEN

The Duke of Kent was killed in August, in a plane crash near Dunbeath in Caithness. Verity rang to tell Clemency, her voice high with excitement.

'He was meant to be visiting the RAF in Iceland and he had the best crew and pilot and they crashed into Eagles Rock. People are saying it's sabotage and Harry's here, looking into it and . . .'

They'd heard the news of the duke's death but not much more and Clemency warned Verity not to exaggerate it. 'Accidents happen all the time,' she said, 'the weather changes suddenly, the pilot gets disorientated, or an engine stalls. You mustn't dramatize it into something sinister.'

'I know all that, but the point is,' her voice was heavy with drama, 'his plane wasn't meant to be over the land at all. He was in a flying boat and he was meant to keep over the water, north west over the Pentland Firth, and the pilot was very experienced.'

Clemency was surprised that Verity knew so much about it. 'Did Harry tell you this?' Surely if he had confided his suspicions to anyone he would not have chosen Verity?

'No. Don't you think it strange?'

'You said Harry was up there. Is he staying in the house?'

'No, we've got the squadron leader,' Verity emphasized *squadron leader* and giggled. 'Harry was at the 'drome. He wouldn't tell me anything but some of the aircrew told me about it.'

'So it's just rumour then?' The duke was the first royal to be killed on active service for centuries, so there were bound to be all sorts of suspicions flying around. But Verity was in Caithness, so the stories she heard might have some truth to them; it was not sensible to speculate.

'Be careful what you say, Verity,' Clemency warned her sister. 'Give my best to Harry if you see him again,' She did not mention Stephano, determined to banish him from her thoughts, though sometimes he crept in, haunting her dreams.

'Harry's left now,' Verity said. 'But if you hear any more about this air crash, you being with all those pilots, let me know. It's quite shaken the place up.'

'It's a tragedy, Verity. He has a family, and think of all the others on the plane.' Was Verity too crass to realize how every plane crash chipped away a little more from their morale? None of them felt safe, quite a few of the women pilots had been killed in accidents: two had crashed close to White Waltham. The worst of these accidents was when something was found wrong with the aircraft: the air vents of the petrol tanks carelessly doped over, closing them; or things wrongly connected, making people wonder whether it was an innocent mistake by an exhausted mechanic or sabotage? So rumours and prurient excitement whipped up by people with no knowledge of flying were hard to take.

Clemency changed the subject. 'Tell me about Mummy, and have you seen Daddy?'

'Mummy's all right and . . . I think Aunt Mattie is in love with Bob, our squadron leader. She's always there waiting for him . . .'

Clemency had to laugh at this; trust Verity to see love everywhere.

'It's true. I told Stephano and he says everyone is capable of love.'

Stephano. His name burnt into her. She said, 'Surely you are not still in love with him, I'd have thought you'd have had at least half a dozen more love affairs since I last saw you.'

'I told you I loved him; I really do.' Verity sounded indignant. 'I see him at Graemeshall when I can, but not nearly as often as I'd like. If only this war would be over we could go and live together in Italy.'

'What about his wife and daughter?' Clemency reminded her tartly.

'Oh . . . wait and see,' Verity said, as if his family were just a small hindrance to her dreams.

The following week Dory and Clemency went up to London. It had been a washout day and no flights had taken off or come in. At five o'clock they were told they could go, so, feeling like schoolgirls let out of class early, they dashed for the train to London. Both had been working hard so they had not been there for a while and they were excited to be meeting friends for an enjoyable evening.

They took a taxi to the flat, opened the front door and nearly fell over a bag lying in the hall. Tony, Dory's father, came into the hall to greet them.

'Daddy.' Dory flew to him. 'Why didn't you say you were coming? It's so good to see you.'

'I didn't know when I was coming, but what luck you . . . both of you, and Wellington.' He bent to rub Wellington's head as he jumped up against his legs. 'You're here too.'

He had that rosy look of someone who had just had a bath; he was dressed in a suit and tie. Though at first sight he seemed to be the same jovial Tony she remembered, Clemency felt that he was different, more subdued. But then, coming back suddenly from a war zone and another country was bound to be difficult to adjust to.

'Does Mummy know you're back?' Dory slipped her arm into his, cuddling up to him as if she couldn't believe that he was really there.

'I've telephoned her; I'll go to Chesterfield tomorrow. I'd have gone straight away but,' he sighed, seeming suddenly old, 'I thought I'd have a night here, a good night's sleep and a bath.' His smile was strained. 'But we could all go out, or do you not want an old codger like me tagging along while you're with your young men?' He tried to make a joke of it but Clemency caught a glimpse of pleading in his eyes.

'No one is as important as you, Tony,' Clemency said. 'It's so good to see you; of course we'll spend the evening with you. We have to take the early train back to Hamble but we have the whole evening.' She was touched by the gratitude in his expression.

'This calls for a drink, I suppose there's no champagne,' he said.

'Maybe there's a bottle in the fridge,' Dory said. 'Oh, Daddy I'm so glad you're safe. We hardly heard from you, but I suppose the post didn't exist or was sent by camel,' she laughed.

Again there was a look about him that disturbed Clemency, but she dismissed it, reminding herself that he'd returned from terrible events in North Africa, after being away for over a year. It would take him time to adjust to his old life; not that it was there any more and might never return.

'That's about it, but I got letters from your mother and a couple from you.'

Dory patted his hand. 'Sorry I didn't write as often as I should have; we're so busy, you see, and time just hurtles by.'

'I understand, darling, you've been doing a vital job. Your mother kept me informed about you. I'm so glad to see you both.' His smile was not reflected in his eyes and Clemency was struck by how empty they seemed, devoid of emotion.

'How long is your leave?' she asked, feeling unsettled by his mood.

'Oh . . .' he looked vague, 'a couple of weeks.'

Dory went to the kitchen to fetch the champagne. Left alone with him Clemency was shocked to see his anxiety. His hands started shaking; he clasped them tightly in a vain attempt to still them. She said gently, 'Was it very terrible?'

He did not answer for a moment but clutched his hands hard together. 'It was war.' He seemed about to say something else when Dory returned, carrying a bottle in one hand and three glasses by their stems with the other. 'I don't want to talk about it, spoil tonight,' he said quietly before turning to Dory, forcing another smile.

'Here we are, you open it, Daddy. What a celebration to find you here.'

'Good to be here, and all the better to find you two girls.' He took the bottle from her and opened it, the cork popped out with a little gush of foam. Dory squealed and held out a glass to catch it.

'I don't want to be a spoilsport, but I'd rather go somewhere quiet to dine,' Tony said when they had finished the champagne. 'I'm sure you've planned to go out dancing, but I'd prefer to turn in early, I've had one hell of a journey to get here.'

'Whatever you want, Daddy, let's have dinner and then if we feel like it we'll go on to the 400 Club. If not we'll come back here with you.' Dory glanced at Clemency to see if she agreed.

'Good idea.' Clemency nodded.

Dinner was rather flat, Tony tried to be amusing and cheerful but as time went on it was obvious that he was very tired and even Dory noticed and suggested he take a taxi back to the flat.

'I will, if you don't mind, but wake me before you go in the morning. Perhaps you can come to Chesterfield,' he said, settling the bill before he left.

When he'd gone Dory said anxiously, 'He's not himself; do you think something dreadful happened, or that he's just exhausted? Finding it hard to settle back?'

'I'm sure that's it. He doesn't want to talk about it, and we understand that. I expect he'll be fine after a few days in the country with your mother,' Clemency said.

It was difficult to adapt to all the changes the war had bought to their lives and finding that people who'd been there in your child-hood, safe and reliable in their familiarity, had now changed added to the insecurity of this frightening, shifting world.

'Come on,' Dory said determinedly, 'let's go and see who is at the 400.'

The club was bursting and both girls were soon dancing. On her way back to their table Clemency saw Harry dancing with a beautiful woman. Her face was like an alabaster mask. He held her close, his expression happy and it smote Clemency's heart. They turned, a perfect pair waltzing together, and she had a good view of the woman, who looked lazily round the room over his shoulder, beautiful and bored. Was this his wife whom he loved but seemed so indifferent to being in his arms? The pleasure fled out of the evening as she suffered for him. She was glad when Dory suggested they went home. She was relieved that Harry had not seen her. She told Dory about it as they went upstairs to the flat,

'Was his wife with him when you saw him at that lunch?' she asked Dory.

'No, he was on his own. Poor man, he deserves better.'

Tony came out of his bedroom to say good-bye to them in the early dawn.

Some days later Clemency got back to the cottage after her day's work to find Dory throwing things into a suitcase, tears pouring down her face.

'Daddy has shot himself,' she gulped through her tears. 'He's not dead, but he might as well be.'

CHAPTER SEVENTEEN

The story of Tony's disgrace came out soon after his 'accident' as his suicide attempt was euphemistically described, but he was past caring or even knowing about it. He had inadvertently led his men into some sort of an ambush and many were killed or badly injured. Not being able to live with the knowledge of his error he had as good as deserted, got back to Chesterfield, his home in Hampshire, and shot himself.

'He'd far rather be dead, I know he would,' Dory told Clemency when she returned from compassionate leave. 'He's a good shot; you'd think he would have managed it, but now . . .' Her face was gaunt with anguish, 'he's like a vegetable. He may make some progress but he'll never be able to live a normal life again and for Mummy it's . . .' She was past tears now; the whole episode had severely shaken her. She, like all of the people who knew Tony, could not believe it of him.

'Everyone's so tired they don't always make the right decisions, anyway, his decision might have felt right at the time,' Clemency said. She wished she could find words to comfort Dory, make sense of it. 'Look at us, it's a miracle sometimes that we land in one piece. You said he was owed leave, he may not have deserted—'

'But he was absent without leave, and he had to have his wits about him to get home, so no one can say he didn't know what he was doing,' Dory said despairingly. Clemency remembered how his hands had been shaking the night they'd seen him; perhaps his hand had shaken when he held the gun, and so the bullet missed its target.

Even when stories came back that Tony's error with his troop was more bad luck than bad judgement and that his courage while serving out there had been exemplary it did not help Dory. 'He should have died fighting, instead of this,' she said. 'That is what he would have wanted.'

'He is still a casualty of war.' Clemency tried to reason with her. 'We rarely hear about those who come back mentally broken. So many lives are torn apart in different ways.'

Dory's close friends formed a group round her and no one blamed her father. They were close enough to the war themselves, hearing the fighter pilots stories of near escapes, seeing the wrecks of planes who'd just made it back. They understood more about servicemen's torment than people in civilian life did.

But watching Dory's doll-like face, set with a relentless determination as she worked, worried Clemency. Winter was upon them, the dusk looming up in the late afternoon, cutting their hours of flying. She begged Dory not to fly in such dreadful weather; they didn't have to, nor were they equipped to do so, but Dory just flew, sometimes taking Wellington, who scampered importantly beside her as if he knew he was doing his bit for the war effort. He was such a keen flyer people joked that he ought to join the team.

It was a relief when Johnnie came home. The powers that be had also become worried about Dory, and she was about to be stood down for a compulsory 'rest' when he turned up. The two of them borrowed a friend's cottage, deep in the countryside, and spent time there alone.

They could hear Johnnie coming before they saw him. He roared up the lane to their cottage to fetch Dory, in his dark-green Morgan.

'Think of him flying.' Audrey saw him arrive from the window. Jane opened the front door as he skidded to a halt and leapt out, his body lithe and graceful, a great smile on his face.

He kissed them all and then Dory was there in his arms.

'I'll take good care of her, hell of a thing to have happened,' Johnnie said to Clemency. Dory hugged them all and got into the car.

'I know you will. It's so good that you're back.' His fellow pilots teased him about his matinée idol looks: auburn hair and piercing blue eyes and a full mouth that smiled often, making every girl feel his smile was just for her. He was over six feet tall and many a girl lost her heart to him, but he only had eyes for Dory.

'I feel I'm running out on you all,' Dory said to Clemency.

'It's called leave and you should have had some ages ago. Now off you go and enjoy yourself.' Clemency stood back as Johnnie started up. Waving with one hand, while the other expertly steered the car out of its tight space he roared back up the lane.

When Dory returned after her leave with Johnnie, she had a glow about her and on her left hand flashed a diamond ring. 'We're engaged, we're going to get married on his next leave,' she said happily. 'Hope I don't get preggers before,' she confided to Clemency later. 'We did "it",' she explained with a giggle. Most of the women were innocent about sex, but now Dory knew it all. 'Once we got the hang of it, it was wonderful.' Her eyes shone. 'I can hardly wait for him to come back.'

Perhaps, Clemency thought, this lovemaking was responsible for making Dory calmer, more fulfilled. She was still passionate about flying but did not seem to need the buzz of it as much as she once had. They were still close friends, but sometimes Clemency felt estranged from Dory, as if Dory had entered another room to which Clemency did not possess the key. It did not surprise her; in fact she felt that she understood it more since she had met Stephano; she recognized a feeling of completeness, of two people fitting so perfectly together. Yet it would not happen to her, not anyway, with Stephano.

Clemency had assumed that Dory might not want to go back to the flat after Tony's accident, to be reminded of that last evening with him. They'd endlessly gone over that evening, wondering if they'd missed some vital clue that could have averted the tragedy. Clemency had thought him changed, but both of them had agreed that that was not unusual; in fact it would have been stranger if he had not changed after the long and difficult time he had been through in North Africa.

But Dory insisted that they went back to the flat when she returned from her compassionate leave.

'Better face it.' Dory's smile smote Clemency's heart. 'We'll invite some of the boys round for a drink before we go out to dinner.'

It had been a difficult moment, seeing Tony's uniform pressed and hanging in the wardrobe, the dressing-table with his set of brushes laid out on a starched cloth, the chair which he sat on to tie up his shoelaces, and knowing that he'd never be well enough to use such things again. It was a relief when their friends arrived. Clemency, watching Dory enjoying herself later, thought how well she hid her anguish.

There was some concern that the Huns might take advantage of the Christmas break and bomb the planes at White Waltham, so they had had to move them to Smith's Lawn at Windsor, which added to their work load. They only had two days off and Dory asked Clemency if she'd come with her to Chesterfield for Christmas.

Clemency had spent some happy times there as a child. The house dated from the time of Queen Anne. It was full of magnificent furniture and pictures, though much of it had been put in storage until the end of the war. They took the train on Christmas Eve, and walked the mile to the house from the station, arriving in the early evening.

As they reached the house Clemency felt tense with anxiety at the prospect of seeing her beloved godfather so changed. She glanced at Dory and saw that she too was dreading the encounter. Clemency took her hand and together they went inside, calling to Wellington who had made off for the overgrown shrubbery.

Clemency was shocked to see how much Grace, Dory's mother, had aged. Her face was haggard with suffering, but she brightened when she saw them. She kissed them both, apologizing for not sending someone to meet them, adding flatly, 'There's no change; you'll find him in his study, Marie is there with him, she's a great help.'

'Marie is one of the Belgian refugees,' Dory explained as they went down the gallery to the study. Grace had put Tony in his study where he used to spend a lot of time, hoping it would feel familiar to him.

Grace did not come with them and when they reached the door to his room, Dory paused, bracing herself for the ordeal. Clemency was afraid of what she would see. Only Wellington, eagerly trotting behind them, seemed impervious to their mood. He waited expectantly for the door to be opened, wagging his tail and looking up at them as if to say, 'what's the matter, can't you open it?' With a glance at Clemency, Dory turned the ornate handle and they went in.

A young woman was sitting beside Tony, who was in his invalid chair; she put down her sewing and got up when she saw them.

'Hello, Marie,' Dory smiled at her and went towards the chair. 'How is he?' Her voice sounded mechanical as though she knew it was a pointless question.

''e is good, 'e eats better.'

Clemency willed herself to approach the chair and face Tony, the man she'd known and loved all her life, who'd been so generous with his presents and, best of all, had given her flying lessons. How should she greet him? Would he know her, or even know that people were in the room?

'Hello Daddy.' Dory bent down, one hand on his shoulder and kissed his cheek. 'I've bought Clemency to see you.' She threw Clemency a pleading, almost despairing look, as if to beg her not to show her fear or her distaste.

Clemency faced him. 'Hello, Tony,' she said. His face was gaunt; there was a vivid red scar from his hairline and over the top of his skull. His head had been shaved and his hair was growing back in patches. The bullet had lodged in his brain. Fortunately the old gardener had found him and Grace had not seen him until he was bandaged up. The wound now was healed enough not to appear too horrific. But Clemency was shocked by his face, it was like a waxwork, recognizably Tony but without life; only his eyes seemed restless, darting glances here and there, but whatever they sought they did not see or did not register, and that she found the most pitiful of all.

It had not been like Christmas at all. Dory found some decorations in the attic and she put some up in Tony's room.

'Christmas, Daddy, do you remember?' Her eyes glistened with tears. Marie blew her nose, missing her family and the Christmases she'd had back home. Dory put the rest of the decorations back in their box, feeling that her gesture to cheer everyone up had had quite the opposite effect.

'Tony is a war hero all the same,' Clemency said as they walked back to the station. 'Everyone said how brave he was before the incident. He can no more help it than could the soldiers in the First World War who suffered from shellshock.'

'Not every one sees it that way,' Dory said, 'but his war, his life is over and so, it seems, is Mummy's.' She sighed. 'It's ironic really. Before the war she used to complain that he was never at home, and now he always will be. I feel guilty that I don't help her more. I know she'd like me to give up flying and go home and help, but I can't, not yet. When the war's over and Johnnie and I are married we'll live close by and by then,' her face lit up with hope, 'Daddy may be much better.'

CHAPTER EIGHTEEN

To Clemency's surprise her father had answered the telephone when she rang them at Christmas.

'I trust you're well,' he'd said briskly, and she could picture him standing tall and straight, holding the receiver as if it were a weapon. 'Dreadful business about Tony. How's Dory taking it?'

'She's coping, she's engaged to a fighter pilot, but it's so hard for Grace,' Clemency told him.

'I can imagine.' There was a pause, then he said heavily, 'I'll go and see him when I can. Here's Verity, better be quick before we're cut off. You ought to come home, there's plenty to do here.'

'Goodbye, Daddy.' She wished he'd said something to assure her that he loved her. But she knew him too well. His pride would hinder him from forgiving her for catching him with that Joan, and despising him for being with a woman inferior to his wife.

'How are you?' Verity, giving her no time to answer said quietly, 'I'm still with you know who. They bought a Catholic priest over for mass at Christmas. I suppose I may have to convert. I see him when I can, and . . .' On she went and at last, when she paused for breath, Clemency couldn't help asking,

'Is he well? Has he heard from his family?'

'Yes, they get parcels from home now. I've seen a picture of his wife, she's quite plain, but the child is sweet.'

'That's not the point, Verity, she is his wife and—'

'But I am with him so he loves me. It's a more passionate love than he had with her.' She giggled.

Clemency sighed with impatience at Verity's naive view on life. Couldn't she see that Stephano might enjoy being with her while being so far away from his family, but when it came to going home he'd go back to where he belonged. What if Daddy was listening to this conversation? The telephone was on the landing, making it easy to be overheard.

'I hope you are being sensible, Verity,' she said. 'Don't forget he's a POW, and married, so it will be impossible for you to marry him.'

'Don't be so sure,' Verity said, leaving Clemency despairing of her sister's inability to face the truth.

Clemency had four Spits to deliver that day. It was a clear, brittle day in March; the pale sun was lifting the drabness from the winter countryside. Her first three flights went well. Her concentration was directed to her flying; she was enjoying the sound of the Merlin engine, the compact intimacy of the Spit, away from the troubles of her heart. But on the last flight, when she was almost at her destination, she flew into a bank of cloud. At first, it didn't bother her; she'd fly straight through it and the airfield at Cosford would be ahead, but it went on too long and was too dense and without instruments she had no idea where she was.

Her choices were to turn back, or push on flying blind, which, apart from some guidance from RAF friends, she knew little about. The ATA stated that one was never to go over the top of the clouds, but if the rules were never broken far fewer planes would be delivered. She could turn round and hope that the sky was still clear behind her, but she'd nearly finished her day's work and was so close to the airfield. She'd been asked to deliver four planes and four she would deliver.

Feeling rather reckless she climbed to get above the cloud, to fly over it to where the sky would be clear again. She climbed higher but still it was dark. A sliver of unease crept into her, triggering an aching loneliness. She was unable to see anything, or to communicate with anyone. If only she could see another plane; just something to give her hope. Still she climbed, searching for the light. She reached the top of the cloud; she was at 12,000 feet and had no oxygen, she was foolish to fly so high without it.

She glanced at her watch, by dead reckoning she was above the airfield; she must not overshoot it. The cloud thinned, she dived into it. The Spit, nose facing down was going faster and faster straight for the ground. She felt cold, fatalistic; was this to be the end? Would she crash, be smashed to pieces in her plane? She could straighten out but then she'd overshoot Cosford, and if the cloud had covered everywhere she'd be forced to try and land or ditch the plane and bale out. They'd been told with unemotional precision that, owing to the shortage of ferry pilots, if there was a choice it was better to save oneself instead of the plane.

With one eye on the altimeter she began to pull out of the dive. Then, by a miracle, there was a gap in the cloud and she saw that she was in the circuit of the airfield. She felt limp with relief and exhilaration; she'd done it, by sheer luck and bloody-mindedness she'd got here. Dear little Spit, it had brought her through. She switched all her attention to the landing. She touched down: a little bump, then she was there.

'Where have you come from?' demanded a mechanic who came to meet her. 'We were told no one would make it, all planes are grounded or turned back because of the weather.'

'Well, I've made it.' She got out, no doubt the flying taxi would be grounded. She'd have to take a train back.

The mechanic grinned at her. 'You ladies are the devil.'

It was very late when she got back to the cottage. She tiptoed in, not wanting to wake anyone, then she fell into bed and slept. Only Audrey was there at breakfast and she was going to London, as it was her day off.

Pleased to have the place to herself Clemency hogged the bathroom, washing her hair and relaxing in the permitted four inches of water. Dory had had a plane to deliver to Prestwick and had friends near by, so she'd probably spent the night with them, gorging on farm-fresh food. Jane was ferrying various bigwigs across the country, and might be cut off somewhere by the bad weather. It happened so often; sometimes you had to put down halfway to one's intended destination and wait there – in a funk, they called it – until the weather changed.

She set off for the airbase on her bicycle. When she arrived, she went to the board to read her schedule for the day. Yesterday she'd reported to the base that she'd got to her destination and would take the train back, so they expected her to be there. She might be called up and scolded for flying 'over the top', so she kept out of the way of the officers in charge.

She checked the board for her name. She was just under Dory's, but Dory's had been rubbed out. Her heart stopped; it must be a mistake. She read through the other names, all of them were there but Dory's.

Not Dory, it couldn't have happened to Dory. She'd flown to Prestwick so many times before; she was so experienced, she wasn't a reckless pilot taking stupid risks. But why had her name been rubbed out? Had something happened to Tony and she'd had to rush home?

Jane was coming towards her, her face taut with grief; she put her arm round Clemency and led her away.

'It hasn't been officially confirmed yet, but someone saw her fall into the sea. Something must have happened to the plane and she didn't bale out in time.' She paused a moment, waiting for the news to sink in, then added quietly, 'She had Wellington with her.'

CHAPTER NINETEEN

It was as if her emotions were anaesthetized, Clemency's brain was like a machine programmed into carrying out her work. She had planes to deliver and that she did, forcing herself to focus her mind on collecting the papers, checking her route and setting off. She dared not think, afraid to unleash horrific images of Dory struggling to bale out, or burning to death, or wounded and left floundering to drown alone in the sea. Death happened, just fate or luck gave you another day, another week, another decade. There were too many of them gone, young and vital people cut off too soon. This was the price of war and there was no point in wondering if it was a price too high.

Tomorrow she and some of the others were to return to White Waltham for a month's training with Class IV planes – known as the heavy twins as they had two engines. Today she was to deliver a Miles Master Mark 1 to Debden and as there was no plane to fly back, drop a Spit at Colerne for MU. She dropped her chit at the Ops room. There was nothing to report; perhaps they'd heard about Dory, but no one said anything. She got back to base and was immediately told there was a P1W, a Priority One Wait, a Lysander which must be delivered urgently to Chattis Hill, back in Wiltshire. It was known as the 'secret airfield', where Spitfires were tested. She'd been trained to take orders so, without questioning it, she got into the Lysander and set off.

It had been a clear morning but now, in the late afternoon, she could see the cloud beginning to bank up ahead; she should get there before it closed in. She didn't care, her emotions were so battened down that she had no fear, no apprehension. A part of her warned her to take care, knowing that it was dangerous to lose the

SHADOWS IN THE SKY

safeguard of fear.

She flew on, in another twenty minutes she'd be there. She studied the pattern of the land beneath her, the railway line cutting through the earth, the gleam of rivers following their ancient courses. The cloud got thicker, obscuring the land, but it had been the same yesterday and she had got through it. A thought pushed into her mind: while she had been battling with that dense cloud, frightened and alone, was Dory already dead? Had Dory known that her time had come? Her plane dropped a little, she pulled herself together; she must get there, this was a priority delivery, and yet she dreaded finishing the flight for she'd have hours in a train back home with too much time to think.

She was through the cloud but she had overshot the airfield. She turned back into the grey fathomless mist, counted to twenty, then dropped low. There it was among the trees. She skirted the trees, which were supposed to hide the airfield and turned to the approach of the runway. Straight ahead, landing gear down, skimming the earth and she was down. She taxied to the dispersal point. It had started to rain, great drops were splashing down. An airman came to meet her, holding a tarpaulin over them as they ran together to the operations room. She handed over the chit; there was nothing to report. The officer smiled at her. 'Thanks. Good flight?'

'Fine thanks.' The telephone rang and throwing her an apologetic glance the duty officer picked it up. Clemency turned away and a feeling of utter desolation hit her like a sledgehammer. She didn't know anyone here; she went into the mess but it was empty. She held her nerve. She'd have a cup of tea, then get to the railway station. She fetched her tea and saw, through the window, the Lysander take off. No doubt someone important was inside who needed to get out in secret.

The door opened behind her, bringing in the heavy patter of the rain, the sound of boots on the floor. She turned and there was Harry and another man, shaking off the rain from their clothes.

'Harry.' Whenever she needed someone he was there. She clutched the back of a chair beside her and held on while the room spun. She hadn't realized what an effort this day had been, as she had forced herself to clamp down her emotions.

'Clemency, what a wonderful surprise! Just the person to cheer us up in this downpour. This is Mac.' He gestured to the man beside him.

'Was that you landing the Lysander? Great landing,' Mac said. He had dark laughing eyes that for a moment brought back Stephano, making her blush.

'I'm just having a cup of tea, then I'll make for the train,' she said.

'Wait awhile and I'll drop you at the station,' Harry said. 'You don't want to go out in this and anyway I should think that's it for flying today, isn't it?'

'For me, yes.'

Mac sat down opposite her, Harry beside her, but almost as soon as they were settled Mac was called away, leaving Harry and Clemency alone. She was so tired; the sturdy barrier she'd struggled to shore up her emotions was cracking. Harry studied her face. 'You look exhausted, no let-up with work?'

His obvious concern for her broke though her resolve.

'Dory is dead, she was killed over the Irish Sea yesterday.' Then she cried; great, gulping sobs racked her body. Other people were coming in now, chatting, laughing, the opening door letting in the wet cold. She struggled to control herself, but she could not stop. Harry got up and pulled her into his arms, holding her. He led her away, she stumbled with him, her head down, hiding her face. He opened a door; they were alone in a small office room.

He handed her a handkerchief. 'I'm so sorry.' He held her close.

'And Wellington.' She cried even harder.

He did not say anything, he just held her. One of the buttons on his jacket bit into her face and she pushed her cheek hard against it, trying to dispel the pain in her heart. Slowly she became of aware of him, the wool of his jacket, the smell of him, the feel of his arms holding her, even his silence was eloquent.

Embarrassment flooded her, how could she have let go like that in front of everyone? It was bad form, especially for a woman pilot whom many thought too emotional to be left in charge of an aircraft, and what must she look like? All blotchy and wet-faced. She hid her face in the crook of his neck; it was warm, slightly damp from the heat of him and for one mad moment she wanted to kiss it, to feel the skin under her lips, taste it with her tongue. She sprang back, wiping her eyes with the heel of her hand, blowing her nose on his handkerchief.

'I'm sorry, so sorry Harry. I'll go now. I—'

His arms encircled her waist. 'Don't go.' His voice was rich with emotion. 'I understand. Too many people have died and Dory was special.'

It was so comforting here in his arms. 'I . . . I didn't think Dory would die. Stupid of me.'

His smile was sad. 'No, just hopeful. You cannot allow yourself to think it.'

A great weariness hit her and she leant against him. 'I don't think I can go on.'

'Yes you can. You love flying and you're good at it. You'll go on flying for Dory.'

His voice filled her with courage. She told him then about Tony and how now poor Grace had lost her daughter too. He listened, sitting back on the desk watching her while she paced around that small room. She finished, 'Sorry to burden you with all this. I'd better get to the station.'

'Must you?' There was a slight wariness in his gaze. 'Can't you have dinner with me? There's an early train tomorrow that should get you back on time.'

His request, so simple, so natural hung in the air. Whenever people met each other, caught away from their base, they spent time together, shared a meal, a drink; just colleagues passing the time. But she sensed that he was asking more of her. Yet there was no demand there, no feeling that she must now pay the price for her outburst.

'Where would I sleep?' she whispered.

'There's a friend's cottage not far from here. I often bunk down there.'

'I must let them know at Hamble; they might not let me stay.' She did not mention that she was going on a training course and need not be at White Waltham until mid-morning.

'I'll see they do,' he said, 'unless . . .' He paused, stretched out his hand and, with his little finger, linked hers, his signet ring glowing against her skin. 'Unless you would rather go back. I can drive you to the station.'

He's married; the words marched into her mind like religious elders to warn her, forbid her. 'I . . . I'd love to have dinner with you,' she said in a rush, hungry now, she'd barely eaten today. She'd have dinner with him and play it from there.

He took her to a scruffy restaurant near by. 'Sorry it's not the Ritz,' he said smiling, 'but the food's not bad.'

They were easy with each other, talking of many things, though as the evening progressed Clemency felt a tension between them, or maybe it was just her imagination as her own apprehension increased as to how the evening would end. She had drunk a couple of glasses of wine and she felt soporific and lazy. It had come out in the conversation that she was going on a training course the following day, so now she had no excuse about having to rush back on a night train. He told her that he and Mac had been waiting for her plane to arrive, 'to give someone a ride.' She knew not to ask who it was or where he was going.

He asked about her family and she told him about Verity and Stephano. 'She'll be terribly hurt when the war ends and he has to go back,' she finished. 'He misses his wife and daughter so much.'

'We can't think too far ahead. Who knows what will happen? We can't allow ourselves to live in the future.' He took her hand in both of his. 'We must live for the present, you know that.'

'Yes.' She thought of Dory. The pain of her loss lodged in her like a wound. She'd had plans to marry Johnnie and go and live near her parents. You couldn't make plans in wartime, it was tempting fate.

They finished dinner but still they lingered, both in their own way wary of the next step. She had to sleep somewhere; she could fall asleep here over the table, she was so tired, but part of her was alert, wondering how to get out of spending the night with him, wondering if she wanted to. Perhaps he wouldn't touch her because he was married, or she wasn't his type. If only Dory were here to talk to, joke about it. The tears rose again and he, who had been watching her, guessed at the turmoil in her.

He said, 'Come on, we must go. Can't sleep here.'

He paid the bill and they went out to his car, he opened the door for her and she got in. As he went round to his side she rehearsed what she should say. *Drop me at the station, better get the dawn train.* Or, *I'll sleep on the sofa . . . if there is one, what about your wife?* But she said none of these things and they sat there cocooned together in the car in the black of the night, a sliver of light from the covered headlights tracing out the lane, the trees towering above them and here and there a star twinkling in the sky.

After about a mile he turned into an opening in the hedge. 'Here we are, it's a dear little place, a refuge from the harshness of life.' He stopped the car. She could just make out the humped shape of a cottage. He opened her door and took her hand.

'Watch out, you might fall over a flowerpot, they are everywhere though most of the plants are dead.'

She wondered whose cottage it was but she didn't ask. His hand was warm around hers and she felt safe. He opened the front door and stood back for her to go in. He picked up a torch that stood just inside, saying they must get the blackouts up before they could put on the lights.

The room was small, furnished with a couple of easy chairs and a sofa, and bulging bookshelves. A staircase led up from a corner of the room. There were some watercolours on the wall, depicting golden summer days, wheatfields at harvest time, a river lazy in the sun, all painted by the same artist – a woman, she guessed. Was this her cottage? Who was she? He'd said a friend; how good a friend?

'There is only one bedroom and that is upstairs,' he said. 'You can have that if you want to, I'll sleep down here; it won't be the first time.'

Unreasonably she felt hurt. She'd been in this situation before: men and women having to spend the night in the same place because of bad weather or no transport, and there was nothing odd about splitting up and sleeping in different rooms, though she had to admit that this was the first time she'd been alone with one man.

'Thanks.' She went towards the stairs.

He did not move from where he stood by the fireplace. 'Will you be all right alone?'

Her hand was on the newel post, one foot on the bottom step. He was giving her a choice: if she went upstairs he would not follow her. He said he'd slept on the sofa before; had he asked other women here, or had it just been a male colleague? There was no time for this sort of interrogation; as he had said, in wartime you couldn't make plans.

'You're married.' Why ever had she said that? She bit her lip. 'I mean, well ...'

'You can just tell me you don't want to and I will understand,' he said gently.

He had told her how his wife behaved, and had Clemency not seen her bored expression as she danced with him? He had said at dinner that they must live in the present in case they had no future. They were here together now; it was so quiet, as if they were the only people in the world. She felt so lonely; there was such a huge void in her life now that Dory was dead. She wanted him, wanted to be in his arms and to be kissed by him. She took a step towards him.

'I ... I don't know what to do.' Then, feeling that that sounded as if she couldn't make up her mind where to sleep, she blushed and mumbled, 'I ... I mean I don't know how to.'

'There's nothing to it, or in fact there is everything to it.' He came towards her slowly, as if she might take fright and run away, but she stood there waiting for him, her body yearning for his arms to be around her. He took her in his arms and bent and kissed her on her mouth, softly at first, then more urgently. Then he picked her up, carried her upstairs and laid her on the bed. He switched on a lamp, it glowed in the darkness, creating the illusion that she was in a warm nest.

'Don't be afraid,' he said, gently undoing her clothes, slipping them off her. 'I think you'll find this better than flying.'

She felt no shame as she lay there naked before him, watched as he tore off his own clothes and then lay beside her, taking her in his arms. As their bare skins came together it was like an electric shock. She had never believed it would be like this, that two bodies could fit so perfectly together.

'I love you,' he said, 'I think I always have, but now I'm sure.'

'I love you,' she said, because she supposed she did; surely you couldn't feel like this, want to do these things unless you loved the person? In the dark as she lay with her head over his heart, his arms round her, she thought of Stephano and felt ashamed. How could she think of him, an enemy, when a British war hero loved her?

He woke her at dawn, he was already dressed in his uniform, his hair brushed down; he appeared the epitome of a smart RAF officer in command. Had she imagined that naked lover who had shown her the heights of desire? He put a cup of tea down on the table beside her.

'Time to get up.' He bent and kissed her, a gentle kiss, not like the passionate ones he'd given her last night.

'Thanks.' She struggled to sit up, pulling the sheet round her breasts, shy suddenly. Was he now regretting their night and all that lovemaking? They were both lonely in their own way but it had been more than that, hadn't it? He'd said he loved her and she had said the same, but maybe that was what people said as they devoured each other in passion. She leant back against the bedhead examining his face for traces of the desire he'd shown last night, but he was taking down the blackout, drawing back the curtains staring out at the grey sky as if assessing it for the day's work. She wanted to ask him what happened next, would they make love the next time they met? Would they plan to meet up again?

'I'll leave you to dress. I'll cook you some eggs and bacon. Are you hungry?' He stood by the door stiffly, polite as if he were a waiter in a hotel taking her order.

'I'd like that. Thanks.' She waited to get out of bed until she heard him go downstairs. She had a bath in the icy bathroom, drying herself on the single towel that she found thrown over the wooden rail. As she dressed she told herself that she must learn to be more sophisticated over such things. Dory and Johnnie had been going to get married; they loved each other and had waited a long time before they had actually made love. She knew that other girls went to bed with men whom they were not going to marry; there was a fast set of men and women who, she felt, bedded each other as though it were just another feast to be enjoyed before their lives were cut short. She wished Harry had singled her out because he loved her, but that was naive of her. He was married, so they could never be together. Last night had been a special time, a magic time. He had shown her with exquisite skill and tenderness the mystery of lovemaking. She should be grateful for that; they'd needed each other last night but now, in the cold light of day, he was, in a kind way, telling her what she already knew, that there was no future for them together.

When she went down to the kitchen a plate of eggs and bacon and a jug of coffee were on the table. 'We haven't much time,' he said, 'your train leaves in half an hour.'

'Have you had your breakfast?'

'Yes, I got up earlier. I . . .' he paused, she could feel the weight of something important hanging in the air, but he went on, 'I have lots on today. Got to get going.'

His mind was on his work and she understood that. She knew not to ask him what he was doing today, it could be secret and lives could be in danger. She remembered he'd been sent to deal with the Duke of Kent's death, and yesterday he'd arranged that flight for someone in the Lysander.

The station was only ten minutes away and as they drove she sensed that he was on the brink of saying something, when ahead they saw a man on a bicycle. Harry slowed down. 'That's Mac, off to the station too,' he said. 'Better wait until he's out of sight then I'll drop you round this bend. You'll see the station ahead of you.'

She sneaked a look at him, his mouth was taut, the muscles tight beside it. She understood that it was better not to be seen together; people suspected that amorous adventures went on but it was safer not to leave a trail. He stopped the car and, feeling she must play her part, she sprang out and went to the boot to take out her parachute bag.

'Don't get out,' she said, thinking it would not do if someone else saw him standing there in the road with her. 'Thanks.' She attempted a smile, determined to succeed in her role as a sophisticated woman, not looking at him as she passed his side of the car.

'Clemency. I . . .' he called through the window, but she walked away, her heart aching.

Then she turned round just once, calling, 'Mustn't miss the train or I'll get shot. 'Bye.'

CHAPTER TWENTY

The service for Dory was held in the ancient, flintstone church where she'd been baptized and where she and Johnnie would have been married. The church was packed; many of Dory's friends had been able to get here.

Clemency went with Jane and Audrey. It wasn't a funeral as there was no coffin, no part of Dory there. She and Wellington were at the bottom of the Irish Sea, with countless others from both sides who had lost their lives there. Grace called the service a 'thanksgiving', which broke Clemency's heart. In peacetime the shock of her untimely death, so young, would have hit harder but there had been too many young deaths now to mark it out as something unique. There was a stoic weariness among the congregation. Not one of them had been spared the anguish of losing someone close to them.

It had been a month now since Dory had been lost and Clemency had struggled to lock it away, but Dory, and indeed Wellington, were not so easily forgotten and memories would break out, sometimes making her smile but more often weep. She'd been through the tragic ritual too many times since the beginning of the war. When someone died their things were collected up and either sent to their families or, if there was no one, handed out to their particular friends. A tidying away of a life, done quickly and efficiently so as not to dramatize it. The hardest thing had been clearing up Wellington's bed, his 'toys': a well chewed ball and a rubber bone, secreted by him under the blanket in his basket. Clemency had had to leave it for Audrey to do while she stood outside by the Solent, the wind rippling across the water, drying her tears.

Sitting now in the church, struggling with her emotions before the service had even started, she saw Grace come in with Tony in his chair, his brother Michael and Marie. She had gone down to Chestefield to see Grace a week after Dory was lost. She'd driven there in Dory's Humber – Dory had told her to use it whenever she wanted to. Halfway there she'd worried that it could be a mistake. Grace, seeing it arrive might be filled with hope that Dory had not died and would jump out, with Wellington yapping with pleasure to be there. Should she turn back and return another day on the train? But she'd told Grace that she was coming, and she had to be the one to return Dory's things and mourn her loss with Grace.

A middle-aged man, a younger version of Tony had opened the door. 'I'm Michael, Tony's brother,' he told her by way of introduction. As he stepped back into the hall he dragged his leg painfully. 'Just a war wound,' he said. 'I'm out of action so I'm here to help out. Tragic about Dory, a dear girl.'

'Yes, I . . . we miss her.' Clemency couldn't say any more. Last time she'd been here she'd held Dory's hand, knowing how she dreaded seeing the empty husk of her father. How quickly life changed and how unfair it was that Grace had lost so much.

She pulled herself together, this was how it was in war and there was nothing anyone could do about it.

She found Grace almost numbed with grief, although every so often she burst out, 'That bloody flying, and to take Wellington? I suppose he hadn't got a parachute so she wouldn't leave him and save herself.'

There were no magic words that would soothe their grief. She shared Dory's love of flying but they could all have just as easily been killed during a night out in London, or been in the Café de Paris when it was bombed.

Grace told Clemency to use the flat in London whenever she wanted; she'd probably sell it after the war but she did not want to make any decisions now.

'Take her car and anything else of hers you might like.' She refused to see the things that Clemency had bought from Hamble, telling Marie to take them to Dory's bedroom and leave them there.

Clemency protested about the car, but Michael said, 'Take it. Grace has no use for it.'

All the while Tony sat in his chair, sometimes agitating his hands, glancing fearfully round the room. Did he know his beloved daughter was dead? Perhaps the one good thing about his disability was that he did not.

Now in the church she watched Dory's family slowly progress up the aisle to the front pew. Grace, dressed in a black coat, Michael, limping badly, pushed Tony's chair. Tony seemed quite animated, looking round bemused but as if he knew the place.

Clemency was sitting at the end of the fourth pew from the front with Jane and Audrey next to her. Someone squeezed in beside her and, glancing up, she saw it was Johnnie. He kissed her cheek. His face was ashen, his blue eyes, usually sparkling with humour, were bruised with pain. He'd been overseas and she hadn't heard from him since it had happened. She took his hand and held it tightly, biting the inside of her cheek to stop crying out at the waste of it, the end of their hopes of marriage, the children they might have had together, and at the whole damn futility of war.

Together they somehow got through the service, the hymns of hope promising eternal life, the prayers, the eulogies that tried to conjure up Dory, but, well-meaning though they were, Clemency felt they did not do her justice. Childishly she blamed God for snatching her away too soon.

Johnnie could not stay for the tea laid on at Chesterfield. He kissed Grace gently, as if she might break.

'Johnnie,' she laid her hand on his cheek, 'oh, Johnnie, what can we do?'

Johnnie had come with a couple of friends from his squadron who had just returned from Iceland. Clemency and Dory knew them both and after they had made their farewells they went and waited for Johnnie in the truck. He kissed Clemency goodbye, holding her close in a sudden hug.

'We'll see each other about.' His eyes were bright with unshed tears. Dory stood between them yet neither could bring themselves to mention her. She had gone, leaving them behind.

'I'll look out for you.' Even in his anguish his looks were extraordinary; a perfect face, straight nose, beautifully shaped lips, and those blue eyes and long lashes. He had a face that it was a pleasure to look on, to watch as his expressions changed, never once spoiling its beauty. Women – men too – were struck by his looks, and his nickname 'matinée idol' was an apt description. What a couple he and Dory had made, and their children – she couldn't think of that.

'I'll be away awhile, but I'll keep in touch. Take care.' He kissed her again and, with a passable attempt at a smile, he turned to join his friends in the truck.

'Keep safe.'

She watched him stride towards the truck as one of his friends called, 'Come on, idol, put the girls down.'

Johnnie said something rude back, got in and they drove off.

'My,' said Jane, who'd joined Clemency, 'what a man. It's so tragic how it ended for him and Dory, but he won't be alone for long.'

'No, but I don't think he'll ever love anyone as much as he loved her.' Clemency was left with the familiar void of loneliness, a terror of knowing how fragile life was.

She'd half-wondered if Harry would be at the service. She hadn't heard a word from him since their night together, but, she reasoned to herself, although married people had affairs in these strange times; the sin was in being found out. He might jeopardize his job, his future rank and his marriage if their night of passion became known.

Sometimes in the loneliness of the night she wondered whether he regretted going to bed with her. She'd often said to him that she didn't want commitment until after the war and he'd agreed with her. She was making too much of that night, the few hours of pleasure snatched in troubled times, leading nowhere.

She could have talked it over with Dory; she couldn't discuss it with anyone else. It would be best to keep quiet about it, not make it sound important and risk its becoming a scandal, but often she thought of that night and his tenderness.

But still she thought of Stephano, the one man who had really ignited her emotions without touching her. She'd experienced a *coup de foudre* – had been struck by lightning. She might love Harry; she was certainly fond of him, but she hadn't felt that urgent magnetism, that feeling that she must be part of him. But a saner side of her warned her such emotions were madness. She could never be with a POW, an enemy of her country, a married man with a child.

The three of them did not stay long for tea at Chesterfield. They drove back in silence, each lost in their own thoughts. Tomorrow was another day; would they last through it? Just a tiny mistake or a distraction, made through exhaustion or a sudden blanket of cloud, and they too could be snuffed out like Dory.

CHAPTER TWENTY-ONE

Clemency missed Dory in the cottage and in the mess, though with their different shifts and leave days people were often not about. But she'd always been there in the flat in London and going there without her was hard.

Friends begged her to come to London, and she needed to see them, get some light relief from the gruelling round of work. She could almost hear Dory telling her to go, that she owed it to her to enjoy life while she could.

Jane and Margot, another ferry pilot who sometimes took Dory's place in the cottage, came with her that first time. To her relief Mrs Stanley, who 'did' for them had done her bit and tided most of Dory's and, indeed, Wellington's things away, but it was heartbreaking to see Dory's coats hanging on the pegs in the hall and Wellington's leads on the hook by the door.

The drawing-room held so many memories of fun and laughter: evenings with Teddy and Charles, both gone now, so smart in their uniforms. Sometimes they would open a bottle of champagne or mix a martini while they decided where to go for the evening. Now she was the only one of the four of them left; she must not waste a moment. She was seized by a surge of energy that lifted her spirits, as if her dear friends were somewhere in the shadows, urging her on.

Their three escorts for the evening, Peter, James and Alec, came to pick them up and they went to the Dorchester for dinner.

Clemency glanced round to see who else was there. At the table opposite them was a woman, she'd seen before but couldn't place. She was dining with an officer in uniform. Her dark hair was looped back with diamond clips, and it was obvious from the way she leaned in to whisper to him, or touch him with one delicate hand while the other held her cigarette holder, while her carmine lips sinuously exhaled the smoke, that she was working at seducing him.

'Who has caught your fancy?' Alec teased her.

'That woman, I've seen her before, I'm trying to think where.'

Alec inspected the woman. 'That's Flavia, known as Anemone. If a chap gets too close she draws him in and swallows him whole.'

'Is that true?' Margot craned to look at her.

'Poor Harry. He's off doing his duty and Flavia's always got her claws into some chap,' James said.

'Harry Chatwin?' That's where Clemency had seen her, dancing with Harry.

Peter nodded. 'Last time I saw him was at the Savoy on Teddy's last evening out.' Peter was in the same squadron as Teddy and had flown with him the day he was killed.

Clemency studied Flavia surreptitiously, hating her for playing around while Harry was away working so hard for his country. Since their night together she had occasionally been tortured with guilt for sleeping with a married man, but now she felt exonerated. Harry deserved some love. Watching the woman with this officer Clemency doubted whether Flavia cared for anyone but herself.

'Harry's a good fellow, has some ties to my squadron,' James said. 'He doesn't deserve such a wife, but what can you do? Some women are just out for a good time. There is plenty of opportunity if you look for it.'

'Oh yes,' Alec teased him. James hit back with a choice remark, leaving Clemency furious with Flavia for treating Harry so badly.

Flavia got up from her table and the man she was with rose too, giving Clemency a chance for a good look at him. He was in the army and not a patch on Harry. His blubbery mouth seemed to Clemency's overworked imagination to be salivating at the thought of the night ahead. Without knowing why she followed Flavia to the powder room.

Flavia was touching up her make-up in front of the mirror. Clemency hovered behind her. Flavia ignored her, her attention on her own reflection. Clemency said sharply. 'I know Harry, your husband. He stayed with us in Scotland.' Her own reflection in the mirror reflected the fury in her eyes.

'How nice for you.' Flavia, the Anemone went on applying lipstick to her overpainted mouth, pursing it as if ready to suck in her prey. She twisted her lipstick back into its gold case, massaged her lips together, leaning closer to the mirror, tilting her face this way and that with a look of self-appreciation. Close to, Clemency saw that she was quite old. Her skin was fine but a web of wrinkles fanned out at the corners of her eyes and ran down beside her mouth.

'I think he is a wonderful man; so brave, so loyal.' Clemency tried to appear nonchalant. Jane and Margot had joined her. They regarded the scene with surprise.

'He is wonderful, darling,' Flavia drawled, 'trouble is he's never here.' She snapped her evening bag shut, whipped round to face Clemency, her eyes cold. 'So what's a girl supposed to do?' She swept out, leaving Clemency dumb with anger. She moved to follow her, but Jane laid a restraining hand on her arm.

'Leave her. She's a bitch. Everyone knows it. But why are you so hot and bothered about it?' Jane regarded her intently, Clemency turned away; she must be careful or they'd guess that she had been to bed with Harry. She could hardly justify accusing his wife of going out with another man if she had been in his bed herself.

'Sorry. Don't know what came over me.' She hadn't seen Harry since that night and she missed him. After feeling him so warm, so alive beside her, lying close, skin to skin, she was left with a kind of coldness that she suspected would only leave her when she made love again. She remembered Dory saying, after her weekend away with Johnnie, 'Imagine waking up every day of your life in the arms of the person you love and making love. Once you've done it, it is so hard to live without it.'

She reminded herself of her vow not to fall in love until after the war. She thought of Johnnie, so broken without Dory and so many other girls she knew whose fiancés and husbands would never come back. Or, if they did, like Tony, were completely changed for ever. Then there was Stephano, his face as clear now as if he stood before her. Her heart beat faster. To her amazement and chagrin Verity was still in love with him. She had telephoned a couple of days ago and Clemency couldn't resist asking her.

'Of course I'm still in love with him. I keep telling you he's the one. Why don't you listen?'

They went to the 400 Club; it was full of people they knew. A couple of fighter pilots, Tom and Geoffrey, who were on leave from Iceland, joined them. Geoffrey asked Clemency to dance. He had an endearing puglike face and was amusing. They waltzed together and when the dance was over he said gravely, 'Sad about Johnnie.'

She felt as if she'd been punched in the stomach. 'Johnnie? Not Johnnie Elliot?'

'Didn't you know? Shot down. Terribly burned.' Seeing her distress he squeezed her to him. 'I'm so sorry, Clemency, I thought you knew.'

'No. What happened?'

'Happened last week but I only heard yesterday. Bloody Hun got him, he fought back but his Spit caught fire. He got out but he's badly burnt. He's in hospital, in good hands in the Queen Victoria.'

'Oh God, not burnt.' Pilots dreaded being burnt, trapped in the cockpit. Spitfires carried such high-octane fuel that they could ignite quickly, envelop the pilot in flames before they could bale out.

Geoffrey looked grim. ''fraid so. He was escorting a convoy. He's in the care of Archie McIndoe – couldn't be better. Hope they'll patch him up.'

The fun went out of the evening as the news went round. Everyone knew Johnnie and a gloom settled over them, but then Alec made a joke about barbecues and the others did their best to laugh. If the girls had not been ferry pilots they would have thought the joke in dreadful taste but they knew, as indeed Johnnie would know, that jokes conquered fear and none of them could afford to lose their nerve.

The last time she'd seen Johnnie had been at Dory's service, his perfect face, matinée idol. She couldn't bring herself to ask Geoffrey if his face was burnt. She struggled to banish images of him grotesquely maimed from her mind.

The next day Clemency contacted his family. His sister told her that he was badly hurt but fighting back.

It was some weeks before they were able to visit him. They heard through a friend of theirs, Lavinia Bevington, who was nursing at the Queen Victoria Hospital, that he was now up to receiving visitors and would like to see her and Jane. They scrounged enough petrol coupons to go to East Grinstead to visit him.

'I'm dreading this, but that's selfish of me, isn't it?' Jane said as they drove through the Sussex countryside to the special burns hospital. Clemency remembered Johnnie talking about his fear of being burnt, telling her that he, and indeed others, carried a pistol, preferring to shoot themselves than burn to death but, whatever had happened, Johnnie hadn't used it.

Professor Archibald McIndoe was the saviour of these men, making them as presentable as he could. The 'Guinea Pig' club was formed, its members being the pilots who'd suffered burns and the club was so named because its members were guinea pigs for the new treatments the professor tried on them. Clemency was afraid she would distress Johnnie if she couldn't control her horror at seeing his injuries which, she felt, would seem worse on such a beautiful man. Dory would not have flinched, she was tough and she loved him. There were stories of men who, unable to stand their own looks and the pain of their injuries, blew their brains out rather than live with them, or became so twisted and difficult in their characters they chased away the most loving of women.

They were shown in to the hospital garden. It was a warm day and various men were sitting there, many on their own, most of them covered in bandages. Clemency and Jane didn't know where to look; they were crushed with sympathy for these shocking relics of such golden youth, though they knew sympathy was not what the men wanted. So the two women walked tall, smiling at the men as they passed, as if they were all at a party, forcing themselves not to show their pity and disgust and both of them deeply ashamed of such feelings.

'Clemency, so glad you came.' There was Lavinia, crisp in her nurse's uniform.

'Oh, Lavy, it's so good to see you.' Clemency hugged her, filled with relief. If Lavy could cope so could she. 'We've come to see

Johnnie. This is Jane Glover.'

'He's waiting for you over here.' Lavinia looked sad. 'Bloody about Dory.'

'Yes.' Hurriedly Clemency blinked away her tears. It wouldn't do to break down now, but it was all so terrible. She pulled herself together; she was doing this visit for Dory. 'How is Johnnie?'

'Coming on. He's jolly brave. They all are here.' Lavinia seemed unfazed by the dreadful sights around her. Briefly Clemency remembered the wounded being brought in from the bombing in Wick and she shuddered; she was not cut out for such sights; she felt far more comfortable in the clean fresh air of the sky.

'Here he is.' Johnnie was sitting on a bench, reading a book, holding it with bandaged hands. His profile was perfect, that smooth brow and the lean cheek. His hair was shorter now but still curled in that engaging way round his ear. Clemency felt a shot of relief; his face was not harmed.

'They're here, Johnnie.' Lavinia reached him, laying her hand on his shoulder. He turned and Clemency had to bite the inside of her mouth to stop herself crying out. The other side of his face was gone, or it was there, but not recognizable as a face. The skin was puckered and raw, his eye shone out from damaged lids, his head was bald a few tufts of hair sprouting from the red skin, but his mouth was untouched.

'You don't see me at my best.' He struggled to get up. 'Sorry.' He held out his bandaged hands. 'I can't shake hands with you.'

'Johnnie.' Clemency, afraid of causing him pain by inadvertently touching one of his wounds, kissed his smooth cheek, forcing herself not to flinch. There was a smell about him that almost made her gag: destroyed skin, ointment, she didn't know what. She longed to cry, to scream at the inhumane destruction of war. Was it worth all those lives lost and destroyed?

Jane managed herself better. 'So good to see you,' she said, sounding as if she meant it.

But the conversation that used to flow so easily between them had now dried up. What could they say? *What a lovely place this is*, when being here brought so much anguish? Lavinia saved the day asking about their flying and Johnnie joined in, making jokes about their skills. Clemency watched how often he glanced at Lavinia, as if she were his support, and how tender she was towards him. Was it just her nursing compassion or was there more to their relationship? Dory's absence hit her savagely. Johnnie must have picked up her feelings, for he said, 'I miss Dory terribly but perhaps it is for the best that she wasn't lumbered with me like this.'

'She wouldn't have seen it like that,' Clemency assured him. 'She loved you, knew what could happen. After all it could have happened to her too, and what would *you* have done? Oh, I'm so sorry I didn't mean . . .' she floundered, ashamed of her outburst.

Johnnie said, 'None of us dwells on it, you know that. Don't know how I would have behaved if she'd been left like this.' He waved his bandaged hands, his mouth was taut. He fixed Clemency with his eyes, one still so clear, the lashes long and silky, the other grotesque and for a moment she thought of Harry, and wondered what his wound looked like under his patch.

'You would still have loved each other,' Clemency said fiercely, wanting Dory here, wanting them still to be together.

'We'll never know.' He threw a pleading glance at Lavinia, who smiled lovingly at him.

Clemency banked down her feelings of despair; it shouldn't have ended like this, with Dory dead and Johnnie burnt, but she must curb her tongue and not upset him further.

'It's good to see Lavy here.' She turned to Lavinia.' I thought you were nursing in St Thomas's?"

'I was but then I met the maestro, as we call Professor McIndoe, and I was so impressed with his work that I came here to work with him. It's such a special place.'

'Can't think why you'd choose to be here among us toasted has-beens, when you could be with glamorous soldiers with just sore trigger fingers and blisters from marching,' Johnnie joked, 'but if my hands get better I'll fly again, see off those Huns once and for all.'

He seemed suddenly to droop with exhaustion. It was time to leave. They'd brought him books and whisky. 'Purely for medicinal purposes,' Jane said.

'We'll come back soon,' Clemency kissed him.

He regarded them both gravely for a moment, 'Don't forget me, don't forget any of us.'

'Of course we won't,' Clemency said vehemently. 'Don't ever think that.'

He smiled a sad smile and lifted his bandaged hands in farewell.

Lavinia came with them to the car. 'He's doing well, though you might not believe it, but he so nearly didn't make it.'

'You're in love with him, aren't you?' Clemency said.

Lavy smiled, that special smile that lights up the heart. 'Yes, I've always loved him; we've known each other since we were children, but he had Dory and he will always love her.'

'But you are here.' A lump swelled in Clemency's throat. 'I so hope you have a future together, Lavy, I really mean that.'

'I hope so too.' Lavy kissed them both goodbye before going back to her duties.

The two women were deeply affected by their visit; neither of them had seen such horrendous injuries before. Jane said, 'I'm so glad he's got Lavy. I never thought she'd become a nurse, but look how good at it she is.'

'This war has been liberating for us girls,' said Clemency, 'but it's perhaps as well that none of us knew the horrors ahead or I, for one would have run away screaming.'

'No you wouldn't,' Jane retorted. 'None of us would, because we never believe that anything horrible will happen to us.

CHAPTER TWENTY-TWO

Clemency's first job that day was to fly a clapped-out Blenheim to the MU to be scrapped. No one enjoyed flying planes that had been shot down or had been involved in a crash on their last flight, wondering if the aircraft would fall out of the sky with them in it, which would be an ignominious way to go.

It was dull day but with enough visibility and she took off, climbing into the sky, the plane labouring as if it hardly had the strength to do so. She was exhausted, but that was nothing new; you worked hard all day, danced all night if you could, snatched a couple of hours' sleep and then started it all again.

The engine didn't feel right. She listened to it intently. The plane dropped a little, the engine coughed, the oil gauge went to zero: it was packing up. She'd better put down, or bale out.

She looked beneath her, saw a clump of houses and a field ahead. She flew lower, preparing to land, but as she got closer she saw that the ground was full of old cars and posts put there to deter enemy aircraft. She lifted the plane back up. The engine faltered; she was too low to bale out and she didn't dare climb any higher. She was strangely calm; could this be the end for her? She glided on, seeing a wood ahead and just before it a short strip of grass. She had to land there, it was her only chance.

Carefully she steered the plane towards the grass. It touched down, then bounced up on the uneven ground. She was going too fast, she had run out of land, she was into the trees, one wing was torn off. After skewing round the plane had stopped, its nose embedded in a tree. With difficulty she pushed back the cockpit hood and jumped out, falling heavily on to a jagged tree stump. A youth came running towards her, holding a pitchfork as if it were a spear.

'It's all right, I'm English, a ferry pilot.' She took off her helmet, wincing at the pain in her side.

'Cor, miss. Thought you was a Jerry.' He broke into a grin of incredulity.

An older man joined him. Seeing she was hurt he helped her to his house.

'I'm fine,' she said, 'just a bit bruised.' The pain in her hip was excruciating.

She telephoned Hamble and explained what had happened. She was put on a train back to base. When she arrived her hip was worse. She went to the lavatory, undressed and saw a huge bruise spreading. Fortunately her flying suit had protected her from a worse injury.

She reported back to her commander and related the story of her ignominious landing.

'Were you injured? You seem to be in pain when you move.' Her commander had X-ray eyes; Clemency should have known she would find out that she was hurt.

'Just a bruise on my hip, it will soon heal.'

She was ordered to go to the doctor, who, after examining her, insisted that she take time off.

'I'm fine,' she said, but both he and her commander insisted that she must take a fortnight off. This gave her time to go back to Caithness.

The train was cold and draughty and by the time she'd arrived her whole side had stiffened. Nancy, there to meet her in the canteen van, was horrified by her appearance and even Verity, who had been longing to relate every detail of her love life, was shocked at how pale and thin she was.

'Don't fuss, it's only a bruise,' Clemency protested, but she fell gratefully into bed and for a few days she welcomed her mother's care.

'Harry was up here the other day,' Verity told her. She was curled up on the end of Clemency's bed, longing to gossip after managing to curtail her stories while Clemency slept.

'Is he still here?' Clemency wanted to see him again, though it might be embarrassing after their night together. She must behave in a more sophisticated manner; it obviously meant nothing to him – apart from perhaps a sliver of guilt over cheating on his wife. Though she wondered why it should when she'd seen herself how Flavia behaved. Perhaps, and the thought made her sad, he joined her in her games and went to bed with lots of women. She had just been the one for that night.

'Don't know. He asked after you.' Verity eyed her curiously. 'Have you seen him in London, is he one of your beaux?' She giggled. 'A bit old, I'd have thought.'

'I see him occasionally at the 400 Club, where the RAF go.' That would sidetrack Verity who longed to know every detail of her social life.

'It's so tragic about Dory,' Nancy said as they sat together in the study. 'And Tony. Poor Grace, how can she cope?' She shuddered as if she might be called on to suffer such tragedy. 'I'm so glad you're back, darling.' She clasped Clemency's hand. 'You've done your bit. Now you can stay and help out here. There's lots to do.'

Clemency ignored the last bit of her remark. As soon as she could she'd go back to Hamble and keep on working until the war ended, but she wasn't going to say this now.

'I miss Dory so much and it's dreadful about Tony, but his brother, Michael, seems to be there, helping Grace. I think he's been invalided out of the army.'

'Ah, Michael. I'd heard he'd been badly wounded. I'm glad he's at Chesterfield, he's always been in love with Grace.'

Clemency thought of Tony confined to a wheelchair, his mind confused. Would he ever get better? Would he come to realize that Dory was dead and that his brother loved his wife?

Verity talked about Stephano in endless detail. Italy had capitulated and the Italians were out of the war, no longer their enemies. The POWs couldn't leave Orkney, but their status had changed and they'd been given radios and bicycles and more freedom, and paid a wage for their work on the causeways.

'They are building a chapel in one of the Nissen huts,' Verity told her. 'They've covered it with cement, shaped the front in a sort of triangle with pillars and windows and a little bell tower on top.

Stephano showed me his drawings of it.'

'Did Stephano design it?' Just his name on her lips made her heart race. She scolded herself for being so foolish.

'Not exactly, though he had some ideas and he helps with the painting.' Verity giggled. 'He says he'll paint me as a tiny face of an angel and it will always be there in memory of our love. We could see the chapel when we go to see him. He's allowed to go where he likes now, so we're often alone.' Verity's eyes shone.

'The war will end soon and then he'll return to his family.' Verity's enthusiasm irritated her.

'He might stay,' Verity said defiantly. 'Our love is too strong to be broken.'

There was little point in continuing the conversation but two days later Clemency agreed to go to Orkney with her sister.

They bicycled towards Lamb Holm where the POW camp was situated. It was now possible, Verity told her, to scramble across from the Mainland Island as the causeway was now built.

'Do we go to the camp then?' Clemency asked.

'No, we don't need to. We meet on Mainland, you'll see.'

As they cycled along beside the vast area of water, Clemency was surprised to see so many Italians along the way. Verity blew kisses at them. Clemency cycled on; she had taken Stephano's characteristic charm too seriously. When she saw him this time she would not react so strongly.

She was wrong; if anything her reactions were worse. He looked better than when she'd last seen him, more filled out, healthily flushed with working outside.

'Clemency, you've come back to us.' He kissed her on both cheeks as a brother would. For a second she recalled Harry's lovemaking, now she knew what it was about the feel of Stephano's body as it briefly touched hers; his quick kisses and the scent of him meant that she had to summon all her self-control not to snatch at him and twine herself round him.

She had to escape. She took out her sketch book and turned to leave him with Verity. Stephano, seeing her book, said, 'Don't go away, I'd like to see your drawings. You still have not done one for me of Verity, but I've done my own.' He pulled a pad of paper from his back pocket and held it out to her. 'There are two of her in here, and I have pictures for our chapel. Has Verity told you of it?'

'Yes, it sounds . . . beautiful, a place of hope.' She ignored Verity's expression of sulky disappointment with his showing more interest in the chapel than in listening to her.

He came close to Clemency, the pages of his book fluttered in the wind; some were loose and he struggled to stop them blowing away. 'Let's sit out of the wind.' He went over to a wall.

'She can see them later,' Verity grumbled, putting her arm round him.

'*Pazientàre, Cara*, be patient, I want to show her and you too.' He sat down in the shelter of the wall, patting the grass beside him. Clemency hesitated a moment before sitting down close to him so that she could see his work.

Verity sat on his other side nuzzling her face into his neck. He ignored her, holding the pages tight against the determination of the wind to scatter them. They were detailed drawings, first of a hut, then of how it changed with a façade over the front of it. It was much as Verity had explained: the triangular shape edged with curled detail, and two pillars on either side, topped with what looked like *fleurs-de-lys*. There were more sketches of a metalwork screen before the altar and low gates to form part of the communion rails. He pointed out the details, explaining how they would construct it, his accent importing to the words a special flavour. How intimate this was, thought Clemency, the way he shared his joy and excitement with her, his face alight, animated by his ideas.

Verity hung on to him but she did not show much interest in his descriptions. For a few moments as dark eyes darted to Clemency, then back to his sketches, it was as if their glances were weaving a bond between them.

The intimacy was shattered by a cry and a man appeared, calling for Stephano. He gathered up his drawings.

'We have to work, we are paid now, so it is good,' he explained.

'You can't go. We've just arrived.' Verity clung more tightly to him.

'I must go, *Cara*.' He kissed her, unlacing her fingers from his arm. 'I'll see you another time. I'm usually here. We may not be in the war any more, but I cannot go home.' His smile was bitter-sweet.

It struck Clemency that whatever dreams Verity had she would never make a life with him. He didn't belong here, he didn't belong to them. Like a migrating bird, when the time came he'd return to his home and his country, on his own.

The following day she left him to Verity. She was rested now, ready to go back to work. She wouldn't come here again, at least not until the war was over and the POW camp dismantled.

They stayed another day in Orkney. It was cold, the wind relentlessly gusting off the Atlantic. Betty was there, and Judy, Mrs Donaldson's daughter, was back on leave. They went together to a dance in Stromness. It was a relief, though Clemency didn't say it to Verity, that their father's ship was not in. She could now enjoy herself without fear of seeing him with some woman, or with Joan, if she was still around.

Verity became increasingly subdued as the evening progressed. Clemency assumed it was because she hadn't been able to see Stephano again, having heard that he, among others, was to work on some remote farm for a few weeks. She tried to jolly her sister along, pointing out various British young men, but Verity did not rise to it even refusing to dance, though she was often asked to do so.

The boat trip back to Caithness was choppy and they both felt queasy, Clemency felt better as they bicycled home, but Verity took to her bed and lay there listlessly with Nancy fussing round her, scolding her for gallivanting about so much.

For the next couple of days Clemency bicycled around Caithness, seeing friends and sketching, Verity would not come with her.

'I want to stay here,' she said, hunching into herself.

'Do you still feel seasick, or are you moping over not seeing Stephano?' Clemency asked her, wishing she'd snap out of this mood.

'Just leave me alone,' Verity turned away from her.

Verity's malaise irritated Clemency; she swerved between despondency and mild hysteria with her love life. It was time to go back to work. She'd ring Hamble tomorrow; tell them she'd be back by the end of the week.

That evening she was pleasantly tired from her bicycling and the sea air. She got into bed and opened her book, a detective novel by Raymond Chandler that she'd found downstairs. Verity was still wandering around the room.

'It's time I went back to work. I'll ring Hamble tomorrow and go back to lighten their load,' Clemency said to her.

'But you can't.' Verity sank down on her bed, her face twisted in panic. 'I thought you were home for good now.'

'No! Whatever gave you that idea?' Did Verity think she was going to be sucked back into her family where the only excitements seemed to be whether Aunt Mattie was attracted to the squadron leader or Verity's love life, or what Daddy was up to? 'I'm only on leave. I was given more time as I hadn't had any for so long and was injured, but now I'm better I must get back. They need me.'

'*I* need you.' Verity whispered in terror. 'I'm having a baby. Mummy and Daddy will kill me and you are the only person who can help me.'

CHAPTER TWENTY-THREE

'Good night, girls,' Nancy called as she passed their door on the way to her room.

Verity glanced anxiously at her sister as if afraid she would call Nancy in to spill the shocking news. Clemency tensed, listening to Nancy footsteps as she went on along the passage, willing her to come and kiss them goodnight as she used to do when they were children. Then Verity might tell her about the baby and somehow Mummy would make it all right. Though in reality she wouldn't be able to stand the shame, and Daddy's fury.

''Night, Mummy,' Clemency answered from force of habit. Both girls sat like statues listening intently for Nancy to close her door.

More steps on the stairs, heavy this time: the squadron leader must have returned. Aunt Mattie got in a flutter over him, and they'd gleefully wondered if he'd been put in the best bedroom so he could creep into her room at night, but tonight they were in no mood for jokes.

When all was quiet Clemency hissed at Verity, 'How could you? I told you to be careful. Are you sure?' They were both too innocent about the facts of life; their parents had not mentioned them, except in a sort of euphemistic way. But she had no right to blame Verity, after that night with Harry. He'd said he'd be careful and she had not become pregnant, but what would she have done if she had?

Verity was crying. 'I love him. He loves me. We didn't do it very often. I asked Judy; she knows as it happened to her. I missed the curse once and Betty said that was fine, stress and stuff often mucked up your cycle, but then I missed it again. It's now ten days late for this month, and I talked to Judy and she said if it's over a week late after missing it for a month I may well be. My breasts hurt, I feel sick, but I haven't been sick, so maybe I'm not.' She threw Clemency a pleading look, but if she expected her sister to reassure her she was mistaken.

'Have you talked about it to Stephano?' How would he react and what could *he* do about it?

'No. I didn't think I could be until I talked to Judy the other evening. I thought the curse would come any day but now it's ten days – no, eleven. What can I do?' She pressed her hands over her stomach, either in a gesture to push out the baby or to guard it.

There were ways to get rid of babies: hot baths, gin; some girls whom Clemency knew had tried it, though she couldn't remember whether it had worked. Or, if the man was about, they got married quickly. She'd heard rumours of back-street abortionists, but they sounded dangerous, and anyway she hadn't a clue how to find one.

'What can I do?' Verity repeated. 'Do you think he'll divorce his wife and marry me?' Her voice lifted with hope.

'He may not want to divorce his wife.' Clemency's emotions were spinning now that the first shock was over. She banked down a surge of jealousy as she pictured her sister and Stephano making love, but she didn't envy Verity this disgrace. Their parents, especially Daddy, wouldn't stand for it. Would they send Verity away to one of those homes for such girls, or disown her? It smote Clemency's heart to see her sister slumped on her bed, tears streaming down her face; no longer the femme fatale but just a young and frightened girl.

She would have to look after her: there was no other way out of it. She could imagine Daddy's fury. Even though his own behaviour was deplorable, his excuse was that men were men and couldn't help such urges – urges he would not explain – but women should remain pure. It would be an added disgrace that a POW had fathered the child, even though Italy was no longer in the war, and by a man whose family was unknown. If Verity had been engaged to a suitable man whom she then hastily married, it could be successfully hushed up; many a large baby had been born 'prematurely'.

Verity blew her nose. 'You must take me to London. We could live there until the baby is born, then when Mummy and Daddy see it they'll love it and everything will be all right.'

'But where would we go? If we go home the neighbours will know, and Dory's flat is the same, and other friends . . . they all know Mummy and Daddy. We'd have to go somewhere away from everyone we know.'

'Can I come to your cottage in Hamble?'

'No, it's full, and we couldn't have a baby there.'

They talked long into the night. Clemency said Verity must see a doctor to be certain, but the only doctor they knew was a friend of Aunt Mattie's and would be bound to tell her. Judy, who after all had been through it herself, had said missing two periods after having been to bed with someone meant you were pregnant, and Clemency had to agree.

Verity fell asleep at last, worn out with exhaustion, without reaching any conclusion. The best outcome would be if she had a miscarriage, Clemency thought, wondering how common they were. Perhaps stress might bring one on. If Verity did miscarry Nancy would cope and no one need ever know, but hoping would not solve it. Verity had insisted that she would not try and get rid of the baby with hot baths and gin. The baby was part of Stephano; she loved it already, and she convinced herself that when he saw the child he would divorce his wife and marry her.

It was impossible to sleep and when dawn came Clemency had cobbled together a plan. She would return to her unit and look for somewhere for Verity to stay. The baby – as far as they both could work out – was not due until around June and Verity should be able to keep her condition secret for another month or so. Then she must say she was coming to London to stay with Clemency to do some war work; she could say she had found something clerical she could do at the base. If necessary Verity would have to escape in the same way that she had. She could get herself to Wick and catch the train to Inverness, then take the sleeper to London, where Clemency would meet her.

The next morning they walked along the headland. The sea was dark and glutinous and the sombre clouds hid the sun. Clemency told Verity her plan, though even as she explained it, it sounded too complicated, too difficult to achieve.

'And what if Stephano wants me to stay? Marries me?' Verity broke in impatiently.

'That cannot be decided until after the war and he goes home. He can't divorce his wife and marry you just like that while he's in Orkney. I think it would be best not to tell him. He might get into trouble, getting a local girl pregnant, perhaps even be sent to prison, court-martialled or something. '

'Do you think he will be?' Verity eyed her fearfully. 'Might they shoot him?'

'No . . .' Clemency was doubtful, 'but he might be punished, sent somewhere else. I don't know.' She took Verity's hand. 'Don't tell anyone, and that includes Betty and Judy. I know Judy's about to return to her unit and won't be back for ages, so she won't say anything, but tell Betty it's a false alarm. People talk and Mummy or Aunt Mattie might get to hear about it, or more likely Daddy if he's at Orkney.'

'I suppose you are right, but I must see Stephano. Surely he'll guess, anyway?'

'By the time you show you must be in London,' Clemency said firmly. 'I'll find somewhere for you to stay but for now do all you can to keep it secret . . . even from Stephano. Understand?'

'What would I do without you? I knew you'd help.' Verity whimpered as they hugged each other. Clemency felt weak with anxiety, where could she find a safe place for Verity to stay without their parents finding out and what would happen after it was born? She'd had her twenty-first birthday in July, not that there been time or inclination without Dory, for much celebration, so she could do what she wanted without her parents' consent, but Verity would still be under twenty-one when the baby was born.

Clemency was back at Hamble by the end of the week. Burdened with Verity's problem she'd longed to engage her mind with flying, but now she was back she found that the joy had waned. It was winter again and the long, cold train journeys back from airfields depressed her. She still had friends at Hamble, Jane, Audrey and Margot were the closest, but she missed Dory more than ever. She would have known what to do about Verity and the baby, or anyway Clemency could have shared this problem with her. It was so daunting having to cope with it all by herself.

The war was taking its toll on everyone. People were tired of the food shortages, the shallow baths that never warmed you up, the blackouts and, worst of all, the anxiety for those who were near and dear and in the thick of it, or the raw grief of their loss. Clemency danced and dined in London, determined to enjoy herself, but each time it became more difficult and the spaces left by those who had gone became wider and colder.

News came through that Johnnie and Lavinia were to get married. Clemency was happy that he had someone to love him, but it should have been Dory by his side. Grace had adored Johnnie and Clemency was sure that even though she would be glad for him she'd feel the blow of his making a home with someone else. She owed them a visit, she'd go down to Chesterfield and see them.

As she stood on the front doorstep at Chesterfield she could sense Dory there, and Wellington dashing about the garden, but she didn't turn round being unable to bear seeing the deserted garden. Grace welcomed her and Clemency was surprised at the change in her. She no longer looked so drawn, so fragile, there was a glow about her she hadn't seen before.

'Oh, Clemency, how good to see you.' Grace kissed her warmly. 'Just in time for tea. We'll have it in the sitting room with Tony.'

'So how is he?' Her joy must be because he was better.

Grace shrugged. 'Little change, more *compos mentis* – well, sometimes. I don't think he understands about Dory, but I've told him anyway.' She made a gesture of helplessness that tugged at Clemency's heart.

She didn't think Tony had made any progress at all. He seemed physically well, perhaps he looked at her with more interest, but with no recognition. It was Michael who had changed and at once she sensed the electricity between him and Grace. He'd been seriously wounded, but only physically, and Clemency remembered Mummy saying that Michael had always been in love with Grace. Now it seemed that Grace loved him. What would Dory have made of it, and Tony?

After dinner the three of them sat in the drawing room. It was an elegant room with long windows and delicate moulding bordering the ceiling. Dinner had been pleasant: good food and a fine claret, the conversation easy.

Grace turned to her. 'Strange how life changes, isn't it?'

The only light was from the glow of the fire in the grate and the soft gleam from some table lamps. They sat cosy in the shadows and Clemency sensed that Grace was about to confide something.

'Yes. So sad without Dory and of course with Tony . . . being as he is.' Clemency felt she had to say it, though she sensed that Grace had meant something else.

Michael coughed. 'Sad, very sad.'

Grace smiled at him. 'You were wounded too.'

'But only my leg, and my insides mashed up a bit. My head's all right, thank God, but Tony . . . I see it as a war wound, just as mine is, but his is much worse,'

'Tony will need care for the rest of his life and we will always care for him here. He is my husband and Michael is his brother, we would never leave him.'

'Of course you wouldn't.'

Grace went on, 'So, Clemency, my dear, we don't think it wrong to . . . well, Michael and I are like husband and wife, though we never will be in law, as I couldn't possibly divorce Tony.'

'I understand.' Her news did not shock her. Michael loved Grace and it seemed a good solution. 'I'm sure Dory would understand too.' She sensed that Grace was only telling her this because she had been so close to Dory.

'I hope she would,' Grace said. 'I've told you, so if you hear any gossip you know the truth. Michael will give up his flat in London; he can stay at his club if he needs to, and after the war I'll sell the flat in Victoria.' She wiped away a tear; Michael got up and put his arm round her.

'It's all right, my dear, it's all right.'

But it's not, Clemency thought, Dory should be here listening to this, not me.

Grace, feeling relieved that that was over, asked Clemency about her family, and the warmth of her voice and the comfortable feeling of sharing confidences made her burst into tears.

'My dear, have we upset you?' Grace looked anguished.

'No, you haven't, it's . . .' Clemency blew her nose, 'it's just . . . I don't know if I should tell you, but I don't know what to do.' She paused; what if Grace were to tell her parents?

Michael, embarrassed at such a show of emotion, said he was just going to lock up the house. Grace and Clemency were left alone.

Grace said gently, 'Now's he's gone I'll say that I'm sorry if I've shocked you. Without Dory . . . you're the closest I have to her.' She paused. Clemency struggled to contain her tears as Grace went on, 'I know I've broken my marriage vows but it was a godsend, Michael being discharged and turning up here. He's got no ties and . . . he's always had a soft spot for me, so do you think it is very wrong?'

'No, I don't, and Tony will have the best care from you both.'

'He will, we both love him.' She regarded Clemency intently. 'But my news seems to have sparked off something in you. Is it missing Dory, or something else? You can tell me anything, Clemency. I won't be shocked, I've no right to be.'

Clemency hesitated, still undecided whether she should tell Grace her secret but she'd come no nearer to doing anything about Verity's predicament. There was a lot of work on but even if there hadn't been she would have had no idea where to start. It would be such a comfort to confide in someone older and more experienced than she was.

'It's Verity,' she started, 'sh . . . she's fallen in love with an Italian POW in Orkney, I know they are no longer our enemies, but she's having his baby and he's married and. . . .'

'That is serious.' Grace frowned, 'I can't imagine your father being very pleased about it.'

'That's it, and it will kill Mummy, for he'll blame her and . . .' Clemency sighed. 'I said I'd help her, but—'

'When is it due?' Grace interrupted her.

'June, I think, I don't have much free time but I must find her somewhere to go where no one knows her or our parents. I've heard there are homes for such girls, but I don't know where.'

Grace thought for a moment, then she said, 'You remember Nanny? She died, as you know, but her sister, Elsie, lives in

Hammersmith. She might take Verity in. We may have to concoct a story about her husband being killed, but I think she's pretty broadminded; Nanny was, after all. I'll write to her. I'd have her here but I don't think that is right without your parents knowing, and they'd be sure to find out.'

'Would you ask her? That might solve everything. You're so kind, many people wouldn't want to have anything to do with it.' Clemency grasped Grace's hand in gratitude.

Grace squeezed her hand; her eyes were gleaming with unshed tears. 'At least she's alive. I wouldn't care what trouble Dory was in if she were still here with us.'

'Of course you are right. I think when, if, we ever get through this war these sanctimonious codes of behaviour might be relaxed and people might stop being so judgemental.'

'Oh, they'll be judgemental about something else,' Grace said, 'that's human nature. But I'll write to Elsie tomorrow, see what she says.'

'Thank you, it will give us a breather and when it's born . . .'

Grace said, 'It might not survive, so many don't, you know; two of mine were stillborn, but if it lives she can have it adopted. She couldn't possibly keep it, not in the circumstances. Silly girl.' She sighed, shook her head. 'With so many nice young men up there why couldn't she have kept to her own kind?'

CHAPTER TWENTY-FOUR

Clemency still found herself storing up a joke, an incident that she knew would amuse Dory before remembering with a sickening jolt that Dory was no longer around to tell. But there were other friends, like Jane and Audrey, who were courageous, kind women who could be depended upon and they had known and loved Dory too. Sometimes they would laugh together over something, usually concerning Wellington, that kept Dory's memory alive. But how she missed her. If only she were here now to discuss Verity's misfortune with Clemency.

Verity often telephoned her at the cottage, always in a panic, which was made worse as she hadn't seen Stephano for ages. It became increasingly difficult to keep her family problems secret from Jane and Audrey.

It wasn't as if they listened purposely as she crouched by the telephone in the cramped corner by the stairs, but they could not help noticing her distress.

The three of them were in the cottage one cold November evening, relieved to be here in the warm and not stuck in some 'funk' near some god-forsaken airfield. Verity telephoned, she was in a state. Surely someone would guess her condition and what if they were snowed in until the spring, when her pregnancy would be obvious? Clemency struggled to placate her, reassuring her that she could hide herself under a bigger jersey for another couple of weeks.

When she returned to the sitting room, it was obvious that Jane and Audrey had been discussing these frantic calls and her reaction to them. With a quick glance at Audrey, Jane said, 'You can tell us to mind our own business, but we both feel there is something bothering you. Do you want to share it? You know you can trust us but you haven't been your usual cheerful self since you came back from Scotland.'

Clemency sank down on a chair. How could she be cheerful with this terrible problem eating into her? Elsie had said she would take Verity in, but naturally she had to be paid for her trouble. Verity had no money – she frittered away the small allowance Daddy gave her. Clemency had a little money; she earned six pounds a week flying, Daddy gave her an allowance, and she had a few savings but for how long would she have to support her sister? There would be no money from Stephano and they couldn't marry. The child must be adopted but she didn't know how long after the birth that would be. Only then could Verity return home and get on with her life.

'You don't want it to interfere with your work ... and your health. You don't look well at all,' Audrey said with concern.

Fear twisted in Clemency. 'No one's said anything, have they? I mean they won't stop me flying?'

'No,' Jane said, 'not yet, but you said you had a near shave landing that Hawker the other day. You know it only takes a small shift in attention to cause an accident. For your own safety you must be vigilant.'

The last embers of a fire glowed in the grate. Outside the wind raged, rattling the windows. Clemency felt safe in this cosy atmosphere, safe from the elements but, more importantly, safe with her friends, the urge to confide in them overwhelmed her.

'It's Verity, my sister. Dory knew her, so she'd understand how she got into this appalling muddle. She's very pretty but frivolous and thinks only of parties, boys and love.'

'Don't we all?' Audrey chipped in.

'We do, but I think we have more sense. We're all involved in an important job that takes up most of our time. Verity thinks war work is being nice to men and unfortunately she's fallen in love with an Italian POW in Orkney.'

'They are no longer our enemy,' Jane said.

'I stayed with an old Contessa in Florence; the people I met were charming, so attractive.' Audrey's eyes shone.

Clemency took a deep breath. 'He's married and has a child. He loves them and after the war he'll go back to them and . . .'

'These things happen in wartime,' Audrey said. 'People are lonely, far from home.'

'There are complications . . .' Clemency hesitated, then snapped out, 'She's pregnant.'

Both girls looked shocked. 'Oh no.' Jane said. 'That is serious, what do your parents think?'

'They don't know. They'd be horrified.'

'At first they would be, but they'd help her, wouldn't they?' Audrey said.

'No, I don't think they would. Oh, Mummy would but Daddy . . .' Clemency tailed off, feeling ashamed of having to explain about her father. 'Daddy . . . seems to think there is one rule for him and probably men in general and one for us. He behaves badly, he's attractive to women and . . . well, never mind, but *we* must be pure as snow. He won't put up with it, especially as she's been with a POW.'

'But your mother . . .' Jane said tentatively, 'surely she—'

Clemency interrupted her. 'She adores my father and is completely under his thumb. She'll do what ever he says, to keep his love.'

'So what will happen to Verity?' Jane asked.

'Through Dory's mother I've found somewhere she can stay in Hammersmith. She'll say she's a widow. Sadly there are a lot of them, so she should be believed.'

Clemency had been to see Elsie on her last day off. Having heard from Grace that a young, expectant mother needed a home Elsie had not probed into the story. If Grace . . . Mrs Wakeham, was asking her if she could help then that was all she needed to know.

Make sure she's wearing a wedding ring, had been the only reference she made to Verity's condition.

'Surely your parents will find out?' Audrey said. 'When's it due?'

'Early June. Verity must get to London. I'm going to say she's needed for some clerical work in the ATA. Once the baby is born it will be adopted. There is no other way,' she added firmly. There must be no sentimentality over the baby, from any of them.

It was a relief to share the problem with two such sympathetic women. They all agreed that if Verity could be kept hidden until after the birth and the baby given up for adoption, she'd probably get away with it.

Verity telephoned her in tears. She hadn't been able to see more than a glimpse of Stephano for weeks – well, not alone – and now he was in the hospital ship, having had appendicitis. She'd sent him letters through his friends, but had not mentioned the baby. 'I simply can't leave without telling him.'

'But you must. Mummy will guess if you stay there much longer,' Clemency said. 'You must come down in the next week or so.' Perhaps it was all too much and it would be better to leave Verity in Scotland. Mummy had told her that Daddy was away on a secret mission and would not be back for some time. Left alone, Mummy might surprise them and deal with the situation. But Verity, terrified of how they would take the scandal and afraid that her father might use his influence to cause Stephano harm, agreed she'd come down as soon as possible. If she couldn't see Stephano, she would make sure he knew the address of their house in Kensington.

They concocted a story together. Clemency's base was in urgent need of someone to do some clerical work for a few months and she had suggested Verity. They would be together so she'd be quite safe.

Nancy took some persuading and it was fortunate that she could not get hold of Gerald to ask his advice. It was Aunt Mattie, who, after telephoning Clemency and making sure that Verity would be met at the station and be staying with her, persuaded Nancy to let her go.

'I might come down and open up the house,' Nancy said, adding to Clemency's tension. ' I told Verity to wait until the spring, when we could go together, but she says there's some training course she needs to be on? She's not flying too, is she?'

'Oh no, just a secretarial course, she's helping in the office.' Clemency wished she didn't have to tell all these lies.

With her usual talent for finding a man to help her Verity was driven through the snow in an army truck to the station and put on the train to Inverness, where she took the sleeper to London.

Clemency had planned her arrival during her three days' leave so that she could meet her and settle her with Elsie. The evening before Verity was to arrive she went round to their house in Kensington to fetch some things for her.

She rang the bell of their neighbour's house to collect the keys from Mrs Paxton, their housekeeper. Mrs Paxton opened the door cautiously, peering at her.

'Oh, hello love, keeping all right?'

'Yes, thank you, and you?'

'Mustn't grumble.' There was something about the way the housekeeper was looking at her that unnerved Clemency. Before she could ask for the key, Mrs Paxton said, 'She's got the key, she'll drop it back when she's gone.'

'She? Who?' It couldn't be Verity or Nancy; the tension tightened; surely Mummy hadn't come before her? The two women who used to work for them had gone back to their families, so who else was there?

Mrs Paxton looked aggrieved. 'Don't ask no questions and I'll tell no lies,' she said mysteriously before shutting the door. Clemency heard her lock it, as if she was afraid her secret might burst out of her.

Puzzled, she went to her front door and rang the bell. In a moment the door opened, and a woman said in a husky voice, 'Darling, I . . .' when she saw it was Clemency she frowned.

Clemency pushed her way in, seething with fury. 'Flavia! Why are you in my house?'

Flavia was wearing a black silk dressing-gown; her hair was hanging loose down her back. She was shocked at seeing Clemency.

'Who are *you*?' she demanded.

'This is my house. It belongs to my parents. Why you are here. Are you after my father?'

Flavia relaxed. 'I've seen you before, haven't I?'

'You are Harry's wife and my father is married too, and neither of you should be together, so get out now.'

'What if I don't?' Flavia's eyes were hard. 'It is nothing to do with you if your father and I are friends. It's wartime, we must take our pleasure where we can.'

'Not from my family you won't,' Clemency clenched her hands tightly, afraid she might seize Flavia and throw her out on to the pavement. 'Of all the men you could have chosen, why him?' she demanded, fury twisting in her.

'I just met him, darling.' Flavia took a cigarette from a silver case in her pocket and lit it slowly, exhaling the smoke as if she had all the time in the world.

Daddy had told them he was on a top-secret mission. Was this a lie? A story made up to keep Nancy quiet while he cavorted with Flavia? Clemency struggled to stay calm. His ship went all over the place and he could be in London for a briefing or for some other valid reason. Flavia, the Anemone, was always around, luring in any man she fancied.

The bell rang again, quick and sharp, and Flavia, throwing Clemency a pitying look, moved to open it, but Clemency was quicker. She snatched open the door, saw the smile freeze on her father's face.

'Hello Daddy. Busy with top secret war work, I see.' She despised Flavia, despised them both; they were two of a kind, neither of them worthy of being married to such decent people as Mummy and Harry. She was taunted by the image of herself making love with Harry. He had not been in touch with her again, so that night had obviously meant nothing to him.

'Clemency.' Gerald's eyes glittered with anger.

'Come in; don't let's give the neighbours anything more to amuse them.' Clemency stood aside to let him in to the hall. 'If you're on leave why aren't you with Mummy?'

'I have business at the Admiralty. What are *you* doing here?'

'This is my home, in case you've forgotten. You are using it as a . . . brothel.' She got a savage pleasure from seeing his shock at the word. 'For that is what it is. This woman is married too. Her husband is a brave, hard-working man and this is how she treats him.'

'Gerald, I won't stand for such rudeness.' Flavia pushed herself forward, her silk gown opening, revealing black undergarments.

'That's what I think of you. And you, Daddy, are you not ashamed of yourself? Mummy waits so patiently for you. I wish she'd find someone else, someone to take care of her.'

Guilt and anger distorted his face, his eyes shifted from one woman to the other, and Clemency saw how weak he was when faced with such a beautiful and seductive woman as Flavia.

'I thought this was my home,' she said. 'So, surely, I can come here when I wish?'

Gerald struggled to appear composed. 'Usually, yes but . . . not this evening, my leave is over tomorrow.'

'Then we can spend it together, *Daddy*,' she challenged him.

'I'm not staying.' Flavia threw him a glance as if to say, *stand up for me, don't you want me tonight?*

'Good, the door's there,' said Clemency through gritted teeth. 'Give me the key before you go.' If only she could pull that gleaming hair. Where was Harry? Waiting at home for her, or on some bleak airfield in the back of beyond? She wanted to ask but she could not give herself away, for was she not as bad as they were?

'Gerald?' Flavia tried again and Gerald attempted to bluff his way out of the situation.

'It's not what you think; Mrs Chatwin has come to ask me about her husband. He's—'

'In her nightclothes? And why would she ask *you*? He's in the RAF not the Navy. You can't fool me, Daddy. Get her out of here and don't ask her back.'

'How do you know her husband? I suppose he flies with you,' Gerald said sarcastically.

'He billeted with us in Scotland.' She was not going to say any more.

This obviously shocked him, afraid no doubt that his liaison with Flavia would get back to Harry as well as to Nancy. If it was discovered that you were sleeping with another man's wife, it was a serious offence.

He forced a smile. 'Darling, don't let's quarrel over this silly mis-understanding. Shall we all go out and have dinner?'

'Don't bother,' Flavia said. 'I'm leaving. I'll find someone else with more guts,' she eyed him witheringly, 'and no tiresome children.' She picked up a fur coat that was lying on a chair and put it on. Gerald helped her, trying to make amends.

'Go and find me a taxi,' she said, 'and send my things on.'

Clemency went upstairs to fetch the items that she had come for. As she passed her parents bedroom she saw a silk nightdress lying across the bed, and in the bathroom there was a collection of cosmetics. Sweeping the whole lot into a wastepaper basket she ran downstairs with them, pushing them at Flavia just as the taxi arrived.

'Take your rubbish with you,' she shouted, and ran back upstairs to pack. As she reached her father's dressing-room she remembered that he kept money in the bureau. Hearing them still talking downstairs she slipped into the room and felt behind the bureau for the lever to open a concealed drawer. She pressed it and it opened. There was about fifty pounds there; she snatched it and rammed it down her bra. It was for Verity, and, thinking of the money he must have spent on Flavia and Joan and others of his fancy women, she felt no qualms about taking it to help his own daughter.

She picked up handfuls of Verity's clothes and shoved them into a suitcase, hardly thinking that soon Verity would not be able to fit into them. Gerald came up the stairs calling for her, but she didn't answer. He charged into her bedroom.

'How dare you insult my friends,' he shouted. He raged on, each word hitting her like a stone. In his fury he didn't seem to notice that she was packing. He paced round the room, swearing that she was the most ungrateful child, and ended up by saying why wasn't she more like Verity?

She shut the cases, saying quietly, 'You wouldn't want me to be like Verity.' But he didn't seem to hear her. She went downstairs and he followed her, ranting all the way. Here and there she caught words about the danger he'd been in, the horrors he had seen, but she was too angry and disgusted with him to let it move her. Though later, when she'd got back to Dory's flat, her emotions battered by the scene, his distress at the terrible things he had been through hit her. The brutality of war had affected them all, pushed some of them to the limit and beyond.

Infidelity was not right but in such testing times, when loved ones were lost or far away and people cried out for a touch of kindness, it was understandable. Hadn't she found it herself that night with Harry? But even as she knew this the child in her protested in horror: not Daddy and Harry's wife? Surely that was the worst insult of all?

CHAPTER TWENTY-FIVE

Clemency's first sight of Verity smote her heart. She was walking alone, lugging her suitcase towards the ticket barrier where they'd arranged to meet. She was like a scared child, nervously glancing about her as though she had never been to London before. Then she caught sight of Clemency and her face relaxed in relief. She waved, filling Clemency with dread as she realized how much her sister depended upon her.

Verity clung to her. 'It was so cold, and crowded with airmen and soldiers coming down on leave.'

Clemency expected Verity to say she'd fallen in love on the journey, but she did not. She was exhausted and near tears.

'I'll get us a taxi and we'll go straight to Elsie's,' Clemency said. 'You'll like her,' she added, catching Verity's expression.

'But you'll stay?' Verity's mouth quivered; she clung to Clemency's arm while the other passengers streamed past them.

'I have to return to work tomorrow but I'll settle you in and come and see you as often as I can. In theory I have three days off in every two weeks.'

'Every two weeks?' Verity echoed in despair.

'It's going to be hard, Verity. I'm sorry but it is. If you don't stay hidden Daddy and Mummy will hear of it.'

'I know.' Verity's eyes filled with tears. 'If only I could have seen Stephano, told him I was coming here, but he's in hospital. I sent him a letter to explain, not mentioning the . . . you know. When it's born I'll go back and find him. I'm sure when Mummy and Daddy see it they'll love it and so will Stephano.'

This was not the time or the place to tell her that she must have the child adopted, that being the only way to avoid a scandal and ruining her reputation. Instead Clemency said, 'You're tired. Let's get to Elsie's. Take things as they come.'

Elsie Maddox lived in a small house off the Fulham Palace Road. Verity grabbed Clemency's hand as they stood together outside her front door, blinking back her tears. Clemency squeezed her hand reassuringly, wishing someone would support her in this ordeal, but at least Verity had got here without Mummy finding out that she was pregnant. They only had to get through the next few months, then an adoption agency would take over. 'The ring,' she remembered. She fished in her pocket and handed it to Verity.

She rang Elsie's bell, filled with sympathy for her poor, silly sister, but then what did any of them know about lovemaking and babies? The whole charade was kept secret until one married, which was ridiculous, criminal even. Encouraging men and women not to be alone together was not enough; they should be taught the facts of life before ignorance ruined lives.

If there hadn't been a war and she hadn't mixed with the people she'd met she would not know anything either. Harry, dear Harry, had shown her, answered her questions and taken care not to leave her pregnant. Thinking of Harry brought back that terrible scene with her father and Flavia, and she shuddered. Verity felt it and, not knowing her thoughts, imagined she was about to be confronted by a wicked witch.

'What is it?' Her voice was fearful.

'I'm just cold.' It would not be fair to tell Verity about that scene now. It was sickening that Daddy, who behaved so badly himself, would be so unforgiving at Verity's predicament, leaving them to seek help with strangers.

The front door opened and Elsie stood beaming at them.

'Welcome, come in. You must be tired. We'll have a nice cup of tea,' Elsie urged them to make themselves at home in the scrupulously tidy room with its plain furnishings and a collection of carefully arranged china ornaments.

To Clemency's relief Verity seemed to relax. Later she remarked that Elsie reminded her of their nanny: warm and reassuring, always there. When Clemency left a couple of hours later she felt more optimistic about their shocking situation.

*

It was a relief to get back to work. So much concentration went on the flying that it crowded out Clemency's worries. She had done what she could for Verity, so she mustn't keep on worrying that someone who knew their parents might see Verity and tell them about the baby. If it happened she would deal with it . . . somehow.

Verity soon complained of boredom. She could not go out with friends dancing, or to the cinema in case she was seen and her condition revealed. Elsie did her best to keep her occupied with making things for the troops and accompanying her to draughty halls where she gave lessons in first aid. But worst of all she pined for Stephano, filling her telephone calls to Clemency with unlikely scenarios of their living happily ever after.

A letter for Verity was forwarded on from their house to the flat. Clemency took it round to her. It was a sharp day in March and they walked together in the local park. Verity's pregnancy was obvious, though she was not very large. Elsie had taken her to her doctor; he had not questioned her story of being a young widow left pregnant. He thought she was due at the end of June, or even the beginning of July, and Verity, too embarrassed to go into the exact dates she'd been with Stephano, took him at his word.

'Let's sit. I've something for you.'

'A letter? You have a letter from Stephano?' Verity shrieked in excitement, then quietened and said desperately, 'You have, haven't you?'

'I don't know who it's from. It could be from Betty.' They sat down on a bench and Clemency handed the letter over. Verity opened it; it was from Stephano. Clemency watched a group of boys throwing stones at a tin, wishing she could hold his letter and read his words herself.

'He's missing me, but he's got my letter, wants me to hurry back when I can. He's better, doing farm work.' Verity turned to her sister smiling. 'That's not so hard as working on the causeways, is it? If only I could see him.' She cried a little; her emotions seemed to be all over the place. 'I'll write back at once, send it to Betty.'

Clemency had been going to broach the subject of adoption this morning, but now with Verity's emotions heightened with

171

the receipt of her letter and thoughts of Stephano, she decided she would bring it up on her next visit. The doctor had said she was due at the end of June, so there was plenty of time. She'd mentioned it to Elsie, who'd guessed that Verity had never been married. She knew of a good adoption society connected to the church, and now it seemed that they had more breathing space than they had thought. Clemency would contact the church society through Elsie and have the whole thing set up before she told Verity about it.

A couple of weeks later Clemency found she had a Lancaster to deliver to Wick the following morning. This was a special order; she was then to wait a couple of days and fly down a wing commander who was coming in from Iceland.

'You live up there, don't you?' her controller said. 'You can visit your family.'

Clemency telephoned her mother to warn her of her impending arrival. She decided not to tell Verity until she was back, but Verity telephoned her that evening and it seemed churlish not to tell her.

'You must go to Orkney and take a letter to Stephano,' she insisted.

'But I'm leaving early tomorrow. I won't be able to fetch it from you.'

'Then I'll dictate it and you must write it,' Verity sounded frantic.

Clemency sighed; she should never have mentioned it, knowing that Verity would beg her to go and see Stephano. Perhaps, she shamefully admitted to herself, this was why she *had* told her? She copied down Verity's emotional letter, slightly tempering some of her wilder remarks. The letter finished by saying she would be back in the summer with a present for him. Clemency wondered whether it was prudent to say such a thing, but she let it go.

There wouldn't be much time to go to Orkney. It might arouse suspicion, to be seen searching round for Stephano. But with Verity's letter she had a valid excuse to find him; besides, she reasoned with herself, it would give her a chance to find out more about what sort of man he was and if, as Verity was convinced, there was a chance that once he knew he'd fathered a child he would support her.

But it's going to be adopted so it doesn't matter what he's like, a little voice nudged her annoyingly.

It was April; a clean, clear day with few clouds and the flight filled her with joy. She was told to report back in forty-eight hours to pick up her passenger and fly him down south. Alice wasn't there so she walked into the town and found a taxi to take her to Aunt Mattie's. She had telephoned ahead and Nancy was in the house, waiting for her.

'So how is Verity? What is she doing?' Nancy greeted her.

Clemency couldn't remember the story they had decided upon. She was afraid that Verity had told Nancy things she knew nothing about, and that she might inadvertently give her away.

'She's fine, she sends her love.'

'I thought I'd come to London, open up the house and then we can all live in it. I never see your father. He seems to be more in London than here.' Nancy said with a sigh.

'Don't come now, it's still cold. Come in the summer,' Clemency said hurriedly. It would be a disaster if Nancy took it into her head to come before the baby was born and safely away with its adoptive parents.

'It's not nearly as cold in London as it is here,' Nancy countered, 'and I could see your father, he says he was in London recently, reporting to the Admiralty. Do you ever see him? '

He must have telephoned home to check that she hadn't told Mummy about Flavia. Clemency said vaguely, 'No, but maybe he's back at Scapa Flow. I'd like to go to Orkney tomorrow, just for the day, see some friends. Come with me, see if Daddy is there.' This was a shot in the dark but if he was there and was faced with Nancy he might be ashamed enough to give up his womanizing, for a while anyway.

'I can't go tomorrow. But why must you go? You've only just come and you say you've got to go back in a day or so.'

Clemency was saved having to make up some excuse by Aunt Mattie's return. Later she telephoned Betty to ask if she could arrange for someone to pick her up at Stromness and to say that Verity had a message she wanted her to give to her friends.

'How's Verity and her new job? Is she enjoying it?' Betty asked. 'I haven't heard from her. I miss her. We used to have such fun.'

'She's very busy; she sends her love. I had a plane to deliver at Wick so I'm here for a couple of days. I thought I'd come over and see if my father's ship is there and bring messages from Verity.' She was aware that Mummy, pottering around in the kitchen close by, could hear every word she said.

Betty, an expert on romantic subterfuge, giggled. 'I think he works on the land now. I don't see much of them. I'm busy here and I have a fiancé in the Seaforth Highlanders. I spend what time I can with him.'

Early next morning Clemency bicycled up to Scrabster and found Sandy about to leave for his daily crossing. He nodded when he saw her, his face impassive, and they crossed over in silence.

She told Sandy she'd be back before he started his homeward journey. Andy was there to meet her with his truck; he looked disappointed when he saw that Verity was not with her.

'She'll be back soon,' she said briskly. 'Has Betty told you where to go? I have to see some of the Italians. They are probably in the direction of Lamb's Holm.' It was easy to persuade Andy that she needed to see them in some official capacity. Much though she longed to see Stephano, she would not ask for him by name. If she didn't see him among the others she would just hand over the letter to someone else and hope that he would get it.

They set off along the road. Barrage balloons were bobbing in the air like vast whales. They reached a farm. Andy slowed down. 'They be Italians.' He gestured towards a group of men working in the fields. 'Be back in an hour. Got some deliveries to make.'

'Just wait a moment.' Her heart was fluttering now that there was a chance she might see Stephano. If he wasn't here she'd hand over the letter and that would be the end of it. She didn't want to be left here. She jumped down on to the road. Picking her way through the mud she walked across the farmyard towards a man working in the field. He smiled when he saw her.

'Verity!' he exclaimed. 'Go,' he pointed towards a barn on a piece of wasteland. 'I tell Stephano.' He turned from her and strode across the field calling for Stephano.

Andy had not waited; she saw his van going on up the lane; how irritating he was. She felt vulnerable and cold, standing here in the piercing wind on the edge of the field with the other Italians staring at her, some waving and smiling. She turned towards the barn, realizing that the man had mistaken her for Verity. It would be galling to see Stephano's disappointment when he saw she was not her sister.

It was a relief to get inside the barn away from the wind. It was dark, lit only by a shaft of daylight through the open door. Bales of straw for the livestock were stacked in the corner. She sat down on one, suddenly weary.

'*Cara*, is it really you? You are back.' Stephano came into the barn. She stood up, poised to say she was Clemency. But he ran to her, snatching her into his arms, kissing her passionately, murmuring words of love. He kissed her mouth, deep, demanding kisses, holding her as if he would never let her go.

She must tell him she was not Verity, but oh those kisses, the surge of desire in her body. She tried to pull back but he would not let her go. His kisses devoured her, he picked her up, his lips still clamped on to hers, carried her a few steps then laid her down on some straw out of sight. Again she tried to escape but his hands were on her breasts, and then her slacks, pulling them off. She must stop him, but she had lost control of her body. Her hand slipped under his shirt, feeling the roughness of his skin, the hair on his chest, and she couldn't stop herself. She was someone different, in another time, and nothing else mattered but the feel of his body on hers. She arched herself against him, clinging to him with her legs, all her energy going into this lovemaking. Then it was over. They lay together, exhausted, in the shadows. She held on to him, hiding her face from him. It would be unbearable if he realized she was not Verity; she listened to his endearments, inwardly weeping that they were not for her.

Someone called, it sounded like a warning. He kissed her quickly, pulling her clothes over her then struggling into his own. 'Come again . . . tomorrow? I am helping here for a few more days.' The call came again, a bird's call made by a man, and with one last kiss he left her.

She lay there in the straw, the glow of their lovemaking receding, filling her with desolation. But what if the farmer came in and found her like this. She dressed hurriedly, combed her hair with her fingers and crept to the door. A truck had arrived and the men were getting into it; they must have finished their work and were being taken on somewhere else. She saw Stephano look back, lift his hand in farewell, and blow her a kiss.

She retreated into the barn, her heart pounding. What had she done? But he had thought she was Verity. He had been so overcome with passion, and no doubt he knew he had very little time, as he couldn't be away from his work for long; there had been no chance to explain. She heard the truck leave. She peered out again. A man, probably the farmer, opened the door of the farmhouse and went in. Furtively she slipped out of the yard to the lane and sat on the grass verge, waiting for Andy. To her relief he arrived a few minutes later and she told him to take her back to Stromness. She'd wait there until it was time for Sandy to leave.

She stared out at the passing landscape without seeing it. The delicious soporific feeling of her body being sated by love was now being eaten away by anxiety. What would happen if she became pregnant too? She had blamed Verity for being too easy, but what about her? Hadn't she been to bed with Harry and now Stephano, both married men, and one of them her sister's lover? She had no right to criticize anyone now, not even Daddy. But even as she scolded herself she marvelled at that sudden surge of passion. She loved Stephano, there was no denying it, but she would not come back here again and seek him out. She had stolen a moment with him and she would have no more, but she would never forget it, never stop loving him.

Then she remembered that she had not given him Verity's letter. It was too late now. He must never see it, for then he would know of his mistake and it would break his heart.

CHAPTER TWENTY-SIX

She got to Wick airfield early, to escape her mother and her endless questions about Verity. Why had Verity, who hadn't shown much enthusiasm for war work, suddenly decided to go south to do it?

'It's all your fault,' Nancy grumbled, 'for going off yourself and boasting about all your goings on in London.'

'I did not boast, I talked more of my job; not that any of you would listen with your ridiculous prejudices that women cannot be pilots.' She was hurt at her rebuke. How would Mummy feel if she knew the real reason why Verity had had to come to London?

She was now tortured with the thought that she could be pregnant too; both of them being pregnant by the same man, a married, once POW, was too dreadful to contemplate.

Aunt Mattie came to the rescue. 'Come along, Nancy, stop harassing Clemency. Perhaps it is a good thing that Verity is following her example and getting down to something specific at last.'

The taxi arrived and Clemency kissed them both goodbye, saying she must not be late as she had an important person to fly down south.

'I'll let you know if I come down. I'm sure I'd see more of your father there than I do here. He seems to be at the Admiralty quite often.' Nancy smiled. 'They must think much of him, mustn't they?'

'Let's see what happens. He may be back up here any time.' Clemency kissed her mother and felt sad for her, for being so besotted with a man who cheated on her.

It was cold, the sky was waking up and the sea was metal grey. Her body was restless, fired up after Stephano's lovemaking, though, she reminded herself, it was not she whom he loved but Verity. She felt guilty, but it wasn't absolutely her fault; he was so strong, she couldn't get away, not that she'd tried very hard. She'd never talk about it unless – and she was struck with dread – she was pregnant too.

Once she had reached the airfield her mood changed completely. She was no longer the anxious woman yearning for a lover she could not have, she was now the experienced pilot. She signed in, the Lysander she'd flown up a couple of days ago waited for her.

She waited in the mess for her passenger to arrive. She heard the plane that was bringing him land and a few minutes later she was told it was time to go. She walked out to the plane feeling a momentary sadness at leaving Caithness. She mustn't come back until Stephano had gone; she didn't trust herself to stay away from him. She turned her thoughts to the route home; she reached the plane, and there was Harry.

'Clemency,' he greeted her before she had time to utter a word. 'What luck! Are you my ferry pilot?' He smiled, his face grey with exhaustion.

'Harry.' For a moment her professionalism faltered, her body became fired with remembered desire. She felt herself blushing, and aware of the amused glances from the mechanics, she said briskly, 'So you're my important passenger.'

'So it seems. Are you disappointed?'

'Of course not.' She knew she sounded brusque but she was afraid someone would guess that they had been lovers. Her body felt warm but it was Stephano's kisses that sparked her desire. She asked the mechanic a few questions just to show she was a professional and had no private life.

'Shall we go?' she said.

'Ready when you are, but . . .' he smiled, 'would you mind if I flew? Not because I don't trust you, you fly superbly, but because I don't get much chance to do it now. Would you feel safe with me?'

She'd been looking forward to this trip, knowing that once she was behind the controls she'd feel calmer, more in control of the events in her life. But Harry looked so eager that she could not disappoint him.

'Of course I would.' Even with one eye he'd fly well, she'd known pilots with one arm fly, had even once seen two one-armed pilots arguing about which arm it was better to be without to manage the plane better.

'I'm better at flying than dancing,' he said as they started off.

Harry took off like a bird, straight up into the sky, turning in one elegant curve to head for home. They soared over the rugged landscape, the sea gleaming below; he set the course flying down over the country to the south,

For the first few moments neither spoke; she was waiting for him to speak first. For all she knew he liked to fly in silence, but then he said, speaking loudly over the noise of the engine, 'I'm so glad to see you again. I've been away.'

Unless someone volunteered the information you asked no questions.

She thought of Flavia sleeping with her father and burnt with guilt and anger, as if she had had a part in it. Did he know about it? Perhaps it had happened when he was away and he'd only just returned and ... her mind spun, dreading him finding out, dreading him questioning her.

'I wanted to say how much that night we spent together meant to me. I felt bad about it in the morning, as if I might have inadvertently taken advantage of you when you were so vulnerable after losing Dory. You know I'm married and I couldn't think how to put it, and then there was Mac at the station and I thought it better for you not to be seen with me. I hope you understand.'

'I understand. It was a beautiful night.' She wanted to say more but her body was now tormented with the memory of another man's lovemaking and she felt as ashamed as if she had betrayed Harry.

'It *was* a beautiful night.' His face was tender as he turned to her. 'One I shall never forget. If things were different . . .'

He was married to a woman who did not deserve him, but when the war was over Flavia might settle down again with Harry and they would have children and live a respectable life.

'War disrupts everything,' Clemency said. 'We live on the edge, but when the war is over we'll pick up the pieces and get back to how we were.'

'I wonder if we will? Too much has happened, too much has changed. The men coming back from the war will be different people and so, to some extent will be their wives. I fear many will find they cannot go on together.'

She thought of her parents. Would her father come back and carry on as before? Or had he had too much freedom now, with Nancy safely out of the way in Caithness? Though maybe she was tired of it now and would carry out her threat to return to London. Clemency's heart went cold; however could she keep Verity away from her parents until the baby was born and adopted?

If only she could tell Harry about Verity, but that would not be fair. He might be shocked; anyway it would irritate him, as he thought Verity rather silly, thinking only of falling in love.

'We must wait and see,' she said lamely, 'remember how we said we couldn't make plans in wartime.'

'Yes, at that dance in Wick. How long ago that seems.'

'So many good people dead.' If only Dory were here with her laughter. She asked Harry about the war and how much longer he thought it would go on. Now that at last America had joined them things were going better.

The sky ahead was clear, stretching on into infinity. There were just the two of them alone in this beauty, understanding, as they were both pilots, the powerful thrill of it. Harry must have felt the intimacy too, for he said, 'This will be another beautiful event for me, just us, the plane and the sky.' Then, as if shy of his emotions, he laughed. 'I won't be flying again for a while, so this is very special. Thank you.'

'I'm glad you're enjoying it.' She felt shy too, not knowing what she should say. There was something between them but they had no future together, even if they both got through the war. But what future did she expect?

'I'm away for some time, but I hope we meet again,' he said as they approached the airfield. He landed smoothly, smiled at her. 'Safe landing.'

'Beautiful landing.' She was sad that they had arrived back in the bustle of life. In a moment he would be gone. They came to a stop and were surrounded by airfield crew. The flight was over; they were just two colleagues with a job to do.

'Good landing, sir, spot on.' The cheery face of a mechanic greeted them.

They both got out, exchanged a few words with the crew, who then took charge of the plane. A young RAF man came towards them. Clemency could see a car pulling up. They had a split second together before Harry was whisked away.

'Stay safe, my dear,' he said quietly before he walked away.

CHAPTER TWENTY-SEVEN

Clemency kept putting off seeing Verity after her visit to Orkney. She was so ashamed of herself and yet part of her seemed energized by her lovemaking with Stephano, but she had to face her. She lied, hating herself when she saw Verity's disappointment, but how could she tell her the truth? She had betrayed her sister anyway.

'I didn't see him, but I saw one of his friends and gave him your letter.' They were walking together in the park; she walked a little ahead so that Verity could not see her face.

Verity's eyes brimmed. 'I wish you'd seen him, told him I loved him.'

Clemency hugged her, torn with guilt. 'I'm so sorry.' If only it would all end happily for Verity, the two of them and their child together.

As the pregnancy progressed Verity became more tranquil, content to sit about listening to the gramophone and dreaming of her life to come with Stephano.

'Let her be until it is born; it's bad for the baby if the mother is agitated,' Elsie said when Clemency shared her fears with her of the outcome of the birth.

'But she can't keep the baby. Our parents, especially my father, will never stand for it. I'd better get in touch with the adoption society.'

'Life is changing,' Elsie said. 'Who knows how this war will end?'

The second letter from Stephano came some weeks after Clemency had been with him. To her great relief she was not pregnant, but whenever she saw Verity she was plagued with guilt. She had hoped to intercept his letters, steam them open to see if he had written anything that would expose their lovemaking, but this letter had been send direct to Elsie's by Betty.

'I have a letter from him at last.' Verity's face glowed, 'Most of it is about his work on the chapel, but this bit is odd. I don't understand it.' She read it out. '"I dream of that afternoon when you came to the farm, loving you in the hay." But I wasn't there.'

To hide her consternation Clemency pretended to search for something in her handbag. 'You did meet him there sometimes, didn't you? He must have muddled the days, or his English tenses.' Her heart was heavy. Verity must never know that Stephano had mixed them up.

'I suppose so, but working on this chapel has changed him,' Verity went on. 'It's as if he's thinking more deeply, his mind seems more on his painting than on me.'

'He is excited about the chapel, so he's sharing it with you.' What if, when Verity was alone, dissecting every word of his letter, she guessed her betrayal?

'That must be it.' Verity sighed. 'I wish I could tell him about the baby. If only it would be born and I could go back and show him.'

Clemency hugged her; silently promising she'd do everything she could to help her sister through this ordeal, to atone for her treachery.

Verity's rolling fantasy was to return to Orkney with the baby. Stephano would love it instantly and love her even more. He'd leave his wife and marry her. Her fantasy stretched to their parents loving it too, and accepting Stephano as their son-in-law.

To add to the ordeal, Nancy was becoming restless. She'd understood that Verity was only going to London for a few weeks and, as the weeks turned into months, she threatened to come down, open up the house so they could all live there together.

'I wish she would come,' Verity said. 'I'm sure she'd understand and make Daddy see and when it's born . . .'

'No, Verity, we must stay strong, keep her away until it is born. Daddy might be unkind to her, make her feel it is her fault.' It might be harsh to say it but it was true. Gerald, the great womanizer, would not be disgraced at home.

*

News came that their father was ill. It sounded like some sort of mental collapse. His ship had been badly damaged in a bombing raid and only his courage had saved it and his crew, but he had paid for that by having a breakdown. He was with Nancy and Aunt Mattie in Scotland.

'Mummy will be pleased to have him all to herself,' Clemency said, tortured with images of Tony and his botched suicide attempt. She had not yet told Verity about that dreadful scene with Flavia in their home; she could not bear to talk about it, relive it again.

'But how ill is Daddy?' Verity was scared. Her father was such a forceful character in her life, she had convinced herself that when he saw his grandchild he would support them, even help Stephano get free of his wife and marry her.

Clemency, not getting much information from Nancy, who was in her element, fussing round him, talked to Aunt Mattie.

'He's just overtired, and who can blame him with all the responsibilities he has? He needs a good rest and feeding up and he'll get it here. I suggest Verity stays in London for a little longer,' she advised, as though Verity was due back any moment. 'All her comings and goings will only aggravate him.'

Perhaps his erratic love life was partly to blame, Clemency thought sourly.

'Daddy must not suspect anything while he is ill,' she warned Verity, thinking of Tony, who had been pushed to the limit in North Africa. It did not surprise her that men like him and Daddy, who had so much responsibility without much respite, could, in the end, take no more.

But it was a relief to know where he was. He was safe and his illness would mean that both their parents were kept out of their way for a while. It was getting close to the time of Verity's confinement. Elsie had borrowed a Moses basket and shown Verity how to make some small garments, which were put away in tissue paper until needed. Clemency approached the adoption society that Elsie had recommended and had arranged a meeting for the next time she came to London.

She braced herself to discuss the situation with Verity. The usual

184

practice, she understood, was to have the child in one of the society's homes and then not long after the baby would be handed over to its new parents and Verity could walk free. It would be very hard for her at first, so Clemency decided she'd take some leave then and take her away somewhere like Devon for a holiday to help her get over it.

But before she could attend the meeting with the adoption society, the baby was born. Possibly Verity had got her dates wrong, or he was early, but in the middle of May Elsie telephoned her at the cottage to say the baby boy had arrived and both were well. She would talk to Verity about adoption herself; prepare her for it before Clemency could visit her.

Clemency arrived at Elsie's house a few days later. Verity was radiant; the birth had been quick and not too painful. Anyway it was worth it, for wasn't he – Lucian, a name she felt sounded right for a child half Italian and half English – the most beautiful baby ever born?

Clemency, who had little experience with babies, was stunned when she saw him lying there in his basket. He was the image of Stephano, with dark hair and eyes and his father's expressive face. She'd imagined he would be just a pink blob that could be passed off as anyone's child, but he was obviously Stephano's and obviously Latin, so they'd have to rethink their story of an English husband dying for his country.

'Pick him up. Isn't he lovely?' Verity cooed, scooping him up herself and thrusting him at Clemency.

Clemency, afraid she'd drop him, clutched at him, regarding him fearfully. She was surprised at how heavy he was, warm and solid in her arms. He watched her with his dark eyes, twisting her heart as she thought of his father.

Elsie had talked to Verity about adoption, but before Clemency could broach the subject, the words tangling in her head, Verity burst out, 'I'm not giving him away, he's mine, mine and Stephano's, and when he sees him . . .' Her face shone with hope.

Clemency looked away, not able to bear that misguided joy. She must harden her heart and do what was best for everyone.

'I know this sounds cruel, just as you've given birth to him, but it would be better for him if he went to a loving family, a father and a mother with money coming in.' Her voice sounded flat and unconvincing. It had shocked her to see how like Stephano he was; already he seemed to have a character all of his own that stole their hearts made them love him. It would be impossible to keep him in the circumstances, and yet she did not want to give him up either, even though he might get a better life with a stable, loving family. He was something good to have come out of so much suffering.

'He's staying with me, he's mine.' Verity held him close. 'As soon as I can I'm going to Orkney to show him to Stephano. It is up to him to decide what to do.' Her face was hard, determined, a mother fighting for her child.

Perhaps her parents could forcibly take him from her, but Clemency realized she couldn't be the one to part them. She didn't want to think about how it would end but both she and Elsie managed to persuade Verity to wait a few more weeks before going to Orkney; Lucian would be older and it would be easier to travel with him.

Clemency heard that Johnnie was to marry Lavinia. She couldn't make it to the wedding as she was working, but she went to visit them in their house in the country. The work on the side of Johnnie's face and his hands was remarkable, but still his appearance shocked her. Perhaps if his whole face had been burnt it would not have reminded people of how extraordinarily beautiful he had been. She and Jane arrived at the house to spend a night and he came out to greet them.

'If you can bear it you can kiss my good cheek,' he said cheerfully, one side of his mouth slightly curving with a smile, the other side tight after the skin grafts. Clemency kissed him, swallowing the lump in her throat. How cruel was fate to do this to him, to all the other young men burnt in their planes. Lavinia joined them. Clemency suspected she had waited until they had got their greeting over, knowing how much Clemency wished Dory were here instead of her.

Clemency did feel that; she couldn't help it. Such dreams Dory had had, marrying her beautiful Johnnie and living in the country with a houseful of children and Wellington's puppies. But Lavinia was a kind person, she obviously adored Johnnie and he seemed fond of her, though it was difficult to compare this with his time with Dory. He was a different person from that devil-may-care man who was so enthusiastic about life, so passionate about flying and killing as many Huns as he could. He was in pain most of the time and his hands had lost much of their mobility, yet he never complained, and they all spent a happy weekend together. Just before she and Jane left Clemency found herself alone with him.

'Oh Clemency . . .' He was sitting in their small drawing room overlooking the garden, 'we never thought it would all end like this, did we?'

'No, we didn't.' Her eyes filled with tears. Dory would always be there between them, her shadow touching them. She felt it sometimes when she flew, the sky stretching on into infinity, and she liked to think that Dory was still there somewhere, just out of sight. She said this to Johnnie, feeling a little foolish, but he smiled.

'I often felt her there, and my other friends too. So many people have left their shadows in the sky. But dreams . . .' He sighed. 'What is the point of them when they are torn to shreds before our eyes?'

'They give us pleasure and perhaps even courage to go on while we have them.'

'But then they destroy us.' He stared out at the garden and she saw his guard slip for a moment and reognized the full terror of his pain. She went to him and put her arm gently round his shoulders.

'I am so sorry how everything has worked out, but you have Lavinia, and she loves you very much.'

'Yes.' He turned to face her. 'Yes, I am lucky there . . . but,' he lowered his voice, 'I will never stop loving Dory, and I can only say that to you.'

She kissed him, her head resting on his, her heart too full for her to speak. They heard the creak of someone coming down the stairs and she moved away. He swallowed, said cheerfully, 'You know where we are, so you must come again; we're always glad to see you.' He got up and gave her a quick hug, before going to the door, calling for Lavinia, leaving Clemency anguished.

*

Nancy kept the girls informed about their father's progress and soon they were able to talk to him. When they asked him how he was he ignored the question, saying he was going back to his ship as soon as possible. He would not admit to having been ill but passed his weeks off at home as recovering from a back injury.

'His back does ache so,' Nancy said defending him. 'He's returning to his ship next week, so I thought I'd come down and see you both.'

Clemency's heart raced. It was almost June and there was nothing to stop her mother from coming south now.

Verity, once so certain that her parents would fall instantly in love with Lucian was now not so sure. She vacillated between elation and despair, one minute convinced that Stephano would marry her, the next despairing of ever getting to see him again.

When Verity took Lucian out in his pram she found that people remarked at how dark his eyes and hair were when she was so fair. She realized it would not be easy to pass him off as an English man's child. But they could not keep his presence secret from their family for much longer, and now Nancy, at a loose end without a sick husband to care for, made her plans to come to London.

Clemency thought it better not to confront their mother with Lucian straight away. She discussed it with Elsie, who said, 'You two girls go and meet your mother and I'll look after him for the day. Give her a few days before you tell her, but I'm sure she'll love him, he's such a dear.' She smiled fondly. 'Your father, when he returns, will come to accept him too, I expect.'

Both girls longed to see their mother and yet they dreaded it.

'What if Mummy and Daddy insist that I have him adopted before I can get to Stephano?' Verity was becoming very anxious. 'I'm not twenty-one; can they take him by law?' She stuck to her conviction that Stephano would marry her, because she could not bear to think what would happen if he did not. She had not heard from him for some weeks and she began to make plans to go to Orkney to find him.

'Let's not worry until it happens.' Clemency hugged her. She would not have believed that she could love a baby so much; a

SHADOWS IN THE SKY

baby that wasn't even hers. She would do all she could to ensure that Verity kept him. Now that she, Clemency, was twenty-one, surely she could adopt him and they could live somewhere in the country.

Another menace hit London. The city had been fairly safe from bombs since that terrible night in May in 1941, but now there appeared this new horror: flying bombs, which also hit North London. The government did its best to reassure people that the most densely populated parts in the south of London were safe. Nancy had already arrived, or Clemency could have used these attacks as an excuse to put her off for longer, but Nancy telephoned them from the house in Kensington, begging them to come round to see her. Her arrival coincided with Clemency's three days off, so she and Verity went together.

'Do I look different, will she guess?' With the showdown almost upon them, Verity's optimistic expectations of her parents accepting Lucian were fast fading.

'Just say you've been working hard if she says anything,' advised Clemency.

How much Verity had changed, grown up; her figure had reverted to normal, so no one could guess that she had been pregnant, but she was no longer so scatty and shallow-minded.

'Remember, not a word about Lucian until we think the time is right. Talk about your work – remember what I told you about the clerical work at Hamble,' Clemency reminded her.

Nancy's pleasure at seeing them filled them both with guilt. Verity mouthed *shall we tell her?* but Clemency shook her head; let Mummy enjoy being with them again before she had to face it.

Mrs Paxton had come in and taken off the dustsheets and the house looked lived-in again, but Clemency wished she had come round herself to see if Daddy had left any incriminating evidence of his exploits. Perhaps Mrs Paxton had done it; Clemency felt mortified, wondering what the housekeeper might have thought, and if she'd gossip about it.

'Now you are here can't you stay the night, move back in?' Nancy looked brightly from one to the other.

Clemency blurted, 'We've got something on tonight.' Verity had to get back for Lucian. 'A work thing,' she added.

'Oh, must you?' Nancy looked disappointed. 'It's Sunday tomorrow and I'd like to go to the Guards Chapel for the service. I'd hoped you two would come with me so we can celebrate being together again?' She regarded them eagerly.

'Oh I . . .' Verity eyed Clemency with horror. Elsie, who was usually free to look after Lucian, was going to visit her injured nephew in the country that day. It had been planned for some time.

'Please both come, unless you're working, that is,' Nancy pleaded.

'We'll try.' What could they do with Lucian? Should they tell her now? Neither sister dared look at the other, but each felt the weight of the news that must soon be revealed. Which one of them would tell her? But before either could start Nancy told them how difficult it had been caring for their father, her face becoming tighter with strain, as she went on to describe his illness.

'He went back to his ship far too soon . . . I don't think he should have gone at all. It's so bad out there at sea. The bloody Huns bomb the convoys without respite. I hate to think of him there.' She took a handkerchief from her sleeve and blew her nose. Clemency put her arm round her, glancing at Verity; both sisters felt that it would not be fair to burden their mother with their news just now.

Verity agreed to go to church with her. Although they had not had time to discuss it, Nancy, having questioned Verity about her war work, imagined that she had very flexible working hours, so she expected Verity to go with her. She was hazier about Clemency's job, so she did not question her when Clemency said she'd come if she could, but that she did not know her schedule yet.

'You must say I had to deliver a plane urgently; she'll believe that.' Clemency said when they'd left. 'I'll look after Lucian.'

'It's all much more difficult than I thought,' Verity moaned, 'but I must tell her this week, and then go to Orkney. Stephano must see his son. Do you think Betty could get him to her house and I could telephone him?'

'Perhaps, but just wait a little longer.' If Mummy got to know Lucian there was a slim chance that she would be strong enough to

cope with Daddy's fury. It was a gamble, but one they would have
to take.

Clemency took Lucian to Dory's flat. Jane and Audrey had the
day off and they cooed over him as he lay in his basket. A couple
of pilots, Henry and Clive, arrived to take them out to lunch;
Clemency said she was minding Lucian for a friend.

'Dear little fellow,' Clive said. 'Looks Italian, or maybe French.'

'I think his grandmother was Italian,' Clemency said quickly.
'She . . .' Her mind was whirring to think up some story, but then
there was an almighty explosion, somewhere close.

'One of those bloody flying bombs,' Henry said. 'They make
such a noise you can hear them from miles away.'

They tensed, waiting for more to fall, wondering whether they
should go to a shelter now, or were they they too late?

There were no more explosions and the men wanted to go out
and see what had happened. Jane and Audrey went with them, but
Clemency stayed in the flat to feed Lucian; the noise had unsettled
him and she concentrated on soothing him.

Half an hour later they were back, white-faced and dazed. Jane
burst into tears, taking Clemency into her arms.

'It fell on the Guards Chapel,' she said. 'It's done the most
frightful damage.'

CHAPTER TWENTY-EIGHT

Clemency stared at them all in bewilderment, as if she were a spectator of a drama she didn't understand. Then her brain connected, Verity and Nancy had been in the Guards Chapel. She was seized with panic and super-human energy.

'I must go and find them,' she cried. She was at the door in a moment, but Clive caught her, held her in his arms.

'My dear, everything that can be done is being done.'

'They may be trapped, calling out and I . . . We . . .' Why didn't they come with her, sense the urgency?

'We wouldn't be allowed near the site. Stay here, I'll go and see what I can find out.' Clive's face was ashen, he caught Jane's eye. How Clemency hated that; they were ganging up on her, keeping something from her as if she were a child.

'I'm coming with you, they may be trapped,' she repeated desperately, fighting to keep control over her emotions. She must remain calm; she'd be useless if she panicked. She struggled with Clive, but his arms enclosed her like a vice. 'Let me go, please let me go.' She was crying now, she could not leave Mummy and Verity to suffocate alone.

Lucian, woken by the noise, began to scream. Clemency had forgotten him and she was torn between going to him and rushing out to save his mother. Audrey picked him up. Suddenly Clemency's knees buckled, both Verity and Nancy might be dead. Henry caught her and helped her to the sofa.

'We'll go and find out all we can. Stay here,' Clive said, going to the door.

Clemency tried to get up to follow them, but Henry said, 'Please stay here, Clemency. We'll be back with news as soon as we can.'

SHADOWS IN THE SKY

'I can't wait here. I must come and help.' She struggled again to get up, but Jane held her back.

'You can't,' she said firmly. 'They can't allow relatives to help. Imagine if an untrained pilot tried to fly. You know what it would be like.'

'But I helped at the hospital in Wick . . .' The scenes of the broken bodies made her retch; it couldn't have happened to Mummy and Verity. Maybe they hadn't gone to the chapel after all. Hope flared, then died.

'You said you felt useless that day,' Audrey reminded her.

'Don't imagine anything until you know,' Jane said. 'These scenes are chaotic, it takes time to sort out.'

Jane was right but Clemency's agitation increased. Perhaps they hadn't gone to the service after all, or they were in hospital and hadn't been able to inform her, but even as she made excuses, the probable reality took hold. How would she let Daddy know and who would care for Lucian?

The two men returned, their faces grave. Clive, used to breaking news of his soldiers' deaths to their families, squatted beside her.

'It's very bad there; it may take some days to dig everyone out. The bomb fell right in the middle of the concrete roof . . .' He paused to allow the information to sink in.

'Then we must go and dig them out,' Clemency said

Clive put his hand on her knee. 'I know it's early days but I cannot find their names among the survivors. Some personal effects from some of the . . . dead have been found, and you could come and see if anything belongs to them. Then you will know.'

She felt deadly calm now; she lived on the edge of death, ferrying planes, being among the fighter pilots, knowing how many had been lost.

'Take me,' she said. She turned to Audrey. 'Do you mind keeping Lucian until I get back?'

'No, we'll be fine.' Audrey, who had a collection of nephews and nieces, was good with children.

Henry stayed with Audrey while Jane and Clive went with Clemency.

'If I don't find anything of theirs they may still be alive under the rubble. I must find where they are and talk to them while they wait to be rescued.' Clive and Jane said nothing.

Both women were shocked when they saw the destruction before them. Where the chapel had once stood was now a heap of rubble. They were not allowed to approach too close. Firemen and other workers were painstakingly working through the devastation.

One ambulance stood idly by while the mortuary vans were in heavy demand. Blood-soaked blankets covered some twisted shapes lying on the ground, muffled sounds of people screaming under the rubble made Clemency clutch at Clive's hand.

'They could be alive, calling out,' she cried, and tried to get nearer but Clive held her back and led her to a makeshift shelter where the effects of the victims who had been found were spread out. It was a pitiful collection: small pieces of jewellery, bags, prayer books, shoes, and there, sitting by itself, was the beautiful wooden bracelet Stephano had made for Verity.

'That's Verity's, but it could have fallen off.' Clemency picked it up and examined the delicate carving and the tiny heart that Stephano had made.

Clive caught the eye of a woman from the Red Cross who was on duty here; she gave a little shake of her head. 'No.' He tightened his arm round Clemency. 'They found it on her. I'm so sorry, Clemency, but I doubt she . . . either of them, suffered.'

It was not true, how could they be dead? Even when they found the torn remains of her mother's scarf, one she had given her for her birthday, Clemency did not believe it. But other people were crying, turning away, clutching some object to them in despair. If they had lost someone dear to them why should she not have done so?

'Are they there?' She started towards the shapes under the blankets that were waiting to be lifted into the mortuary vans.

Clive led her away. 'Don't go there, they may have been removed already. They'll be identified by their belongings, they number them as they find them. You have the bracelet and the scarf. Those are enough to tell us what happened to them.'

Time passed in a blur of pain and it was only the support of her friends and the need to tend to Lucian that kept her sane. It seemed that the people closest to her had been snatched from her: Teddy, Dory, Nancy and Verity. Only her father remained, and she clung to that, yearning for him to get home to comfort her.

He was given compassionate leave and she waited for him in their house. It was painful going back that first time after Verity's and Nancy's deaths. Jane offered to come with her but Clemency refused; this was something she had to do alone.

Her mother's clothes lay on the chair in her bedroom, her cosmetics were arranged in their pretty bottles on the dressing-table, waiting to be used. She could just detect the lingering mist of her scent, Worth's *Je Reviens*. She remembered it enclosing her when she was a child and Mummy kissing her goodnight before she went out to dinner. *Je Reviens* – I return. She would never return now.

The memory of Harry's wife taunted her: her sexuality, her pitying, mocking eyes. Why wasn't she dead? She deserved to die, Mummy and Verity had not. She got up abruptly and went down-stairs, angry now with her father for betraying her mother with such a woman, with any woman. How would he feel now that Nancy was gone?

Clemency was on compassionate leave, but she longed to return to work, go back into the routine of flying and the power of the sky, to be able to think of something else besides this appalling tragedy and the complications that now ensued, especially concerning Lucian.

She must tell Stephano about him. He was the boy's father and now his only parent. But how could she achieve it? A letter might not get to him, and it was a cruel way to tell him something so momentous. She owed it to him and to Verity to go to him. She had to be the one to tell him about Verity and their child. Yet she was tortured by the guilt of her betrayal of Verity with him.

Elsie was shattered by Verity's death. She was happy to care for Lucian, though Clemency, encouraged by Jane and Audrey who felt he would help her in her grief, was often with him. He grew more like Stephano every day. This pleased her one moment, enraged her the next. If Verity hadn't loved Stephano, had his child and come here to have it secretly she and Mummy would be alive. If Daddy were not so strict she'd have stayed in Caithness and been safe. Yet it was not Lucian's fault that he had lost his mother and did not know his father.

But Daddy must know about his grandson. Surely, after his initial anger, he would find comfort in Lucian? He was part of their family, part of Verity; he was all they had left of her. She would not tell Daddy straight away; she was worried about his mental state and whether Mummy's and Verity's deaths would push him over the edge. It might be best to just appear with Lucian, trust to Verity's conviction that, confronted with this beautiful child, he could not fail to accept him.

A taxi stopped outside the house. Clemency took a deep breath. She must be strong for her father, but when she opened the door and saw him standing there lost and haggard, she could not control her tears.

The funerals were arranged. The church was full of family and friends, furious at the mode of Nancy's and Verity's deaths in a church during a service, even though it was known that the bombs were pilotless and fell where they would. Verity and Nancy were just two more people among the hundreds killed. Many others had died there that morning, though that was little comfort.

Her father's grief frightened her. He sat alone for hours staring into space. She tried to tempt him with whatever tasty things she could find but he barely touched them. Whisky he drank willingly, and when the few bottles he had in his cellar had gone he drank anything else he could find.

'Why were they there, in that chapel? Why did they come to London at all?' he kept asking her in despair.

Aunt Mattie came down to look after him. She told him that Verity had come down to do 'war work' and that Nancy had come down to see them both.

'But what work did Verity do? Don't tell me she wanted to fly too?' He glared at Clemency and she, exhausted by the pain of it all, shook her head and left the room, dreading telling him the truth.

Perhaps she should tell Aunt Mattie about Lucian and ask her to break it to her father? Once or twice she'd been about to when something interrupted them. Aunt Mattie said that she must think of returning home and that she would take Gerald with her if he wished, so Clemency knew she couldn't put it off any longer. She must bring Lucian here and tell Daddy the whole story.

She told Aunt Mattie that she was bringing someone round to the house and not to mention it to her father.

'Why? Is it someone he doesn't want to see?'

Clemency hesitated; she ought to tell her aunt; but no, better to bring Lucian. Once they'd seen him they would love him, would understand. 'This person is special. I'll be back soon,' was all she offered to her aunt. She left before she could be questioned further.

She dressed Lucian in a light blue and white romper suit, making him look even more enchanting. He was more alert now; when he was taken out he attracted a lot of compliments, so surely he could not fail to charm his grandfather?

Elsie said awkwardly, 'You know I love him, but I can't look after him much longer. My arthritis plays up terrible in the winter and he'll soon be on the move. It will be too much.'

Clemency was taken aback by what Elsie told her. 'I'm sorry, I should have thought,' she said guiltily

'You've got so much on your plate. I thought I'd give you plenty of warning, and when your father sees him,' Elsie smiled lovingly at Lucian, 'he'll welcome him as part of the family. You'll see.'

'I hope he will,' Clemency answered doubtfully. Surely after what had happened it would turn out all right? Daddy would get in a nanny and they'd bring him up together. But Stephano must be told he had a son; when should she tell him? Daddy would know what to do. It would be a great relief when it was all out in the open.

She took a taxi back to the house, opened the front door and went in, carrying Lucian. Aunt Mattie came into the hall. Upon seeing Lucian she gasped.

'What . . . ever. . . ?

Clemency said quietly, 'This is Lucian, Verity's baby.'

Aunt Mattie was stunned into silence. Clemency went on, 'She was in love with a man in Orkney. Lucian is their child. Daddy's grandson.'

'No, it's . . . it's not possible.' Aunt Mattie stared at the baby in horror.

Clemency knew that she should have warned her, but however it had been done Aunt Mattie would have been shocked. She went into the study before she lost her nerve. Her father was sitting in his chair staring out of the window. He did not turn round when she entered but Lucian gave a little yelp.

Clemency blurted, 'Daddy, I've someone for you to meet, he . . .'

Gerald turned round and frowned when he saw Lucian.

'Daddy,' she came closer, crouched down before him so he could see Lucian properly, 'this is Verity's child, your grandson.'

Lucian waved his fists cheerfully. Gerald stared at him, then at her, 'What do you mean, *Verity's* child?'

'What I say. She fell in love with someone in Orkney and she had his child. That's why she came down here, so that no one would know, but now she's . . . gone he's all we have left of her, and we must bring him up as . . .'

'Enough!' Gerald shouted making Lucian jump. 'Verity would never do such a thing, but you . . . Now I see it, I see it all. It's your bastard. That's why you ran away from home or . . .' he hesitated, realizing that if she'd been pregnant when she left to fly, the child would be much older, 'leaving home, doing a man's job, you forgot your morals.'

'That is not true, he's Verity's, I promise you.' She gulped back her tears, she hadn't expected this.

Lucian began to cry and Aunt Mattie, having heard Gerald's shouting, came into the room and took Lucian from her, holding him awkwardly before sitting down with him on her lap.

'I cannot believe that my daughter would do such a thing and then blame it on her dead sister,' Gerald raged, his lips ringed with spittle. 'Don't think you can palm that child off as hers, I will have nothing to do with it, and what race was his father? I will not have him here.'

Clemency sank back on her heels staring at him in despair.

'He is Verity's.' Did he hate her so much that he would not believe her?

'Go away and take your bastard with you,' Gerald roared. 'Go now and never let me see you again.'

'Gerald, I think . . .' Aunt Mattie bleated from the sofa.

Gerald ignored her. 'You're nothing but trouble, Clemency, wanting to take a man's job by flying. You know what they say about women pilots, you've lived up to it and now you have disgraced the family by having a child out of wedlock.'

The anger rose in her. 'I don't know what foolish people say about women pilots but Lucian is Verity's child. His father is called Stephano and is in Orkney. The child is the image of him. I'll find him and you can ask him about Verity.' She got up. 'You hate me because I caught you with other women; you even brought one here when you should have been with Mummy. Mummy loved you too much. That was her weakness and you were not worthy of it.' She went to Aunt Mattie and bent down to take Lucian from her.

'How dare you speak to me like that.' Gerald rose from his chair and came towards her, his arm raised to strike her.

'Gerald, let's talk about this rationally.' Aunt Mattie got up and put her hand on his raised arm. 'It's been a shock; rest awhile, then we will discuss it.'

'There is nothing to discuss,' Gerald retorted. 'Did you worry your mother with this? Is that why she went to church and was killed?'

'No, we didn't tell her. We had to do everything secretly because of you and your warped morals. Verity should have stayed in Caithness with Mummy and had the baby there.' Holding Lucian tightly to her, afraid that Gerald would strike him, Clemency left the room. His anger when he was first confronted with Lucian did not surprise her, but never had she thought he would accuse her of using Verity's death to hide a disgrace of her own.

Lucian nuzzled his face into her cheek. He was all she had left of her family but his grandfather didn't want him and he didn't belong to her. She would have to find Stephano and ask him what to do.

CHAPTER TWENTY-NINE

That scene with her father was almost worse than anything that had gone before.

To her surprise, however, Aunt Mattie did not condemn her. Lucian had melted her heart, and as Clemency snatched him up from her to flee from the house she followed them into the hall.

'Your father is distraught; he is taking his anger at their deaths out on you because you are alive. I wish I had noticed Verity's condition; she had become more subdued, but I never thought of *that*.' Aunt Mattie looked embarrassed. 'But if ever you need a home, you know where I am.'

Clemency hugged her, mumbling 'thank you' before running down the street, not wanting to look back and think of all she had lost.

She could not stay in London, the V bombs, or doodlebugs – one of the nicknames the Londoners gave them – frightened her and she had Lucian to think of.

Jane understood her concern. 'You've been through so much and now you're responsible for Lucian. Take a few months out, then you'll be in a better state to plan for the future.'

At the funeral, Grace had said, 'Come to Chesterfield whenever you want to, and bring whoever you want with you, there's plenty of room.' Her smile comforted Clemency, so she packed up and went to Chesterfield.

Lucian changed the atmosphere in the house; he was new life, hope in a devastated world and as each day passed he grew a little more and smiled with such disarming charm that their hearts healed as much as they ever would. The months slipped by,

Christmas came and went, and Clemency stayed on, knowing she must make plans for the future.

Clemency told Grace about her father's reaction to Lucian.

'Foolishly, I was so sure that when he saw him, he'd love him, because everyone else who sees him, is charmed by him,' she said sadly.

Grace was horrified. 'All I can say in his defence, is that grief sends you mad, distorts things. Give him time and he'll understand.'

'Should I take him to his father?' Clemency asked Grace later. 'Or will it break up his marriage?'

'Lucian needs to know where he comes from and that he was made in love. When the weather is better take him to Stephano; he has a right to know about him, and to make his own decisions about his marriage.'

'What if he takes him from us?' Clemency dreaded this and yet she could not bear to hurt Stephano. She loved him, but, she was not like Verity, who had fantasized of living with him after his wife and daughter had somehow disappeared.

Grace said gently, 'Lucian is his son. If he acknowledges him he must have a say in his future.'

Aunt Mattie had written to Clemency telling her that Daddy had gone back to sea and that she'd meant what she said about having her and Lucian to stay. Clemency had no excuse now not to go to Orkney.

Lucian was walking round the furniture now, holding on as he went. She drew him, quick sketches of his chubby cheeks, his laughing face, the way he proudly strutted about. She loved him as her own, but she owed it to Verity to take him to Stephano.

In the middle of March she took Lucian on the sleeper to Inverness and then on to Wick. Aunt Mattie had got hold of a cot and, to Clemency's surprise, seemed unperturbed by the disruption to her domesticity. She put them to sleep in Nancy's room, which she'd rearranged and which now held nothing of her. There was nothing left of Verity either.

The first evening when they were alone in the small sitting room after supper, Aunt Mattie asked Clemency to tell her the truth about Lucian's birth.

'I'm not here to judge. I'm well aware that the war has changed everything,' she assured Clemency.

'It's just as I told Daddy. Verity fell in love with a man in Orkney. Lucian is his, but the man's married. I've met him, he is a good man.' She twisted the bracelet he'd carved for Verity round on her wrist. She wore it all the time now. Lucian loved playing with it. She didn't say that Stephano had been a POW but Aunt Mattie was no fool.

'Lucian's very dark; he has Latin looks. I'd say he was Italian, wouldn't you?' She fixed Clemency with her firm gaze, expecting to hear the truth.

'Yes, he is Italian.'

'It's as well your father didn't know that, though he may have guessed it. But they are not our enemies now. I hear that some of them have left – you must go at once if you want to find him.'

She'd leave Lucian with Mrs Donaldson to whom she had already written, telling her that she had a baby with her and she would explain all when she arrived. She would go alone and find Stephano.

'He's a bonnie boy,' Mrs Donaldson greeted her, 'looks as if his father's one of those Italians. He's not the only one.' She sighed, taking them into the front room where her not so bonnie grandson was playing with bricks on the floor.

'Yes, his father is Italian.' There was no point in lying. Mrs Donaldson might even know Stephano, as the Italians moved quite freely round the island now. 'You've heard . . .' she hated the distress her news caused people, 'that Mummy and Verity were killed in a bomb raid in London.'

'Oh no!' Mrs Donaldson sat down with a thump. 'Oh, my dear, no. They should never have gone there. What happened?'

Yet again Clemency had to tell the story.

'So it looks like you've been left holding the baby,' Mrs Donaldson sighed. 'This war's made a right mess of things, so many fatherless children; don't know how it will all end. Verity and your dear mother . . .' She took out a handkerchief and scrubbed at her eyes, 'getting killed like that, in church on a Sunday, too, what wickedness is that? Well, I hope there's a hell and those Jerries are in it.'

Clemency must find Stephano. Her body sparked with desire as she remembered their lovemaking, but there would be none of that this time. When he saw her in daylight he would see that she was not Verity. She must tell him about Verity's death and the birth of his son; that was her only mission.

Lucian cried when she left and she was tempted to take him with her, but it would not be fair to confront Stephano with his child before she'd told him about his existence. He might want nothing to do with him at all.

She took a taxi to Kirkwall. The Flow was full of ships and aircraft carriers. Was Daddy's ship among them? Now that he was a widower he could have the pick of any woman he wished. She felt sick, wondering who would replace her mother. What if it were Joan or, worse still, Flavia? Perhaps he'd refuse to see his daughter, so it wouldn't matter. Lucian was the focus of her life now.

Her mother had left her enough money to buy herself a mews house and live from day to day, but she supposed she must at some future time get a job to support them both. She missed her flying, but now that seemed like another world. There was no longer such a frantic need for planes and, with the foreign women who had joined the ATA, there was no shortage of ferry pilots now. But there was no point in making plans until she had seen Stephano; he might be able to help them financially. On the other hand, and she must be prepared for this, he might disown Lucian, discard him as yet another casualty of war.

Clemency waited to meet Betty outside the hospital. She'd told her briefly, last night, about Verity's death but not about her pregnancy. When Betty saw her, she burst into tears.

'I told her not to go to London, and your mother too . . . it's cruel – and in church – you'd have thought you were safe in there.'

Clemency said quietly, 'She had a child, Betty. He's Stephano's. I must find him and tell him. Do you know where he is?'

This stopped Betty's tears. 'A baby? That's tough. She did wonder, then she said she wasn't. I haven't seen him for a long time; I expect he's at the chapel; they've made it very beautiful, out of nothing. You'll find him there I shouldn't wonder. Andy will drive you there, he only lives round the corner. It'll give him something to do.'

Betty was practical now. 'It's good of you to come over to tell him. They loved each other, those two.' She smiled sadly. 'Bloody war turned our lives upside down. There are other girls here in love with them, some pregnant, hoping they will marry them.' She shrugged. 'Some luck, I say, once they've gone from here they'll never come back. Why would they?'

With some difficulty Clemency managed to divert Betty from her musings and get her to find Andy, who agreed for a fee to drive her to Lamb Holm and the chapel the Italian POWs had built in their camp.

Now that the causeways were in use, it was much easier to reach the camp. It was close to the water, which lay quiet under the spring sun.

'Tis only a couple of Nissen Huts that they decorated,' Andy said as they arrived. He'd spent the drive cursing the Huns for killing Verity. 'They had a priest so they needed a church,' he continued as if there was no more to it than that.

'Thank you. Will you wait for me?'

Now she was so close to seeing Stephano her heart raced. She dreaded breaking the news to him. The sight of the chapel took her breath away. It was simple but impressive; its pure white façade was picked out in red, and there were two slim gothic windows on either side of the door. Four white pillars, two on each side of the door, supported a pediment, the centre of which was a moulded face of Christ, wearing his crown of thorns. But it was much more than this; it stood there among the dreary Nissen huts that had been their prison for so long, as a sign of hope, a sign that the terrible dark days spent so far from their families would one day be over.

It was humbling standing there and, so slowly at first that she barely noticed, she was filled with a kind of peace, a feeling that however bad life was, however deep the suffering, there was always hope.

'*Signorina, buona sera.*' A man behind her roused her from her contemplation.

'It's so beautiful,' she said.

He smiled. 'Come, see inside.'

She followed him and gasped with wonder. The painting was extraordinary, it seemed at first as though the chapel was built of brick and stone with low walls running round the inside, but looking closely she saw it was a *trompe l'oeil*. An intricate wrought-iron screen separated the altar from the main body of the chapel. A man was finishing painting the ceiling.

'I can't believe it,' she said, 'this beauty, this . . . miracle here in such a sad place.'

It was a few moments before she remembered that she had come to see Stephano. Somehow it seemed fitting that she could break her painful news to him in such a place. More men appeared to do small tasks. As each man arrived she tensed herself for him to be Stephano, there was an ache round her heart as she prepared herself to tell him about Verity and their son.

When he didn't appear she asked the first man she'd seen where he was.

This caused some confusion, as there were quite a few Stephanos and she did not know his other name. She told them that her sister Verity had been close to him, and then one man spoke up.

'*Sì*, Stephano Boldrini and his English girlfriend. I know, you look like her. But he is gone.'

'Gone?'

'Yes, some of us have gone home.'

'Can I find him? Do you know where he lives?' She could not bear it.

A thin youth said hesitantly, 'I come from Lucca. The same town as Stephano. He lives with his wife with her family off the Via S. Giustina. Do you want to write to him?'

'No, I . . .' Why wasn't he here? She couldn't write; she'd have to go there, but travel would be difficult; she'd have to put it off until things got easier.

'I need to go there and find him,' she said. 'I need his address.'

The youth explained that all she had to do was go to Lucca and mention his name and someone would know him. He would be there with his wife.

Clemency left the chapel too dispirited to try and get any more information out of the men. She turned at the door and looked back at the altar, willing this chapel to give her strength.

She must go to Lucca and knock on every door until she found Stephano.

CHAPTER THIRTY

The war ended in Europe in victory but at such a heavy price. Clemency celebrated with her friends in London on VE day, joining the excited surge of people going to Buckingham Palace to see the royal family and Winston Churchill, who came out on to the balcony celebrating with them. There was a heady feeling of excitement and relief, some people singing the songs that had got them through the war, banging on dustbin lids, climbing lamp-posts and statues to get a better view. Fireworks illuminated the darkness with colour.

But Clemency's heart was heavy. Dory, and Johnnie with his matinée idol face complete in its beauty, Teddy, Verity, Mummy and all the other friends that had gone should be here with them. Then she would think of it as a victory.

She had not long been back from her fruitless journey to Orkney. Lucian grew more and more like his father each day, and sometimes she indulged herself with foolish fantasies, imagining herself and Stephano together, watching him grow, though in the loneliness of the night she was haunted by the fear that she might never find Stephano again.

With the end of the war came the end of the ATA. The women pilots who had done so much to help win the war were disbanded.

'I suppose we're meant to go home, marry and become house-wives with nothing more exciting to do than decide what to cook for dinner,' Audrey said bitterly. 'Just because men have come back and left the forces they expect us to stand aside and hand over our jobs to them.'

Jane sighed. 'It seems they've chucked us out when we're no longer needed. We risked our lives, some gave them and all the thanks we get is dismissal.'

The three of them were at Clemency's mews house. Jane had suggested a meeting and they sat round the debris of lunch. Clemency agreed with them. 'Much though I love being with Lucian, I 'd like to work, fly again. I miss that glorious freedom in the sky.'

'Funny you should mention it.' Jane had a mysterious look on her face. 'This is one of the reasons I wanted to see you both.' She paused and they watched her expectantly. 'You could both work for me. I've decided to start a private plane business, fly people to destinations in this country or in Europe, or perhaps even further.'

'You mean it?' Audrey and Clemency exclaimed together. Jane had recently inherited a great deal of money from her mother, but no one had spoken of it.

'I do. I too want to work, want to keep flying. I'll start small with a couple of aircraft and you two and I could pilot them. I don't know how much work we'd get, but it's worth a try.'

This new challenge lifted Clemency's spirits and the joyous prospect of flying again postponed her vague plan of going to Italy. She flew a few times to France and Switzerland, taking business people, or people searching for relatives, or to return to Europe themselves. Elsie found for her a kind woman who came and looked after Lucian and the house.

She began to go out again in London, but it was not the same as it had been. The adrenaline that urged them on in wartime, and the frantic round of amusement had disappeared. People were now faced with a broken world; the country was all but bankrupt, and some relationships that once had seemed so romantic in the magic of the night were now, in the bleak light of day found to have been a mistake.

She wondered where Daddy was. She had cleared out everything she wanted from the family house into her new one, and would not go back again. Aunt Mattie had tried her best to explain about Lucian to Gerald but he'd forbidden her to mention the boy. She tried to excuse his behaviour, explaining how Nancy's and Verity's deaths had all but destroyed him. He was now demobbed and staying with her while he sold the London house. Clemency waited for him to get in touch with her but he did not. Perhaps he was too ashamed to make the first move and she was too afraid that his dislike of her was more than the distortion of emotion by grief so she did nothing either.

She searched too for Harry among the people dining and dancing, but she never saw him – nor, to her relief, did she see Flavia. She remembered that they had a house in Cambridge; perhaps they were there together. She supposed he was alive; she hadn't heard otherwise. Some people were still in parts of Asia or, on coming back to Britain, had dispersed all over the country, struggling to pick up their lives again. Dory's flat had been sold, and Clemency had moved to her mews house off Queen's Gate. Why should Harry be looking for her? They were like so many others, having experienced a flash of romance before going on with their own lives. He loved that dreadful wife and was no doubt back with her.

It was late September. Clemency arrived back from dropping a passenger in France. She checked in at the office. Jane looked up from her paperwork.

'Next week I'm flying someone to Italy. I'll give you and Lucian a lift so you can find Stephano.'

'Find Stephano?' Clemency said stupidly. She had never stopped thinking of him, how could she, living as she did with the mini version of him every day, and yet she had done nothing about it.

'Yes, it's about time. I'm flying to Rome and you can take a train to Lucca.'

Clemency's imagination fired up with foolish dreams. What if things had changed for Stephano and he wanted her and Lucian to stay with him? Then she was hit with despair; she was afraid to go, he might not be there, or worse, he would not see her. Jane guessed all this. She said firmly, 'Lucian is growing up. He needs to see his father and you need to know how much Stephano wants to be involved.'

'I know but—'

'No buts, Clemency. It has got to be done for his sake and for Verity. I know you're scared, but,' Jane smiled at her, 'we've all been scared before and we know the only way to deal with it is to face it and work through it.'

'You're right of course, but—'

'I am. Now, Thursday, be here at nine o'clock.' Jane went back to filling in the flight sheets and Clemency knew that that was that; just as in her days of ferry piloting there would be no arguments over orders given.

It seemed to her that her friends were conspiring together over this trip. Audrey apparently knew a family in Lucca, who would have her to stay.

The flight went well, Jane's passenger, Edward Woodhouse, was obviously a close friend. He'd spent most of the war in Burma; he was someone Jane had kept secret from them all.

'Don't jump to any conclusions; we hardly know each other,' Jane said quietly, but Clemency could see the joy in her eyes. She hugged Jane, wishing her well.

Clemency and Lucian arrived in Lucca at dusk. The little boy had travelled well. Being a child with a sunny nature he'd been fascinated by what was going on and his new surroundings. He squeaked in excitement, occasionally throwing out words: 'car' was his favourite and that covered most vehicles. Clemency had agonized over what he should call her, he made the 'mama' sound but she didn't feel it was right, that was for Verity and she was not here. She tried 'Auntie', but all he managed was 'T', so 'T' she became. The taxi dropped her at a small house just inside the ramparts of the town.

Signora Menotti was about her own age. She spoke good English, having spent a few months in England before the war.

'I'm sorry you find us so shabby, the war . . .' She shrugged, 'it has not left us well.'

Lucian was asleep and Placida – she insisted that Clemency should call her by her first name – showed her to her room. Two little girls watched them shyly from the doorway.

'My daughters Rosa and Florine, Cesar, my husband, is away in Rome.'

Clemency liked her at once and when she had washed and had a small supper, she told her about Verity and Lucian.

SHADOWS IN THE SKY

'It is a sad story, but there are so many the same,' Placida said. 'I don't know his family but I know the address. He lives in a palazzo; there are quite a few of them falling to pieces around these families. They let out rooms, do what they can to keep them; they cost so much to repair.'

Clemency wondered whether she should take Lucian with her or wait until she had broken the news to Stephano. Kind though Placida was, Clemency was worried about leaving Lucian with a stranger. He was going through a phase of being shy with new people and it took him time to feel secure with them. This was another reason why she dreaded the meeting with Stephano. What if Lucian screamed and clung to her refusing to go near his father? He was not very used to men and he might be terrified if Stephano was too emotional, or, and she hated to think it but she was cruelly reminded of her father, if Stephano was furious at seeing him. Maybe this whole thing had been a mistake and she should have waited until Lucian was older and she could explain it to him.

'Wait until he is used to us,' Placida said when Clemency asked her advice, 'then go alone to see his father's reaction.'

Lucian was fascinated by Placida's daughters, and by the following afternoon Clemency felt she could leave him while she went to find Stephano.

'Be prepared for him not wanting to know. He may be afraid of his wife, some Italian men are,' Placida said laughing, 'especially if they have a difficult mother and their wife is like her.'

Clemency tried to smile, but her heart was heavy. She could hardly believe that she was here in his town and might see him, touch him, again.

The palazzo was in a courtyard in a road off Via S. Giustina. It was not far and each step that brought her nearer increased her anxiety. What if Stephano refused to acknowledge her, her and Verity? She imagined Verity here with her now. She would have run all the way, like an eager child, refusing to accept that Stephano might no longer love her. She'd have Lucian with her, dancing along beside her, and she would be convinced that at the first sight of his son Stephano would throw off his previous life as if it were an old coat to be discarded, and go with her. *If only you were here, he would love you.* Clemency thought these words to herself. Tears rose in her throat. Verity and Lucian together would be a winning couple; she was a poor substitute. Her body ached for the passion and tenderness of his lovemaking, but it wouldn't happen now, in his home town, with his wife and her family around.

But what if his marriage had not lasted? What if, on coming home he had found that it was not what he wanted, or his wife had found someone else? She must not allow herself such fantasies. How perfect it would be if he loved her and lived with her and Lucian, but surely that would never be.

She reached the Via S. Giustina and walked slowly down the narrow street, looking along the walls for an opening into a courtyard. There it was, just as Placida had described it: an arch with a dusty window above it, crowned with a pediment and a rusty wrought-iron balcony. She edged a few steps through it and studied the broken paving laced with weeds that pushed themselves through the cracks in the stones. A flight of steps, some broken, led up to an imposing front door, then, further on, there was a smaller door and she saw the back of someone going in. There was an air of decadence about the courtyard that saddened her.

But how could she find Stephano? Should she go to the front door, pull that rusty bell chain, which looked as if it would come apart in her hands, or go to that smaller door? What if his wife, or even his mother or mother-in-law came to the door? What should she say?

She dithered for a moment. Then, afraid that she was being watched through one of those shadowy windows, she returned to the street to decide what to do. Perhaps she should write a letter telling him where she was and put it through one of the doors.

People glanced curiously at her as they hurried past. She'd go back to Placida, ask her what would be the best thing to do. Perhaps Placida would go for her; that might be easier: another Italian to face his family, take him a message, instead of their being confronted by a foreigner.

Convinced that this would be the best way to deal with it she started to go back. A man in the street was staring at her.

'Verity? Is it you?'

'Stephano?' She took a moment to recognize him. His hair was neatly shaped, glossy and dark, his face no longer so drawn; he'd filled out, his clothes were well cut, his shoes polished. Her heart pounded. How attractive he was and how she loved him.

He came swiftly up to her and, taking her arm, led her further up the street.

'You must not be here, how did you find me?' He was stunned and yet he had the presence of mind to get her out of the way.

'You're not pleased to see me?' Why had she said such a thing? It was just what Verity would have said.

'Of course I am, but *cara*, the war is over, this is my home. I will always have such warm thoughts about you but . . .' He pulled her into a small garden and held her close. 'I cannot believe you are here, I never heard from you. I thought you had married a nice, cold, English man.' He saw the wooden bracelet on her wrist and slipped his finger under it, touching her skin, making her glow. 'You still wear this?'

He thought she was Verity. For a moment she was tempted to pretend she was, perhaps she could live out here, somewhere close, see him sometimes. It would be good for Lucian. *Lucian*! He was the reason she was here; she must not forget that. Reluctantly she moved out of Stephano's arms. Oh the scent of him, the feel of him, what wouldn't she give . . . but, no, she must think of Lucian first: Lucian and Verity.

'Stephano,' just his name melted her heart, 'I'm so sorry. I'm not Verity. I'm Clemency.'

He looked gravely at her. 'I thought you were different and yet I had not seen you for so long. We have both changed.' He frowned, looked again at the bracelet. 'So where is she? Why are you here?'

Tears filled her eyes, she held on to him to comfort him, to comfort herself.

'What has happened to her?' his voice was sharp with anxiety.

'She was killed, killed with our mother in a bomb raid, in church on a Sunday.' She told it all to him between her tears.

'My little Verity, how bright she was. How can she no longer be alive?' Tears streamed down his cheeks; he made no attempt to stop them.

After a few moments he said, 'You came all this way to tell me? You are a special person, Clemency; I thank you from the bottom of my heart. I loved her; she was like a light in the dark time I was away from home. I will never forget her. But you know I have a wife and we are happy together, and perhaps one day I will tell her about Verity and your kindness.' Tenderly he stroked her hair back from her face. 'How did you find me?'

She told him about going to Orkney, and again he praised her kindness. For a moment she let herself savour his gratitude; she was so close to him, their bodies were almost touching. It took all her self-control not to kiss him. She must tell him the reason she was here.

'I did come to tell you that but also . . .' She paused, afraid of what she had to say and the words came out in a rush. 'You had a son together, his name is Lucian.'

His mouth dropped open, he stared at her in shock.

'A son?' he said as if the word was alien to him. 'A son? Is this true? Where is he?'

'I brought him to see you; he's two and a half. I thought you ought to know about him.'

He stared at her in disbelief, but she went on, 'I look after him, I love him, he is a beautiful child, but Verity always said she'd bring him to you when he was born so I'm carrying out her wishes. I don't want to cause trouble in your family. You need not see him and I will return to England with him and bring him up, but I felt it only right that you should know about him.'

He was so still, silent as if in shock, staring at the ground, his hands clenched by his sides. She thought: I've done it now, done what Verity would have wanted. Now she could take Lucian home and perhaps Stephano would see him when he was older.

He lifted his face, his expression was intense, his eyes bored into her.

'My son . . . where is my son? Let me see him, I must see him at once.'

CHAPTER THIRTY-ONE

Stephano put his hand under Clemency's elbow and marched her along the street, urging her to tell him where Lucian was.

'Wait, it's getting late. Let me bring him tomorrow. It's nearly his bed time.'

'I cannot wait. You've told me I have a son, now you will not let me see him?'

'Of course you can see him, Stephano, but think of it from his point of view. He is not much more than a baby and we must not rush this.'

There was so much that could go wrong, that could sour this meeting and she struggled to persuade Stephano to wait until the morning. He would not listen, and if a woman hurrying past them had not greeted him, throwing her a disapproving look, Clemency might have lost her argument.

'*Buona sera, signora.*' He bowed to the woman, standing away from Clemency as if he had not been holding her arms and pleading with her.

The woman said something, still staring at Clemency and Stephano answered her, going a little way along the street with her.

Then, he turned back and called to Clemency in English, 'I cannot stay, but you must bring him at ten o'clock tomorrow morning to that garden behind you. You must do it, for I will find you. I must see him.'

There was such agony in his face that she could hardly bear it. The woman was out of sight now and she said, 'Who was that? What did she say?'

He shrugged. 'Just a neighbour, but one who gossips. I must go to my wife and tell her the story. But Clemency,' he retraced his steps and snatched her hands in his, 'You promise me you will bring me my son tomorrow? Look, here, in this garden.' He showed her the arch that gave on to an overgrown garden with various shrubs that had been left to their own devices. A magnolia tree grew crookedly up towards the light, a stone bench stood by the wall.

'Come here tomorrow,' he repeated. 'Bring him to me.'

For one wild moment she was tempted to take Lucian back home to England now, this evening, to the life he was used to, until he was older, but seeing Stephano's pain she knew she could not do it. Lucian was not hers and Verity had been so determined to bring him to Stephano.

Stephano asked her where she was staying. Reluctantly she told him, and the name of the family.

He showed her the way back, just as if he were a courteous man showing the way to a tourist who'd got lost in the tangle of narrow streets. Then, leaning close as if they would be overheard, he said, 'You have come all this way to tell me about him so I trust you to bring him to me tomorrow.' He kissed her cheek and left her, hurrying away.

She talked long into the night with Placida, who had made some enquires about Stephano. He'd been studying to be a lawyer before the war and had now returned to his studies. Donata, his wife, had been left with this crumbling palazzo. Her mother and a few assorted relatives lived there, each in a few rooms.

'At least he is in a good profession with prospects,' Placida said.

The pain of Verity's absence lay heavy. She should be here deciding how best to deal with Lucian's future.

The next morning Clemency dressed Lucian in his best clothes. He looked beautiful with his dark hair brushed into fluffy curls, and his brown eyes. He was in a good mood, chortling at the antics of the two little girls.

She set off late, walking slowly along with him by her side, not daring to think that this might be the last time that just the two of them would be together. He meant so much to her and brought back so many memories.

They reached the street and the entrance to the garden. Clemency paused reluctant to go in, tightening her hold on Lucian's hand. But Lucian, his interest caught by the sight of the trees, pulled her towards it.

Stephano was sitting on one of the stone benches, looking like a discarded puppet, one arm over the back, one leg stretched out, the other bent. He moved restlessly, ready to spring up. His eyes were wild and his expression, which she caught just before he saw them, was full of despair. They were twenty minutes late, had he thought she would not keep her promise and was not coming? Then he saw them. He sprang up, his eyes only on Lucian, his tears welling up.

Clemency held tightly to Lucian's hand, ready to pick him up if he became distressed. He was wary with strangers, often he would move closer to her, clutching her leg or her hand, waiting until he was sure of the new person. Some people he never took to.

She braced herself for him to turn to her, to bury his face in her skirt while holding up his arms to be carried. But to her surprise, for he had never done such a thing before, he let go of her hand and walked a few step towards Stephano, his face beaming, emitting little squeaks of delight as if he knew this man.

Stephano snatched him up. 'My son, *mio figlio*,' he repeated the words again and again, kissing the little boy, holding him out to marvel at him, then hugging him tight again.

Clemency hovered beside them, certain that Stephano's sudden move and now his emotional greeting would scare Lucian and make him cry, but he was laughing, patting Stephano's face with one hand, the other clutching handfuls of his hair. There was no doubt that they belonged together.

After a few moments of mutual admiration, Stephano, still with Lucian in his arms, turned to her.

'Thank you, Clemency.' His voice was thick with emotion. 'Thank you for bringing my son to me.'

'But . . . he's only . . . it's just for you to meet him. Verity would have wanted me . . .' She tailed off, tears in her eyes, remembering how Verity had been convinced that once Stephano, and indeed her parents, saw Lucian they would love him.

'Of course she would, and if she had not died, she would have

217

come herself,' he said. 'How I wish she was here with us, but you are here and I will always think of you.'

'But I understand that you cannot bring him up.'

Seeing them together she realized that there was something about the two of them clasped together that made her feel as though she were an outsider.

'Your wife,' she said firmly, 'she can not be expected to take him in.'

'Oh, but she will. I told her last night about it all, she already suspected that I had found love in my bleak prison and she understood. The war has been cruel; we have all suffered and it is a miracle that she and I are together again. I told her about you bringing Lucian to me and she will love him.'

He kissed the boy, laughing as Lucian covered his mouth with his hands. 'How could she not? He is a baby, no one hates a baby.' He stretched out his free arm and pulled her to him, and for a moment the three of them stood there together in a clumsy embrace, Lucian laughing with delight and patting them both with his plump little hands.

This is how it is, her head told her, how it should be: father and son united; but already the truth of it was painfully squeezing her heart.

'I don't want to lose him,' she said.

'You will never lose him. You can live here with us. There are many rooms. I will never keep him from you, but he is mine and you have so . . . so unselfishly bought him to me.' He kissed her forehead, understanding her grief, but he was firm too. She had bought Lucian to him so that must mean that she expected him to have him.

'Maybe your English men would not want a child born in this way, but we are different. I know it is sad for you, but you knew what was right. Verity wanted you to bring him to me and so you have.'

She wept then, wept for all she had lost, for she could not stay here; she didn't belong and even now, seeing how Lucian had taken to Stephano, she felt she had lost him. Stephano comforted her, telling her she could visit whenever she wanted, and he would write to her every month to tell her of Lucian's progress. When he was older he could come and stay with her in England.

'I will speak of you and Verity often,' he said. 'He will know his story from the very beginning.'

None of this comforted her but she allowed herself to be swept back to his home. Two boys were playing in the courtyard. Lucian laughed at them.

'They are my sister-in-law's sons. Her husband was killed in the war so she lives here now with us.'

He called to the boys and introduced Lucian to them. An older woman appeared, regarding Stephano and Clemency with disapproval before retreating, making Clemency feel uneasy. She couldn't leave Lucian if he wasn't wanted by all of them. Guessing her feelings, Stephano said, 'That is my wife's mother, she is very religious and very shocked, but she will come round.'

'I wouldn't like to leave him where . . .'

He touched her hand. 'Come and meet Donata and my daughter Sabina.' His expression was tense now; no doubt he dreaded this meeting as much as she did. 'It will be all right, you'll see.' He did not sound convinced, but he strode across the courtyard to the side door, which opened into a passage. Ahead was a wide, ornate stair-case and, still carrying Lucian, he went slowly up it. She followed him. If there were any doubt that Lucian would be unhappy here she would take him home. At the top of the stairs Stephano paused at a doorway, as if girding himself with courage. Then he opened the door and ushered her in.

Full of apprehension at meeting his wife she entered and was struck by the beauty of the room. It had a painted ceiling and long windows overlooking a piazza. There were damp patches in parts of the room and the plaster had fallen off over one window. There was a table and chairs, where they ate their meals; an empty box made into a doll's bed lay among vast pieces of furniture, and a few pictures hung on the walls.

'This is our main room,' he said, 'it needs work, but . . .' he shrugged, 'that costs money.'

'The room is beautiful,' she said.

Lucian struggled to be let down and at the same moment a

young woman and a small girl entered the room.

'*Cara*,' Stephano held out his hands to them, 'this is Clemency and Lucian.' He could not hide his pride, which showed on his face as he looked at his son.

Clemency regarded the woman with interest; this was Stephano's wife whose place Verity had been convinced she would take. She was slight and graceful, with dark hair falling round her face. She came forward a little shyly, holding out her hand to shake hers. She did not look at Lucian, who was playing with a rag doll on the floor. Her daughter, seeing this, snatched it from him, gabbling at him, but Lucian had tired of it anyway. He picked up a yellow ball that lay by a chair; seeing this the girl ran towards that too.

Stephano laughed, picked up his daughter and kissed her, pointing to Lucian, no doubt explaining that he was her half-brother. Clemency bent down to pick him up and Stephano said gently, 'This is all so new to him, new to us all, but believe me it will settle down.'

There was a noise at the door and the two boys whom she'd seen in the courtyard ran in, making Lucian laugh and wave his arms at them.

Through all this Stephano's wife stood beside him, saying nothing. At last she turned and inspected Lucian, who was on his feet now, running round the room with one of the boys. Stephano put his arm round her and held her close. He spoke softly and lovingly to her.

It was obvious that he loved her, so there had been no substance to her and Verity's dreams. For a moment she was glad that Verity was not here to witness this scene and she felt guilty that she too had made love to Stephano, but that was a secret that not even he knew.

Donata left the room and returned with some coffee. Lucian fell asleep, there on the carpet. Stephano laid his hand on Clemency's shoulder.

'I will carry him back to your house, then I will fetch you both tomorrow. Gradually he will get used to us and you can leave him, knowing that he will be happy here with us.'

She was not expecting this and she thanked him, comforted that she would have Lucian for a little longer.

'Look, my daughter is mothering him.' Stephano pointed to Sabina, who was laying a blanket over Lucian. 'She will enjoy being the older sister. She is only six, not too much older than he is and,' he smiled at his wife, 'by Christmas there will be another child, so he will have a good family.'

Clemency lay awake for half the night reluctantly accepting that however much she loved Lucian she could not give him all that Stephano and Donata had to offer. She had no man in her life to act as a father to him. His mother and grandmother were dead and his grandfather disowned him. Lucian needed a stable, loving family and here it was, two parents and a sister, another sibling coming, and all these other relatives.

But even accepting this – and as the days passed she saw how happy and at home Lucian was with his family – the parting devastated her. She did not cry in front of him; she held him and kissed him, saying she'd see him soon, but she wept all the way back to Placida's.

Stephano came with her, his arm round her waist, and every so often he kissed her.

'You are so brave.' He wiped her eyes gently with his handkerchief. 'Remember you can come to us whenever you want. There will always be a room for you. You can have it now if you wish.'

She was briefly tempted, but she felt out of place here. Lucian and Stephano belonged together; they could never truly be hers. She had bought him to his father as Verity would have wanted her to do. All she would have of Stephano was the bracelet and that memory of his lovemaking, but even then, she reminded herself firmly, it was not herself to whom he had made love, he had thought she was Verity.

It was a lonely journey home and Clemency's house seemed a sad place without Lucian, but Jane gave her plenty of work and she picked up her life again, cheered by the letters and photographs that Stephano's family sent to her. Christmas passed and she made a plan to go back to Lucca to see Lucian in the spring.

221

Various men showed an interest in her, but she found none of them special enough for a firm relationship. Perhaps her love for Stephano would prevent her loving anyone again, but it did not matter. Surely no one could match him?

Her father wrote, saying he was now living in Malta. Having been part of the convoy that had saved the island from the onslaught of the Axis powers, he'd fallen for it and decided to live there. He suggested that she might visit him, should she care to, but he did not mention Lucian. Even Aunt Mattie sounded happier; her squadron leader was still billeted with her as he had taken a civilian job in Caithness.

One cold February night, Clemency went to a cocktail party. It had been a dull week; there had not been any flying work because of the weather. She didn't know the couple who had invited her very well, but she went to cheer herself up.

The room was crowded with chattering people and, feeling suddenly shy, she decided she'd go home unless she saw someone she knew.

There came a touch on her arm. 'Clemency,' a voice said, 'at last, I've been looking everywhere for you.'

'Harry!' She turned, found herself almost in his arms, then she froze. Surely Flavia would be here and would bear down on them with that supercilious smile of hers.

He saw her expression and took a step back, his face now a mask of politeness. 'It . . . it's good to see you. Is all well with you?'

'Yes . . . y . . . you heard about Verity and my mother. . . ?'

'No. I've been abroad. I've only been back a few weeks.' He led her to a quieter corner and she told him of the deaths of her mother and her sister.

'My dear, I am so very sorry. But are you . . .' he glanced at her left hand, 'are you married . . . engaged? Have you someone to care for you?'

'No . . . I've . . .' There seemed to be so much to tell him. 'It's a long story. Verity had a baby and I've been looking after him, but now he is with his father in Italy. But how are you . . . you and . . . Flavia.' She almost choked on that name.

'She's gone.' He smiled ruefully. 'While I was away she upped and married a rich American. She did divorce me first. I don't know where she is . . . or care.' His face was tender as he regarded her. 'You were always in my thoughts. I looked for you but I couldn't find you. Dory's flat is sold and your house was shut up and those friends of yours whom I knew seemed to have disappeared.'

'I so nearly didn't come tonight, and I was about to sneak off home.' She couldn't take her eyes off him, or stop smiling.

'Let's slip away, go somewhere for dinner. We've so much to catch up on,' he suggested. He took her hand and kissed it. She moved closer to him. How dear he was, how glamorous, how much she loved him. The realization crept into her and settled there.

The wind was cold, the sky was black but glittering with stars. As they hurried along the street, the shop windows glowing back at them, Clemency slipped her hand in the crook of his arm. He bent and kissed the top of her head.

She felt at peace, complete, for the first time in her life. This was the man she loved. Had she not always known it? Even though she had confused the tumult of her passion for Stephano for a lasting love, a love to last a lifetime. The ache of losing all the people she was close to would always be in her heart, but with Harry by her side all would be well.

MARY DE LASZLO